WINE *and* PUNISHMENT

Center Point
Large Print

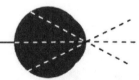

**This Large Print Book carries the
Seal of Approval of N.A.V.H.**

WINE *and* PUNISHMENT

A Literary Pub Mystery

SARAH FOX

CENTER POINT LARGE PRINT
THORNDIKE, MAINE

This Center Point Large Print edition
is published in the year 2019 by arrangement with
Kensington Publishing Corp.

The text of this Large Print edition is unabridged.
In other aspects, this book may vary
from the original edition.
Printed in the United States of America
on permanent paper.
Set in 16-point Times New Roman type.

ISBN: 978-1-64358-097-5

Library of Congress Cataloging-in-Publication Data

Names: Fox, Sarah (Mystery writer), author.
Title: Wine and punishment / Sarah Fox.
Description: Center Point Large Print edition. | Thorndike, Maine :
    Center Point Large Print, 2019.
Identifiers: LCCN 2018055099 | ISBN 9781643580975
    (large print : hardcover : acid-free paper)
Subjects: LCSH: Large type books. | GSAFD: Mystery fiction.
Classification: LCC PR9199.4.F696 W56 2019 | DDC 813/.6—dc23
LC record available at https://lccn.loc.gov/2018055099

WINE *and* PUNISHMENT

CHAPTER 1

The crisp autumn breeze rustled through the colorful maple trees flanking the old grist mill. I stood back from the red-trimmed stone building, near the edge of the road, so I could get a full view of the property. A creek flowed along in front of the mill, gurgling and splashing, turning the old red water wheel, and a wooden bridge led the way from the wide footpath to the flagstone walkway that ended at the building's main door.

Beyond the mill a forest of sugar maples, beech trees, and conifers formed a serene backdrop, birdsong audible even from where I stood. Overhead, the bold blue sky was cloudless, and the early October sunshine brightened the entire scene before me.

It was postcard-perfect.

I'd thought that the moment I'd first laid eyes on the grist mill four months earlier. Now, with the fall colors at their most intense, I often found myself stopping to soak in the view of my new home and to revel in the fact that it was really mine.

That wasn't my purpose at the moment, however. In only four days, the town of Shady Creek, Vermont's annual Autumn Festival would get under way. Although I was new to town, the importance of the upcoming event hadn't escaped me. The residents had made it clear that the festival was Shady Creek's event of the year, and for any local business not to participate was simply unthinkable.

That's why I stood by the road, shading my eyes from the sun, assessing the picturesque building with a critical eye. I lived on the upper floor of the renovated mill, while the main level was dedicated to my literary-themed pub, the Inkwell.

I'd only had possession of the property for three months, and I was determined to make a success of the business. To do that, I needed the townsfolk on my side, and showing anything but enthusiasm for the Autumn Festival would be akin to shooting myself in the foot. Not that I wouldn't have been enthusiastic. I was looking forward to the festival. I was also looking forward to making a good impression on the town of Shady Creek.

"You're looking awfully serious, Sadie."

I dropped my hand from my eyes as Melanie Costas, one of the pub's employees, arrived at my side. Her bleached-blond and electric-blue hair was spiked straight up, and the silver stud in her nose glinted in the sunlight.

"Don't tell me there's something wrong with the building," she said, squinting through the sunlight at the mill.

"No," I assured her. "At least, I sure hope

not. I'm thinking about how to decorate for the Autumn Festival."

"You and the whole town." Mel shaded her eyes as I had done moments ago. "Got any ideas?"

I tucked my red hair behind my ear as I thought about my response. "Pumpkins and decorative gourds, of course. Maybe some bales of straw, and a fall wreath for the main door. A scarecrow too, as long as it's not a creepy one."

"I could put together a scarecrow for you," Mel offered as we started along the pathway toward the bridge.

"Really?"

"Sure. I've made a couple before. And I promise it won't be creepy."

I smiled as we crossed the creek, the water babbling cheerfully beneath the bridge. "That would be fantastic."

Mel was a talented artist, so I knew she'd come up with something great, and that was one item I could take off my to-do list.

"I'll go to the pumpkin patch tomorrow morning," I said, opening the pub's large red door and holding it for Mel. Before following her through it, I flipped the wooden CLOSED sign hanging on the outside of the door so the OPEN side faced outward.

"How's the catapult coming along?"

"Er," was all I could come up with as the door fell shut behind me.

"That bad?" Mel said with a grin.

"With Damien out of town the past couple of days, progress has . . . stalled."

Mel shrugged out of her green military surplus jacket. "I'll come early tomorrow to lend a hand," she promised.

"Thank you. We're going to need all the hands we can get."

Although the entire Autumn Festival was a highly anticipated event in Shady Creek, the most popular part of it was the pumpkin catapult competition held at the end of the nine-day festival. Local businesses and other groups formed teams, with each one building its own catapult. Distance and accuracy were important when it came to catapulting the pumpkins, and the winning team would receive a trophy and, more importantly, bragging rights for the next twelve months.

I'd never anticipated that I'd need construction skills when I'd purchased the pub, but participation in the competition was expected. Luckily, Damien—another of my employees—did carpentry on the side and had designed the catapult for the Inkwell's team. The actual construction had yet to begin, however.

I wasn't overly concerned. Damien would be back to work on the catapult the next day, and I figured that as long as we had one good enough to allow us to participate in the competition, that would suffice. I had enough on my plate without worrying about winning a contest that was all about having fun.

"How about the book clubs?" Mel asked. "Are you having more luck with them?"

"Definitely." I couldn't help but smile. "The first one is tomorrow night. Six people have signed up."

"Sounds like a great start."

That was my thought exactly. The idea of hosting book clubs at the Inkwell excited me to no end, and so far, the local response had pleasantly surprised me. The next night's romance book club had the most people signed up at the moment, but there had also been interest in the mystery book club starting up in a couple of weeks, and I was hoping to organize another one for science fiction and fantasy readers.

As Mel disappeared into the back of the pub, where the kitchen and tiny cloakroom were located, I remained by the front door, surveying the main room. When I'd purchased the building and business, the pub had been quite ordinary, aside from the beautiful historic building that housed it. It was a place for townsfolk to gather and chat over a pint or two, but it wasn't much beyond that. As soon as it had passed into my possession, I'd made sure to change that.

I'd long dreamed of owning my own bookstore, but when I'd arrived in Shady Creek, trying to escape the ruins of my former life in Boston, I'd fallen in love with the renovated grist mill as soon as I'd seen it. When I found out that it was for sale, it seemed like a sign from the universe, and I'd used nearly all of my savings to purchase the mill and business, setting my life on a new course that I'd never anticipated.

Briefly, I'd considered transforming the pub into a bookstore, but once I'd realized that it was a favorite gathering place for the locals, I changed my mind, and instead incorporated my passion for books into the existing business.

I'd been a bibliophile for as long as I could remember; since before I could even read the words on the pages. My dad had read to me every night as a young child, and his home library—though housed in a small room—had seemed like such a magical place to me while growing up. Once I could read on my own, I'd devoured story after story, working my way through books by C. S. Lewis, Enid Blyton, Kit Pearson, and many others. I'd feasted on series like Nancy Drew and the Baby-Sitters Club, and once I'd discovered Agatha Christie's novels, I was hooked on mysteries for life.

My dad had passed away a few years ago, and I still missed him all the time, but I knew I'd never lose the love for books he'd instilled in me. That's why it seemed so right to work books into my new business, even if not in the way I'd imagined while growing up and dreaming of one day having my own bookshop.

Once the purchase of the mill was finalized, I renamed the pub and gave it a literary theme, with drinks named for famous books and fictional characters. I was hoping to add some literary-themed food to the menu soon too, and my extensive collection of books lined the shelf that ran along the upper portion of the exposed stone walls, adding coziness to the pub's rustic charm. The wide plank floors and wood beams were original to the building, and vintage metal-banded barrels had been incorporated into the structure of the bar at the far end of the room, like stout pillars. The lighting in the pub wasn't bright, but I thought the warm glow added to the charm of the place.

Before my arrival in Shady Creek, I'd never imagined myself as a pub owner, but I was enjoying my new role, despite the stresses that came with learning the ropes of the business and staying afloat financially. So far, I was managing, if not exactly prospering.

Behind me, the front door opened, letting in a current of cool air tinged with wood smoke.

"Enjoying the view again?" a man said from over my shoulder.

I turned to see Harvey Jelinek—one of the Inkwell's regulars—grinning at me.

"Hi, Harvey," I greeted as he shut the door

behind him. "I can't seem to help myself."

"I don't think anyone's going to blame you for that. It's a great place."

"It is, isn't it?" I smiled as we headed for the bar. "What can I get you?"

"Just a coffee." He took up his perch on his favorite stool at the end of the bar. "I'm meeting Rhonda here in a bit, and then we're heading to Rutland to have a late lunch with my sister."

"That sounds nice." I grabbed a clean mug and the coffeepot I'd put on to brew earlier.

"It will be as long as my sister doesn't hassle me and Rhonda about when we're getting married."

I filled the mug and slid it across the bar to Harvey. "You two are engaged?"

"No. That's just it. We're not at that point. But my sister doesn't always know how to mind her own business."

"Family can be like that," I said with understanding.

While my Aunt Gilda and my younger brother, Taylor, had supported me every step of the way, my mother and older brother hadn't held back when it came to expressing their negative views about all the changes I'd made to my life in the past four months. Words like "rash" and "shortsighted" had been tossed about. But what had stung the most was my mother's declaration that my new life would fall to pieces within the year, that I'd soon come to see the foolishness of my recent decisions. She was steadfast in her opinion, but I was just as resolute that she was wrong. At least, most days I was.

Two more of the Inkwell's regulars came into the pub then, thankfully distracting me from the unpleasant turn my thoughts had taken. I greeted the newcomers and pulled pints of beer for them as they settled onto stools at the bar. Mel emerged from the back and immediately joined the conversation about football that the patrons had struck up.

I was completely out of my depth with that topic, so I wandered down to the far end of the bar and called out a greeting to Rhonda Hogarth, who'd just arrived carrying a cardboard box. Rhonda lived in the nearest house to the mill—a weathered old Queen Anne—and was the daughter of the man who'd sold me the pub. She was also one of the first friends I'd made in Shady Creek.

"What have you got there?" I asked her after Harvey greeted her with a kiss on the cheek.

She tipped the box my way so I could see the mason jars inside. Each one was decorated with colorful artificial leaves.

"Decorations," she said. "I got the idea from Pinterest and thought you might like some for the pub's interior during the festival. They've got LED lights inside."

She passed me one of the jars for closer inspection.

"These look great," I told her, turning the jar in my hands. I reached inside and flicked on the small light. The leaves glowed, highlighting their autumn colors. "I love them. How much do you want for the lot?"

Rhonda set the box on the bar and brushed her short dark hair off her forehead. "They're a gift."

"Let me pay you something," I protested.

"Nope. You know how I love this place. It makes me happy to lend a hand. That's all the payment I need."

"You're amazing, Rhonda. Thank you."

I took the box in my arms and hugged it to me as Harvey got up off his stool. He put some money on the bar for his coffee and rested his arm across Rhonda's shoulders.

"We'd better be off now," he said.

"Enjoy your day," I said to them as they went on their way.

I spent the next while wandering around the pub with the box of jars, placing the decorative light holders here and there. When I was done, I stood near the bar to admire the effect. I needed more decorations to make the place look truly festive, but the mason jars were a good start.

As the afternoon progressed, the number of patrons in the pub grew. Many were locals, but there were also several unfamiliar faces. With leaf-peeper season underway, busloads of tourists arrived daily, bringing smiles to the faces of all local business owners, including myself. I knew this would be the most prosperous season for the Inkwell, and the more visitors who came in for a drink or two, the more likely I'd be able to make the payments on my business loan in the upcoming months.

After exchanging a few words with one group of tourists, I cleared empty pint glasses from a vacated table.

"Don't you need to leave for your aunt's birthday dinner soon?" Mel asked when I reached the bar.

I glanced up at the Guinness wall clock. "Yes. I'll go get ready once Damien is here."

I continued on into the kitchen and deposited the glasses in the dishwasher. When I returned out front, Damien was making his way behind the bar, shrugging out of his black leather jacket.

"It looks like we're getting a good crowd," he remarked as he passed by me and into the back.

He reappeared a moment later without his jacket, wearing his usual outfit of jeans and a T-shirt, the tattoos on his muscular arms visible. Originally from England, Damien had an accent I loved listening to, but though we'd been working together for weeks now, I wouldn't have called us friends. The truth was that I wasn't entirely sure if he liked working for me or not. He'd come with the pub, so to speak, and had proved to be a valuable source of information and advice on many occasions, but I didn't think he had a whole lot of confidence in me as his boss.

I, however, had plenty of confidence in him and Mel. I didn't often take off during business hours, but that evening I was making an exception for a special occasion, and it was a relief to know I didn't have to worry about leaving the Inkwell in the hands of my employees.

A flash of red caught my eye, and I waved when I saw my friend Shontelle Williams threading her way through the tables toward the bar, unbuttoning her cherry-colored coat. Shontelle, a single mother of an eight-year-old girl, owned the gift shop across the village green from the Inkwell and had quickly become my closest friend in Shady Creek.

"Shouldn't you be getting ready?" she said, eyeing my jeans and V-neck sweater when she reached the bar.

"I'm just about to head upstairs."

I turned toward Mel, but she made a shooing motion with her hands before I could say anything.

"Go," she said. "We've got everything under control."

Shontelle hooked her arm through mine and steered me toward the door marked PRIVATE.

"Call me if you need me," I said over my shoulder, barely getting the words out before Shontelle nudged me through the door.

I hastened up the creaking stairs that led to my apartment, Shontelle's high heels clacking on the steps behind me.

"Did you remember to pick up the cake?" she asked as I opened the door at the top of the stairs and stepped into my cozy living room.

"Yes, it's in the fridge." I went straight to my bedroom and grabbed the blue wrap dress I'd left hanging on the back of the door.

My white, long-haired cat was lying on the corner of my queen bed, watching me with his blue eyes. I paused to stroke his silky fur.

"Hello, Wimsey. Did you have a nice snooze?"

He purred and closed his eyes. I gave him a quick kiss on the top of his head and kicked off my shoes.

"Guess who I saw on my way over here," Shontelle called from the other room.

"I have no idea." I shed my clothes and slipped into the dress.

"That delicious Grayson Blake."

I poked my head out the bedroom door. "Don't you mean Grumpy-Pants Blake?"

"What did you do to make him grumpy?"

"Why do you assume *I* made him grumpy?" I asked, heading for my dresser and the jewelry box sitting on top of it. "I strongly suspect he was born that way." I switched out my silver stud earrings for a set of small hoops.

Shontelle appeared in the doorway and leaned against the frame. "I've never known him to be anything but a courteous gentleman. And one tall glass of delicious."

"Hrmph," was all I had to say to that.

I slipped past Shontelle and headed for the bathroom, where I set about touching up my makeup. My friend's opinion of the craft brewery owner matched that of my Aunt Gilda and pretty much every other woman in Shady Creek. Heck, I hadn't heard a man say anything negative about him either. Sure, he was attractive, and he brewed award-winning beers, but my business—and only—dealings with him hadn't been pleasant experiences. I found him brusque and as prickly as a porcupine. If not for the fact that his beers were so popular with both the tourists and locals, I wouldn't have bothered to sell them at the Inkwell.

Pushing thoughts of the brewery owner out of my mind, I added some color to my lips and fastened my red hair into a twist at the back of my head.

"All ready?" Shontelle asked when I emerged from the bathroom. She'd retrieved the cake from the fridge and held the bakery box in her hands.

"Almost."

I slipped into a pair of heels, grabbed my

handbag, and pulled on my coat. I reached for the door but then spun around, almost smacking Shontelle across the face with my bag.

"Sorry!" I hurried into the kitchen. "I'd better feed Wimsey before we go."

Wimsey came trotting out of the bedroom when he heard the spoon clanking against his food dish. I set his dinner on the kitchen floor and gave him a quick scratch on the head as he dug into his food, purring away.

"Okay, this time I'm ready," I said as I returned to the door.

I locked up, and we headed down the stairs. As we reached the landing halfway down, Mel opened the door to the pub. She cast a quick glance over her shoulder and then slipped through the door, closing it behind her.

"Everything okay?" I asked, continuing down the stairs, noting that Mel appeared uncharacteristically hesitant.

"There's someone here looking for you."

"Who?" I made a move to go around her.

She put out an arm to block me. "I'm not sure it's someone you want to see."

I halted, suddenly apprehensive. "Who is it?" I asked again.

Mel gave me a sympathetic look. "It's your ex."

CHAPTER 2

"Eric?" I took a step back, bumping into Shontelle. "He's not supposed to be here."

Shontelle shifted the bakery box into one hand and put an arm around my shoulders. "Does he know Sadie's here?" she asked Mel.

Mel shook her head. "I told him she was out for the evening, but he seems determined to wait."

"Let him," Shontelle said with authority. "We'll go out the back way."

"Thanks, Mel," I managed to say as Shontelle guided me along the narrow hallway that led to the back door.

It wasn't until we stepped out into the cooling evening air that my stunned mind started working again. As soon as it did, my shock morphed into annoyance and frustration.

"Why can't he let me move on?" I fumed as we hurried around the back of the mill. "I've got a new life now, and he doesn't belong in it."

"Do you think he's here to ask for another chance with you?"

"I can't think of another reason why he'd come all the way from Boston to see me."

We paused, and I peered around the corner of the building. The coast was clear, so we continued on, walking briskly past the pub's front door and across the bridge. I worried that we'd hear Eric calling out to me at any second, but we managed to cross the street without that happening. I chanced a quick glance over my shoulder and saw with relief that there was no one behind us. We followed the road past the wide driveway on the left that led up to Grayson Blake's brewery, and soon we turned right onto a residential street.

Now that we were out of sight of the pub, my shoulders relaxed, and we slowed to a more sedate pace.

"Do you think he'll give up and go home if you avoid him for the rest of the evening?" Shontelle asked.

"After coming all this way? That's probably too much to hope for."

"Maybe I shouldn't have whisked you out of there then. Did you want to talk to him and get it over with?"

"No. That would only make us late for Aunt Gilda's dinner, and I'm not letting him interfere like that. If he wants to wait, he can wait, but I'm not rearranging my schedule for him." I inclined my head toward a small house on our left. "This is it."

I led the way up to the front porch and knocked on the door.

"Please don't mention this to Aunt Gilda," I requested. "I don't want her worrying about me when she's supposed to be celebrating."

The door opened then, putting an end to our conversation. My aunt's gentleman friend, Louie Edmonds, greeted us and ushered us into his house. Gilda was already there, along with her friend and coworker, Betty.

"Happy birthday!" I gave my aunt a hug.

"Thank you, honey. I'm glad you made it."

I relieved Shontelle of the bakery box so she could hug my aunt and wish her happy birthday too.

"I brought cake," I announced once we'd all exchanged greetings.

Shontelle removed a bottle from her large handbag. "And I brought you some sherry." She handed the bottle to Gilda. "I'm told it's your favorite."

"You were told right. That's sweet of you both."

Louie took the cake and sherry to the kitchen, and soon we were all seated at the dining table, eating the delicious lasagna Louie had baked for the occasion, each of us with a glass of wine.

"How's that sweet little girl of yours?" Aunt Gilda asked Shontelle once we'd all had a chance to taste the food.

"She's great, thanks," my friend said with a smile. "My mom's looking after her this evening. They're going out for pizza, so Kiandra's excited about that."

We chatted a bit longer about Shontelle's daughter before Louie turned to me.

"How's business going at the pub?" he asked.

"Really well," I said, trying my best to sound upbeat and unconcerned.

I hadn't lied—the business was going well at the moment, thanks to the influx of tourists—but I couldn't rid myself of the knowledge that Eric was over at the Inkwell, waiting for me to return. As much as I was trying to stay engaged with my present company, it was as if a dark cloud were hovering over me, refusing to release me from its gloomy shadow.

After answering another couple of questions from Louie, I managed to turn the conversation in a different direction, and soon we were chatting and laughing about things that had nothing to do with the pub or my ex-boyfriend.

When we'd all had our fill of the delicious lasagna, I helped Louie clear the dishes away.

"I'll look after the cake," I assured him after we'd stacked the dirty plates on the kitchen counter.

He left me with a set of dessert plates and a knife for cutting the cake and returned to the other room. Alone in the kitchen now, I closed my eyes and tried to banish my ex from my thoughts. It didn't work.

"Want to tell me what's troubling you?"

I nearly jumped out of my skin, whipping around to see Aunt Gilda standing in the kitchen doorway. She wore her dyed auburn hair in an up-do, and the rubies hanging from her ears winked in the light while her brown eyes remained fixed on me.

"Nothing's troubling me." I turned back to the counter. "I'll have the cake ready in a minute."

Gilda crossed the kitchen to stand next to me. "You're not fooling me, honey. I can see plain as day that there's something weighing on your mind."

I cut a slice of cake and set it on a plate. "I don't want to cast a cloud over your party."

"If you don't tell me, I'll spend the rest of the night worrying, so you'd best be out with it."

I sank the knife into the cake again, knowing she wouldn't let the matter rest until I told her what had me preoccupied. "It's Eric. He showed up at the Inkwell earlier."

"He came all the way from Boston unannounced?"

"He probably knew I'd tell him not to come."

Gilda's disapproval showed clearly on her face. She knew all about Eric and our relationship troubles. She'd provided me with a shoulder to cry on more than once after I'd left Boston for Shady Creek.

"Let me guess," she said. "He asked for you to give him another chance."

"I haven't talked to him yet. Mel told him I wasn't there, and I left through the back door so he wouldn't see me. But my guess is the same as yours."

She watched me closely. "And what are you going to tell him when you do see him?"

"The same thing I told him when I broke up with him four months ago. This time we're done for good."

"From what you've told me before, he's not so good at listening."

My shoulders sagged with the weight of my past. "No, he's not. I'm sure he'll tell me that he's changed, that he's attending counseling and won't ever gamble again."

"All of which you've heard before."

"And all the other times it was a lie. Even when he told me he was going to see his counselor, he was really going to the casino." I set the knife down on the counter, unable to focus on the cake. "I tried to help him. I really did. But all the lies . . . they became too much."

Aunt Gilda put an arm around me, giving me a squeeze and patting my cheek. "You did the right thing for yourself by walking away. He had more chances than he deserved, and don't you forget that, no matter how much he tries to sway you."

"I won't," I said, my resolve strengthening. "I love my new life, and he has no place in it. I'll tell him that and send him on his way."

"That's my girl."

I smiled at her. "I'm glad we live so close now. My life is better with you in it on a regular basis."

"Right back at you, honey."

Still smiling, and feeling more positive than I had since learning of Eric's arrival, I finished doling out the dessert, and we both returned to the party.

The cake, layered with chocolate buttercream, was nothing short of scrumptious. I'd ordered it from Sofie's Treat, Shady Creek's only bakery, located at the eastern end of the village green, next door to Aunt Gilda's hair salon. The owner, Sofie Talbot, worked magic in the bakery's kitchen, as far as I was concerned. Her cakes tasted like heaven on a fork, and in my opinion, her pecan pie ranked second only to Aunt Gilda's, which was high praise, considering that Gilda's pecan pie was legendary in our family.

I indulged in a second slice of cake, and by the time I licked the last bit of icing from my fork, I could practically feel the sugar rushing through my bloodstream. It was worth it, though.

After the table was cleared, I helped Louie load all the dirty dishes into the dishwasher.

"Dinner was great," I told him as I slipped the last plate into an available slot. "Thanks for cooking and hosting. I can tell Gilda's enjoyed herself tonight."

Louie smiled his perfect retired-dentist smile and added a handful of cutlery to the dishwasher.

"Making Gilda happy makes me happy, so it was my pleasure."

He urged me to go join the others while he finished tidying up, so I wandered into the living room, where everyone else had gathered. I stood by the front window looking out into the darkness of the night, thinking about Louie's relationship with my aunt. He was older than her by several years, and his neatly trimmed hair was completely silver-gray, but he was still active and in good health, often taking Gilda out for a round of golf or an evening of dancing. I knew my aunt enjoyed his companionship, but I didn't know how deep her feelings for him ran, and whenever I'd tried to fish for that information, she'd deftly dodged the subject.

Maybe she was in the same boat as I was—not yet ready to give her heart to another man. I wasn't ready to trust again after Eric's lies, and Aunt Gilda had known a love that would be hard—if not impossible—to ever match. She and her late husband, Houston, had married at age nineteen and had stayed madly in love right up until Houston's death from a heart attack thirty-three years later.

Looking at Gilda now, though, as she smiled and laughed with Shontelle and Betty, I knew she was happy, and that was what really mattered. I was happy too, generally at least. I wasn't looking forward to seeing Eric, but once I got that out of the way and sent him back to Boston, I could go back to being content, only having the health of my business to worry about.

For the time being, I left my spot by the window to rejoin the others.

"Shontelle and Sadie," Betty spoke up, "I've been meaning to ask if either of you could step in as a judge for the pumpkin pie baking contest at the Autumn Festival. Judith Webster has been judging for years but she's in the hospital with a broken hip."

"That's on Tuesday, isn't it?" Shontelle asked. When Betty confirmed that, she continued, "I'm afraid I'll be minding my store, and my mom has Zumba on Tuesdays, so she won't be able to cover for me."

"Sadie?" Betty turned her expectant eyes to me.

"Sure," I agreed. "That shouldn't be a problem."

"Great!" Betty beamed at me. "I'll get the details to you in the next couple of days."

As the conversation veered off in another direction, Shontelle hooked her arm through mine and tugged me to the far corner of the room.

"You do know what you're getting into, right?"

"Um, tasting lots of pumpkin pie?" I said. "Sounds pretty good to me."

Shontelle gave me a pitying look and patted my arm. "You'll see."

"I'll see what?" I asked before she could leave me to return to the others.

"The competition is fierce, and when I say *fierce,* I mean sometimes the claws come out."

"It's really that big of a deal?"

"Especially among those who've been entering for years and years."

Maybe that shouldn't have surprised me after what I'd heard about the pumpkin catapult competition. "I'm sure it'll be fine," I said, although my confidence wavered with my last words.

"For your sake, I sure hope so."

After a few seconds, I decided not to worry about the baking contest. After all, how bad could it really be?

Back across the living room, I let myself get swept up in the good cheer and conversation, and the time seemed to fly by. It was after ten o'clock when Shontelle got to her feet and announced that she needed to head home.

"I should relieve my mom of her babysitting duties for the night," she explained.

"I'll walk with you," I said, fetching our coats from the foyer closet.

It took several more minutes for us to actually get out the door, between the wrapping up of conversations and the exchanges of parting words.

Gilda gave me a hug before we left, squeezing

me tightly and saying quietly into my ear, "Tell me tomorrow how things go with Eric."

I promised her that I would, and Shontelle and I took our leave. Instead of retracing the route we'd taken to get to Louie's house, we turned onto Hillview Road, following it to the village green. Shontelle and her daughter lived on that street, in a two-bedroom apartment above her gift shop.

The crisp air of the afternoon had turned downright chilly now that night had fallen, and I was glad I'd worn a warm coat. I hadn't thought to wear gloves, though, so I shoved my hands in my pockets to keep them from freezing. Despite the cold temperature, the night was beautiful, with the sky still clear and the stars glinting brightly overhead.

The businesses around the green were closed for the night, their storefronts dark, but the old-fashioned streetlamps lit our way, casting pools of yellow light on the road and walkways. I wished I could simply enjoy the walk out in the fresh air, but I couldn't stop thinking about the fact that Eric was in town. I glanced across the green toward the mill, but all was dark and quiet over that way.

I sniffed the cool air. "Is that smoke?"

"Maybe someone's having a bonfire."

It didn't quite smell like bonfire smoke, but I put the matter out of my mind. A minute or so later, we reached Shontelle's shop, the Treasure Chest, but instead of heading for the door to the side of the shop that led to the apartment's stairway, Shontelle paused in the middle of the sidewalk.

"Here comes your favorite person," she said, a hint of amusement in her voice.

I followed her line of sight to see a figure heading in our direction. The shadowy shape took on more definition the closer it came, and I stifled a groan.

"Evening, ladies." Grayson Blake paused on the sidewalk before us. He offered Shontelle a brief smile but barely glanced my way.

"Evening," Shontelle replied as I forced a smile. "It's a lovely night for a walk."

"Ah . . . Yes, it is," he said, as if he hadn't noticed that was the case until she'd mentioned it.

He too had his hands deep in his coat pockets, and I detected an antsy energy from him, as if he were in a hurry and didn't want to be held up.

"But you're clearly on your way somewhere," I said, doing my best to sound polite, "so we won't keep you."

Shontelle shot a look my way, but I stepped aside to make room for the brewery owner to carry on down the sidewalk. As I moved closer to the curb, a flicker of orange light drew my attention. I gasped and grabbed for the nearest arm.

"Fire!" I managed to exclaim, using my free hand to point westward.

"What? Where?" Shontelle hurried to my side so she could see the flames.

Realizing that it was Grayson's arm I'd grabbed, I quickly released it. As soon as he saw the dancing flames, he broke into a run, pulling his cell phone out of his pocket. Shontelle and I took off after him, hampered by our high heels, but still managing a good clip. When we turned left at the end of the street, we pulled up short, stunned by the sight before us, despite knowing that we were heading for a fire.

On the side street leading away from the village green, the fire was hungrily consuming a building housing two storefronts, flames bursting up through the roof, and dark, acrid smoke billowing out into the cold air. Sirens wailed from somewhere nearby, and a fire truck rounded the corner a second later, its lights flashing, adding to the bright and wavering glow of the raging fire.

As the firefighters jumped down from the truck, the remaining section of the roof collapsed with a booming crash and a frenzy of sparks and flames. There was no doubt that the building was a total loss. The question was, how much more of the town would go down with it?

CHAPTER 3

We stayed well back from the scene, watching the fire crew battle the blaze. A second truck had arrived right after the first, doubling the number of firefighters on hand. As the minutes passed, more townsfolk poked their heads out of their windows and gathered on the street, clustering together to watch the dramatic sight of the burning building.

"At least no one should have been inside at this time of night," a familiar voice said, and I realized that Grayson had returned to my side at some point.

What he said was true. As far as I knew, there were no living quarters above the antiques shop, and the store would have closed hours ago. The second unit of the building was empty, and had been as long as I'd been in Shady Creek.

Rhonda Hogarth and Harvey Jelinek joined the growing crowd of onlookers, craning their necks to get a better look at the fire.

"Does Barry know this is happening?" Harvey asked the crowd in general, referring to the proprietor of the burning store. "What about Frank Fournier?" He turned to Rhonda. "Doesn't he own the building?"

"He does," Rhonda replied. She worked

as a secretary for Fournier Real Estate and Developments.

"I called Barry," a man spoke up. "It took three tries before he picked up, but he's on his way now."

"I'll try to get in touch with Mr. Fournier," Rhonda said, pulling out her cell phone and detaching herself from the crowd.

"It looks like the fire won't spread to the neighboring buildings."

It took a second for me to realize that Grayson was talking to me.

"That's a relief." I put the sleeve of my coat over my nose and mouth as a cloud of smoke billowed in our direction.

My eyes watered, but I could see well enough to tell that Grayson was right. It looked as though the fire crew now had the blaze under control.

Shontelle put a hand on my arm as I lowered my sleeve from my face. "I need to get home."

I gave her a quick hug. "Say hi to your mom for me?"

"I will." She shifted her attention to Grayson. "Good night, Mr. Blake."

"Please, call me Grayson," he said to her. "And good night."

Shontelle flashed him a smile and managed to elbow me in the ribs as she set off for home. I frowned and kept my eyes on the dwindling fire. I knew Shontelle thought I should make the most of having an attractive man standing next to me, but I couldn't bring myself to share her opinion of him. Although, to be fair, he didn't seem grumpy at the moment, and even standing there in the shadows he looked awfully good.

I was wearing heels, but he still had a couple of inches of height on me, and his thick brown hair was stylishly tousled. The emergency lights highlighted the strong planes of his face in flashes of red between moments of deep shadow, and a day or two's worth of stubble covered his jaw. He had the collar of his black wool coat turned up against the chilly air, and while I couldn't see their color at the moment, his blue eyes remained fixed on the decreasing fire.

Maybe, for some reason I couldn't pinpoint, we'd simply started off on the wrong foot. I'd only been friends with Shontelle for three months, but I had no reason to think she wasn't a good judge of character. And it wasn't as if I hadn't been wrong about men in the past. Eric was a prime example of that.

Thinking of Eric reminded me that he could still be waiting for me at the pub. I knew I should get it over with and go see if he was there, but my feet remained rooted to the spot. If he'd waited this long, I figured he could wait a few minutes more.

I glanced at the man beside me and decided to give him another chance. Not that I was interested in having anything beyond a business relationship with him. But it would be nice if we could at least get along.

"How are things at the brewery?" I asked him.

Without taking his eyes off the smoking wreck of the destroyed building, he frowned. "Fine, thank you." His words had a chill to rival the autumn night air, and the set of his jaw was anything but relaxed now.

I bristled. "Heavy on the bitter and short on the sweet."

The words came out before I could stop them. My mother had told me countless times throughout my life to think more before speaking, but at age thirty that was something I'd yet to master.

Slowly, Grayson turned his eyes my way. Now the flickers of red light and shadows crossing his face seemed more sinister than anything else.

"Are you insulting the quality of my beer?" The chill in his voice had deepened, but it wasn't nearly enough to cool the heat of my temper.

"Not at all," I said with seething politeness. "That was directed at you yourself."

I spun on my three-inch heel and marched away with my head held high.

It wasn't until I'd passed Aunt Gilda's hair salon that my fuming dwindled to a simmer, and that had less to do with any diminishment of my annoyance with Grayson Blake than with the thought that I could be moments away from coming face-to-face with my ex, someone I'd never expected—and certainly never hoped—to see here in Shady Creek, Vermont.

The farther I got from the fire, the quieter the night became around me. By the time I crossed the footbridge leading to the old mill, all I could hear was the gurgling of the creek passing beneath me. The light was still on over the front door of the pub, and I was relieved to see that no one waited for me in the pool of light. I tested the door and found it locked, as it should have been at that hour.

I rummaged around in my purse for my keys and opened the door, slipping inside and locking it behind me. Damien had left the light on over the bar at the far end of the room, giving me enough light to see by as I wound my way around the tables. Everything looked as it should, and no shadowy figures lurked in the dark corners. Not that I would have expected Mel or Damien to allow Eric to wait for me in the pub after hours and unsupervised. Still, I let out a sigh of relief as I switched off the light over the bar and climbed the creaking staircase to my apartment.

It was probably too much to hope that Eric had given up and gone home to Boston, but at least I wouldn't have to face him that night. Sure, it would have been best to get our conversation over with, but that didn't mean I was unhappy to put it off until morning.

Inside my apartment, I switched on the light, shed my coat, and dropped my purse on the couch. Wimsey was curled up on the nearby armchair, blinking sleepily at me with his blue eyes.

"Did you miss me, bud?" I asked, picking him up and pressing my cheek against his soft fur.

He purred for a second or two, but then placed one paw on my nose, pushing my face away. He wasn't much into cuddling, although he did humor me on occasion.

I set him on the chair, and he hopped down a moment later, following me across the wide plank floors to the kitchen, where he sat next to his empty food dish and let out a pointed meow. Obediently, I poured a few kitty treats into his dish and set out fresh water for him before heading to the bedroom, where I pulled off my dress—now covered in long white cat hairs.

Once in my pajamas, with my face washed and my teeth brushed, I climbed into bed. Wimsey had followed me into the bedroom, and now curled up at my feet.

"I wish you could explain men to me, Wimsey," I said as I fluffed up my pillows, "because I'm not sure I'll ever understand them."

Wimsey ignored me, crossing his front paws before resting his chin on them, his eyes closing.

With a sigh, I resigned myself to not being able to unravel the mystery of the male of the species, at least not that night. Switching off the bedside lamp, I hoped I could at least enjoy a few hours of peace before I had to face Eric.

I wasn't much of a morning person at the best of times, and knowing I had something unpleasant to face only made me all the more reluctant to leave the coziness and warmth of my bed the next day. A certain someone with blue eyes and a cute pink nose wasn't about to let me laze about for long, though. I had the side of my face smooshed against my pillow, my quilt pulled up to my chin, when I felt four little paws walk their way up my leg and over my rib cage. One of those paws then went tap-tap-tap against my shoulder. When I cracked my eyes open, Wimsey's blue ones stared back at me.

Groaning, I closed my eyes again. "Five more minutes."

Wimsey gave my shoulder another tap, this time adding an insistent meow.

I knew from plenty of experience that this was a battle I had no hope of winning. Accepting the defeat that was staring me right in the eyes, I gave Wimsey a scratch on the head, getting a rumbling purr as a reward. With much yawning and stretching, I managed to stumble into the kitchen in my pajamas, doling out Wimsey's breakfast as he brushed up against my legs, his motor going full tilt.

Once His Lordship was eating happily, I continued my morning routine with a quick shower while my coffee brewed and my bread toasted. Wrapped in a bathrobe, my hair still damp, I stood in front of my open closet. My first instinct had been to grab jeans and a sweater, but I hesitated, wondering if I should dress up a bit.

I quickly nixed that idea. I didn't need to prove anything to Eric when I saw him. I didn't need to go out of my way to make myself or my new life seem shiny and fabulous. My life in Shady Creek *was* fabulous, but that was beside the point. Sadie Coleman on a typical morning in small town Vermont was the Sadie Coleman Eric would get to see.

Hopefully for a very limited time.

After I'd dressed in jeans, a white V-neck tee, and a long and cozy gray knit cardigan, I allowed myself some time to indulge in my first cup of coffee of the day and some reading time. Engrossed in the latest Temperance Brennan mystery by Kathy Reichs, I sipped at my hot drink and nibbled on a piece of toast.

When I'd finished a chapter, I forced myself to stick a bookmark between the pages and close the book. As much as I would have liked to allow myself a second cup of coffee and more reading time, I knew I couldn't procrastinate all day. I spent a few minutes drying my hair and putting on a touch of makeup, but soon after that, I was on my way out the door, pausing to kiss the top of Wimsey's silky head as he settled into the armchair next to the woodstove.

Instead of going out the back door of the old mill, I passed through the pub to go out the front way. I pushed open the red door, half-expecting to find Eric hanging around outside, but only some birdsong and a light breeze greeted me.

Now that morning had arrived, I wanted to get our encounter out of the way so we could both move on with our lives. But I didn't know if Eric was staying at one of the town's B&Bs or at the small inn up the road, and I wasn't about to waste my time tracking him down. I had other plans for the morning, and I was going to stick to them. I'd drive out to the pumpkin patch, load up the trunk of my car with pumpkins and decorative gourds, and return for a spot of decorating and catapult construction before the pub opened in the afternoon.

Across the bridge, I followed the gravel footpath that led past one of the colorful maple trees to the small parking lot at the edge of the mill property. The town didn't allow parking on the streets around the village green, so I kept my aging white Honda in the same lot where any customers arriving by car had to leave theirs. With the pub currently closed, my vehicle was the only one in the lot, and as soon as I caught sight of it, I knew something was wrong.

"What the Charles Dickens?"

I broke into a run, not wanting to believe my eyes, but when I arrived at my car, there was no denying what I saw. Sometime during the night, someone had slashed all four of my tires. My Honda sat low on the ground, useless.

My temper flaring, I let out a loud, "Argh!"

A crow flapped out of the nearest tree, quickly retreating.

I made one circuit around my car, and then another, but no matter how much I fumed or how much I stared at the tires, they remained slashed. So much for my trip to the pumpkin patch.

Still fuming, I stormed my way back along the footpath.

Who would have done such a thing? Eric?

Why would he drive all the way to Shady Creek just to slash my tires? Or was it because I didn't talk to him last night?

I nixed that theory. Despite his faults, this wasn't Eric's style.

Maybe it was teenagers having a laugh, or someone who'd targeted me specifically.

I couldn't think of anyone who would do the latter, except . . .

Could Grayson Blake's dislike of me run so deep that he'd vandalize my car?

It seemed like such a vicious prank, and while

the brewery owner was far from my favorite person, I never would have guessed that he'd stoop that low. But unless it was a random act of mischief, I couldn't think of any other suspects aside from Grayson.

Before I knew what I was doing, I was marching straight past the pub and down the road to the driveway that led up the wooded hillside to the Spirit Hill Brewery. There was one way to find out if Grayson Blake was responsible, and that was to confront him directly. I wasn't afraid to give him a piece of my mind if he deserved it.

I'd almost reached the foot of the driveway when I realized I wouldn't have to go all the way up to the brewery. Grayson was on his way down the driveway on foot, a white German shepherd trotting along with him. The dog couldn't have been very old. He still had a puppy's lankiness about him, and his ears looked far too big for him. The effect was ridiculously cute. Almost cute enough to distract me from my ire, but not quite.

I confronted Grayson as soon as he reached the road. "Did you slash my tires?"

"Did I what?" he asked, sounding baffled.

"Slash my tires," I repeated, enunciating the words.

He stared at me like I'd suddenly grown a second head. "Why would I do that?"

"Maybe because you have a problem with me being in Shady Creek?"

"That's not what I have a problem with." His gaze moved away from me, following his dog as it disappeared down the embankment toward the creek, its nose to the ground. "Bowie!" he called out, but the puppy didn't reappear.

I crossed my arms over my chest. "So you're saying you didn't slash my tires?"

His blue eyes returned to me. "No, I didn't. I'm not some punk. But if you need the number for a tow truck, I know—" A volley of loud barks interrupted him. "Bowie!" he called toward the creek, but once again the dog ignored him.

Grayson left the side of the road, heading toward the creek, and I followed after him. When he crested the highest point of the embankment, he halted and called out to his dog again, his voice urgent and commanding this time. I caught up to him as Bowie came bounding up the bank. Instead of my gaze following the puppy, it locked on something down by the creek.

A man lay sprawled on his back at the water's edge, unmoving on a bed of mud and wet leaves. Even from where I stood, I had no trouble recognizing him.

It was Eric. And the front of his shirt was stained with blood.

CHAPTER 4

I let out an involuntary, strangled cry and took a step forward. Grayson's hand closed around my wrist, halting me.

"Stay here."

Under other circumstances, I might have been irritated by his command, but I was too dazed to argue, and I wasn't sure if I would have been able to make it down the embankment anyway. My legs had gone all weak and shaky, making it a challenge just to stay on my feet. Maybe Grayson noticed that because he nodded toward a tree stump near the foot of his driveway.

"Why don't you go sit down?"

"But Eric . . ." My eyes zeroed in on his bloody shirt and his gray face. "He needs help."

"You know him?" Grayson asked with surprise.

I could only nod in response.

Grayson rested a hand on my upper back and gently turned me away from Eric's body. "It looks like he's been dead for a while now. I'll call the police."

I wanted to protest again, to argue that there could still be a chance to save Eric, but I couldn't get the words out. I knew they weren't true.

"Sit down," he said once we reached the stump.

"I'm not going to faint," I grumbled, but I sat

anyway. I didn't want to prove myself wrong, and my legs weren't going to support me much longer.

As I sank down onto the tree stump, Bowie trotted over and nudged my hand with his nose. I gave him a pat, and he sat next to me, leaning against my leg. I kept an arm around him, drawing comfort from his companionship while Grayson paced along the top of the embankment, his cell phone to his ear.

I still couldn't believe what I'd seen, that Eric could be dead. What could have happened to him? There was so much blood . . .

I tried to will away the image of his blood-soaked shirt and his lifeless face, but I couldn't get it out of my head. My stomach churned, and I had to draw in several deep breaths of the chilly morning air before I could feel confident that I wasn't about to lose my breakfast.

Sensing my distress, Bowie whined and licked my hand. I focused on him, stroking his white fur, and that helped to calm me. I didn't look up from the dog until I heard Grayson's footsteps crunching through some dry leaves as he approached. Bowie bounded to his side, and Grayson reach down to scratch him on the head.

"The police should be here soon."

I nodded but didn't say anything. A strange numbness had crept over me, dulling the sharp edges of my shock, but also slowing my mind. Whenever I tried grasping on to the edge of a thought, it slipped away before I could grab hold of it.

Fortunately, Grayson didn't seem interested in making conversation. With Bowie at his heels, he walked toward the edge of the road and faced toward the center of town, keeping a lookout. It couldn't have been more than a minute or two before he raised a hand and a patrol car came into view, pulling over to the side of the road.

I remained seated as Grayson greeted the man who climbed out of the driver's side of the vehicle, pointing up the gentle hill that led to the top of the embankment. I couldn't hear what they were saying, but I gathered that the officer asked Grayson to hang back while he went to have a look at the scene. A uniformed woman who climbed out of the passenger side of the vehicle followed after her colleague.

The two officers paused at the crest of the hill, but soon began picking their way down the muddy bank, disappearing from sight. They weren't gone for long, and when they reappeared, they both wore grim expressions. The man's gaze landed on me, and he headed in my direction while the woman spoke into her radio, her words inaudible from where I sat.

As the man approached, I got to my feet and pulled my sweater more tightly around me. My legs had stopped shaking, but the numbness remained.

"Police Chief Walters," the man said with a terse nod as he came to a stop in front of me.

"Sadie Coleman," I returned, relieved that I was able to speak without my voice wavering or cracking.

"I understand you and Mr. Blake found the body."

I winced at the way he referred to Eric as "the body," but I still managed to respond. "That's right."

"Do you recognize the deceased?"

My hands, holding my sweater closed, clenched around the soft yarn. "His name is Eric Jensen. He lives in Boston."

"You knew him then."

"He's my ex-boyfriend."

The police chief regarded me carefully. "Any idea what happened to him?"

I swallowed hard as the image of Eric's bloody body flashed in my mind yet again. "None at all," I managed to choke out.

Tears welled in my eyes, and I began trembling again, this time all over. It seemed the numbness was deserting me.

"Do you live nearby?" Walters asked.

"At the old mill," I replied, tipping my head in that direction as I blinked back my tears.

"You're the new owner of the pub?"

"Yes."

"If you're all right to get there on your own, I'll send someone over shortly to take your statement." He consulted his watch. "You don't open for a while yet, do you?"

"Not until noon."

"Then someone will meet you there."

Walters walked off to talk with Grayson as an unmarked car pulled up to park behind the police vehicle. I glanced at the driver on my way back to the mill. The woman who climbed out of the car was nearly six feet tall and dressed in a dark suit, her black hair pulled back into a twist. She removed her sunglasses, and from the purposeful way she strode over to talk with the police officers, I figured she was probably there in some sort of official capacity.

What would happen next to Eric, I wasn't keen to know. It was bad enough to think of him lying dead at the edge of the water. Imagining him getting poked, prodded, and photographed by the police brought fresh tears to my eyes. I tried holding them back, but by the time I was crossing the footbridge to the mill, they had spilled out onto my cheeks.

Glad that no patrons would be arriving for hours yet, I took refuge in the pub. I pulled out the nearest chair and collapsed into it, shaking with sobs. I hadn't wanted to see Eric, I hadn't wanted him to reappear in my life, but I would never have wished him dead. He'd irreparably fractured our relationship with his lies, but he didn't deserve to have his life cut short.

Briefly, I considered keeping the pub closed for the day, but I couldn't afford to lose an entire day's business. Maybe it was better for me to work, anyway. I didn't want to have too much time to think about what I'd seen by the creek.

I allowed myself to sit there and cry for several minutes, but then forced myself to get up and climb the stairs to my apartment. All I wanted to do was flop out on my bed and close my eyes, Wimsey at my side for company, but I needed to pull myself together before the police arrived to take my statement. I wouldn't be much use if all I could do was cry.

I stopped by the armchair where Wimsey was curled up and buried my face in his fur for a second or two before moving on to the bathroom, where I splashed my face with cold water. My cheeks were red and splotchy, but I knew that would fade before long. My red eyes, however, would likely take longer to return to normal.

Feeling marginally better after another few splashes of cold water, I returned to the pub and put a pot of coffee on to brew. While I waited for someone from the police department to arrive, I tried to keep busy so I wouldn't break down again. I polished the bar, even though it was already perfectly clean, and I shifted a few pint glasses on the shelf below the bar so they stood in tidy rows. I was in the midst of dusting the shelf holding my book collection when someone knocked on the front door. It opened right after, and the tall, dark-haired woman I'd noticed at the scene of Eric's death stepped into the pub.

"Sadie Coleman?" The woman had stopped just inside the door, and I realized that her eyes were probably adjusting to the relatively dim light of the pub compared to the bright sunshine outdoors.

"That's me." I set down the feather duster as she walked closer.

"Detective Marquez. I'd like to talk to you about Eric Jensen."

"Yes, of course. Would you like some coffee? It's fresh."

"That would be nice, thank you."

I fetched two clean mugs from behind the bar and filled them both with coffee, sliding one across the bar to Detective Marquez.

"Cream or sugar?"

"Black is good, thanks."

I added both to my own cup and gave it a stir.

"Shall we sit down?" The detective inclined her head toward one of the tables.

I joined her there, sitting across from her as she flipped open a notebook and removed a pen from the inner pocket of her suit jacket.

"I understand that you were in a relationship with Mr. Jensen," she said when she raised her eyes to meet mine.

"That's right." I wrapped my hands around my mug, wanting the warmth for comfort, but I let go quickly when I found that it was uncomfortably hot. "For about four years. We lived together in Boston up until a few months ago."

"That's when you moved here?"

"Almost. I came to visit my aunt after Eric and I broke up, and I decided to stay when I found out I could buy this place."

Marquez wrote something in her notebook. I tried to read the words she was setting out on the page, but I didn't have a good view, and I didn't want to be obvious about it.

"Had you seen Mr. Jensen since then?" she asked as she stopped writing.

"No. I haven't had any contact with him for at least three months now."

"So you didn't invite him to Shady Creek?"

"Definitely not. I didn't even know he was coming until he showed up here at the Inkwell."

"Did he tell you why he was here?"

"I didn't actually see or talk to him. I was on my way out for the evening when one of my staff told me he was here asking for me. I figured I'd talk to him later that night or this morning." My voice wavered on that last word. I took a quick sip of coffee to give myself a moment to recover from the fresh wave of emotion, but all I ended up doing was scalding my tongue.

"So you believe he came to Shady Creek to see you?"

I managed to keep my voice steady when I replied. "I assumed that was the case. He came in here and asked about me, and I don't know of any other reason why he'd come to Shady Creek."

"So he's not acquainted with anyone else in town?"

"Not to my knowledge." I gripped my coffee mug. "His family . . . do they know what happened?"

"I'll be informing them shortly. He had ID on him and a phone, but the battery is dead."

I patted my pocket and pulled out my own phone. "I think I've still got his parents' number in here. And I definitely have his sister's." It only took me a few seconds of searching to find what I was looking for. I pushed the device across the table, and Marquez copied down the numbers displayed on the screen.

"Thank you for that."

Maybe I should have offered to be the one to break the news to the Jensens—whether or not the detective would have taken me up on it—but I couldn't bring myself to form the words. That might have been for the best. I always got along with Eric's parents before, but I had no idea what they thought of me since the breakup. I was still on good terms with his sister, Natalie, but I couldn't bear the thought of being the one to tell her that her brother was dead.

"Do you have any idea when Mr. Jensen left the pub last night?"

"No. You'd have to ask Damien. That's Damien Keys. He works here. I was at my aunt's birthday dinner at Louie Edmonds's place. I left there around quarter past ten, watched the fire for a while, and came back here shortly before eleven. There was no one around by then."

"What time does the pub close on Tuesdays?"

"Ten o'clock."

She made note of that. "Can you tell me how you came to find the deceased this morning?"

I began the story by telling her how I'd gone out to the parking lot to find my car with all its tires slashed.

Marquez's eyebrows drew together. "Any idea who might have done that?"

"Not really. The only possible person I could think of was Grayson Blake."

"The man who was with you when you found the deceased."

"That's right."

"And why would you suspect him of slashing your tires?"

"He doesn't seem to like me much, though I don't know why. That's the only reason, really."

"But you suspected him rather than Mr. Jensen?"

"Eric would never have done something like that. And I really don't know if it was Grayson. He denied it when I confronted him. That's what I was doing when his dog found Eric down by the water."

The detective made some more notes in her book. As she finished up, the pub's door opened, and the uniformed officer I'd seen earlier with Chief Walters came inside.

Marquez took a quick drink of her coffee before setting the mug down and pushing back her chair. "Officer Delaney will take your official statement now." She handed me a business card. "I appreciate your time."

"Detective," I said before she could leave, "what happened to Eric? How did he die?"

"We won't have an official cause of death for a while yet."

"But unofficially? There was so much blood. Was he hit by a car?"

"I'm afraid I can't comment on that at this time." She nodded at her colleague. "I'll leave you with Officer Delaney."

I watched the detective as she left and wished she'd told me more. Maybe the police didn't know what had happened for sure, but I couldn't think of any explanation other than an accident for him to be lying dead down by the creek. The driver could have driven off in a panic, or maybe they didn't even realize they'd hit someone. The impact could have thrown Eric a long way, or he could have crawled to the top of the embankment, seriously injured, not knowing which way he was going, and then rolled down to the water's edge.

Picturing those scenarios made my eyes fill with tears again. I wiped them away with the cuff of my sweater as Officer Delaney took Detective Marquez's vacated seat. Then I pulled myself together as best I could and prepared to give the police officer my official statement.

CHAPTER 5

By the time Officer Delaney left the Inkwell, I was exhausted. It was only mid-morning, and I had a long day ahead of me, but giving in to the temptation to take a long nap wasn't an option. Since I couldn't drive to the pumpkin patch, I'd give Damien a hand with the catapult when he arrived. One way or another, we needed to be ready for the Autumn Festival, even if I wasn't feeling particularly festive at the moment.

Checking the time on my phone, I realized that Damien would likely show up soon. I spent a few minutes searching the Internet for a phone number for the local mechanic, and once I found it, I put a call through to the garage and arranged to have my car transported there and fitted with a new set of tires.

In addition to providing my statement to Officer Delaney, I'd filed a report with her about my slashed tires. I didn't expect anything to come of that, but I figured it didn't hurt to have the incident noted by the police. Now all I had left to do in that regard was to contact my insurance company. Hopefully I wouldn't have to pay too much out of my pocket for the new tires.

As I was about to return my phone to the

pocket of my jeans, I realized that I still needed it. I didn't want Aunt Gilda to find out about Eric through the grapevine, so I needed to fill her in before that happened. I tried calling her cell, but she didn't pick up. Considering the time, I knew she was likely busy with a client, but I didn't want to call the salon phone. That would most likely mean she'd receive the news with an audience. The news of a death in the town would spread before long, but that didn't mean I wanted to have a private conversation with my aunt in less-than-private circumstances.

I could have sent her a text, but I settled on leaving her a voice message. That way she could hear my voice when I assured her that I was okay, and hopefully that would keep her from worrying too much. I did the same for Shontelle, knowing I'd have to provide details to both of them at some point in the near future.

With that taken care of, I wandered out the front door and found Wimsey sitting like a sentinel atop one of the two rustic whiskey barrels located on either side of the entrance. I couldn't allow him in the pub without violating state regulations, but he liked to keep an eye on the place when he wasn't busy snoozing upstairs in the apartment. I'd installed cat doors at the entrance to my apartment as well as on the back door of the building, so he could come and go as he pleased during the day without ever setting a paw in any of the rooms that formed part of the pub.

He was popular with the patrons, and he deigned to being patted by those passing in or out of the Inkwell. I did just that, earning a hint of a purr as I noticed movement over by the shed on the pub's property. The double red doors of the small stone building stood open, and I could see someone moving within the shadowy interior.

Leaving Wimsey to keep watch over his kingdom, I headed across the grass to the shed.

"Morning, Sadie!" someone called out from behind me.

When I turned around, I saw Mel crossing the footbridge. I waited for her to catch up, and as she reached my side, Damien emerged from the shed.

"Any idea what's going on down the road?" Mel asked.

"I was going to ask the same thing," Damien said.

"Unfortunately." I tugged my sweater close around me. "Eric's dead."

That drew startled responses from both of my employees, and a barrage of questions quickly followed. I outlined everything that had happened that morning, wrapping up with Delaney's visit to the Inkwell to take my statement.

"That's terrible," Mel said once I'd finished. "How are you holding up?"

"I'm not really sure, to be honest. I keep going back and forth between grief and numbness."

"If you need the day off, Mel and I can take care of the pub," Damien offered.

I managed a small smile. "Thanks, but I think I'd rather keep busy."

"Do the police know what happened to Eric?" Mel asked.

"If they do, they're not telling me about it. The only thing I can think of is that he was a victim of a hit-and-run." My gaze wandered over to the shed. "Since I can't get to the pumpkin patch, I guess I'm free to help with the catapult."

"I could take you to the pumpkin patch in my truck," Mel said.

"What about the catapult? Don't you need help, Damien?"

"I can get started on my own," he assured me. "I'll probably get it finished today, but if I don't, maybe we can all work on it tomorrow."

"All right, that sounds like a good plan. Thanks, guys."

I locked the pub's front door and gave Wimsey a good-bye pat on the head before following Mel over to the battered pickup truck she'd left in the parking lot. I wasn't able to enjoy the excursion as much as I would have under different circumstances, but it did provide me with a distraction, and for that I was grateful.

An hour and a half later, Mel and I returned

to the Inkwell. As it turned out, it was probably for the best that we'd gone in her truck, considering the size of our pumpkin patch haul. I wouldn't have been able to buy nearly as much if I'd had my own car for transport. We even managed to pick up a few bales of straw from the farm next door to the pumpkin patch.

The sun had been up long enough now to take the edge off the chill in the air, so I dropped my sweater off inside before starting to unload all the pumpkins and gourds. Damien emerged from the shed and gave us a hand with the task, and soon the old grist mill looked far more ready for the Autumn Festival than it had earlier that morning. I still needed to get an autumn wreath for the door, and Mel's scarecrow wouldn't be ready for another day or two, but we definitely had some fall spirit going on now.

I placed one last gourd in the old red wheelbarrow that sat on the lawn, now almost overflowing with autumn bounty, and returned to the truck once more. The remaining pumpkins and gourds would go inside the Inkwell once I cleaned off the worst of the dirt. For the time being, we left them on the lawn around the back of the mill.

By then, it was nearly noon, and two tour buses had already arrived in town, disgorging gaggles of leaf peepers, some of whom would hopefully make their way over to the Inkwell for a drink and a light lunch once they'd checked out the shops around the village green.

At the moment, the Inkwell was without a cook—the one who'd worked at the pub under the previous ownership had moved away before I took over the business—so the only food items we had on offer were premade meat and veggie pies that only had to be heated up, and a large vat of soup, prepared and delivered each day by the local delicatessen. I had plans to make the Inkwell's menu more enticing, but I hadn't yet found a suitable cook.

As I was about to head inside, I noticed the delicatessen's truck heading for the mill, so I dashed inside to retrieve the rolling cart I used to transport heavy items across the footbridge. Once the delivery was complete and the large pot of soup was keeping warm on the stove in the Inkwell's kitchen, I hurried upstairs to change for the workday.

I didn't require Mel or Damien to dress up for work. They usually showed up in jeans, and that was fine with me. I often did the same, but sometimes taking my attire one step above casual helped me to feel like I fit into my new role as a business owner. And I needed to feel that way, because some days the thought of everything I'd taken on scared the heck out of me.

Once in my apartment, I traded my jeans and T-shirt for a gray jersey knit dress with long sleeves. I added black tights, a necklace, and one of my favorite pairs of fall boots, and then I was on my way downstairs again.

"Damien had to go to a dentist appointment," Mel informed me when I returned to the pub, "but he'll be back later to do some more work on the catapult before his shift starts."

"Sounds good. I seriously wouldn't know what to do without the two of you."

"Preparing for the festival always takes a team effort," she assured me as I put a fresh pot of coffee on to brew. "Did you hear about the fight?"

"Fight?" I turned around. "What fight?"

"I should have mentioned it first thing, but I forgot after hearing your news."

"A fight here at the Inkwell?"

She nodded. "Nothing serious. Damien tossed the guys out before it escalated, but Eric got into a shoving match with Carl Miller and Greg Wilmer."

I gaped at her in surprise before I managed to find my voice. "Eric? He isn't—wasn't—a fighter."

"He'd had a few drinks. He seemed nervous when he first showed up. I figured maybe he was worried about how you'd react to him being here."

"He was right to be worried." As soon as I said the words, I felt bad for speaking that way now that Eric was dead, even if the statement was a true one.

Fortunately, Mel didn't seem to think I was too harsh, and continued on with her tale.

"After he'd had a few beers, he started arguing with Carl and Greg—I don't know what about—and when the pushing and shoving started, Damien escorted them from the premises."

Maybe that helped to explain Eric's death. Had he wandered down the road, drunk, and stumbled into the path of an oncoming vehicle?

I pushed down a sudden surge of guilt. If I'd stayed behind to talk to Eric instead of going to Gilda's birthday dinner, maybe he wouldn't have had so many drinks. Even if he hadn't liked what I would have said to him, he might have left the Inkwell rather than hanging around in my establishment to drink away his sorrows.

With those thoughts fermenting in my mind, I gladly headed for the front door, eager to open for business and hopefully keep myself distracted by work. When I stepped outside to flip the sign on the door, four women in their fifties were crossing the footbridge, carrying several shopping bags each. My spirits were still low from the day's earlier events, but I made sure I didn't let that show, greeting the women cheerily and holding the door open as they passed into the pub.

I was going to follow them inside but stopped when I heard a familiar voice call out my name.

Aunt Gilda was hurrying across the footbridge in her high heels, so I let the door fall shut and met her on the flagstone path. As soon as I reached her, she opened her arms and enfolded me in her embrace.

"Oh, honey, I'm so sorry about what happened."

My eyes grew damp as I rested my head against her shoulder, grateful for the comforting hug. She patted my back and then held me out at arm's length.

"How are you holding up?" she asked as she scrutinized my face.

I blinked back threatening tears, not wanting to cry again. "I'm managing."

"What in heaven's name happened? You didn't say in your message how Eric died."

"That's because I don't know."

She hooked her arm through mine, and we slowly made our way along the path toward the pub as I gave her the few details I had to share. When we reached the door, we stopped and I stroked Wimsey's fur as he closed his blue eyes and purred away on his perch.

"It was awful to see him like that," I said, wrapping up my story. "I didn't love him anymore, but I never wanted him to die."

Gilda squeezed my arm. "Of course, you didn't, honey."

I glanced at the pub's door. "Do you have time for a coffee?"

She checked the delicate gold watch on her wrist. "I've got another client in five minutes, but if you need me here I can cancel."

"No, that's all right. I have to work anyway, and I'll be fine."

"You're sure?"

"Absolutely," I said with more confidence than I felt.

She pulled me into another hug. "I'll see you tonight for the book club, but you call me if you need me before then."

"Thank you, Aunt Gilda."

After giving me a kiss on the cheek, she set off toward the bridge again. I allowed myself to bury my face in Wimsey's silky fur for a moment, but I didn't linger any longer than that, instead heading back inside to get to work. Several more tourists arrived over the next half hour or so, and Mel and I kept busy serving drinks, bowls of soup, and meat and veggie pies. A few locals trickled in as well, and I steeled myself for the questions I knew I'd soon face. One thing I'd learned since moving to Shady Creek was that news traveled quickly through the small town. Anyone who didn't already know that my ex-boyfriend had been found dead down the road would hear the story from other patrons within minutes of arriving at the Inkwell.

Somehow I managed to stay composed as I was asked time and time again for specifics on what had happened. I only provided the barest of details, and I told everyone who asked that I didn't know how Eric had died. That was the truth, after all.

Of course, Eric's death wasn't the only hot topic of conversation among the locals. There was also the fire at the antiques shop to discuss. From the sound of things, Shady Creek rarely saw so much drama in such a short span of time.

"Do you think the two incidents could be related?" Susan Purdy, one of the Inkwell's regulars, asked as she sat at the bar. She was nursing a glass of the Malt in Our Stars, one of the first cocktails I'd created after buying the pub. It was made with Scotch, ginger ale, and lemon.

"I don't see how they could be," I said as I pulled a pint for another patron. I slid the full glass across the bar and accepted money from the man before he crossed the room to join his friends at a table. "We found Eric at the edge of the Spirit Hill Brewery property, and the fire was all the way across the green and down the road a bit."

"That's true." Susan took a sip of her drink. "It's just so unusual for Shady Creek to have two major events like that in less than twenty-four hours. I guess it's a coincidence."

"It must be," I agreed. "Have you heard

anything about the fire? Was anyone hurt? Do they know how it started?"

"No word yet on how it started, but luckily no one was hurt. There wasn't anyone in the building at the time, and none of the firefighters were harmed."

"That's good," I said with relief.

Susan left her perch on the stool to go and chat with a group near the middle of the pub. Moments later a new patron claimed her vacated seat.

"Evening," I greeted the man. "What can I get you?"

"Scotch. Neat," he requested in a gruff voice.

"Coming right up."

As I fetched the appropriate bottle from one of the shelves behind the bar, I tried to put a name to the man's face but came up empty. He seemed only vaguely familiar to me, and I wondered if he simply reminded me of someone else. I was pretty sure I'd never seen him in Shady Creek before. He had an imposing figure, tall and bulging with muscles, and his dark, beady eyes sent a hum of unease through me.

"Do you live here in Shady Creek?" I asked as I served him his drink, deciding to find out if I could place him in my memory.

"No."

He didn't look at me when he spoke, and his response was so abrupt as to warn me that he wasn't interested in conversation. At least, I thought he wasn't interested until he spoke up moments after finishing off his drink.

"I hear it was your ex who died down the road."

"That's right." The unease he'd instilled in me grew stronger.

He had his beady eyes fixed on me, and they held no warmth, only cold calculation. He held up his glass to indicate that he wanted another Scotch. I poured him one, and once he'd downed half of it in one go, he spoke again.

"Was he staying with you?"

"No." My internal alarm bells clanged. "Why do you ask?"

"No reason." He flashed what I suspected was meant to be a friendly smile, but to me it seemed predatory and chilling.

I held back a shudder and tried once again to figure out why he struck me as familiar. I still couldn't place him.

"Where are you from?" I tried to keep the question casual.

His expression, not open to begin with, closed off even more. "Here and there."

His accent was far more telling than his answer. Maybe he hadn't always lived in Boston, but he'd definitely spent enough time there to sound like it was his hometown.

He slapped a couple of bills on the bar, downed the rest of his drink, and got up, turning his back on me without another word. I tracked him with my eyes as he navigated his bulky frame around several tables and left the Inkwell.

Although I let out a sigh of relief when the door shut behind him, I couldn't shake the chill he'd left tickling at my spine.

CHAPTER 6

After the day I'd had, I was particularly grateful that I had something to look forward to that evening. I'd been excited about hosting book clubs at the pub ever since I first came up with the idea, and although the day's events had dampened my spirits, they hadn't completely overshadowed my enthusiasm.

Before the members of the romance book club arrived, I flicked on the lights in one of the two smaller rooms off to the side of the main part of the pub. I'd dubbed this one the Christie room, after one of my all-time favorite mystery authors. It had a couple of tables and regular chairs at the back of the room, but there were also some comfy armchairs and side tables clustered around the woodstove.

Framed posters from movies based on Agatha Christie classics like *Death on the Nile* and *Murder on the Orient Express* adorned the walls, while my collection of Christie novels lined the rustic bookshelves. My favorite piece of décor was the portrait of Dame Agatha that hung above an antique table where a vintage typewriter sat. Aunt Gilda had found the oil painting at a flea market in the summer and had given it to me as a gift when I'd taken over the pub. It was perfect for the Inkwell, and I liked to think there was a glint of approval in Agatha's eyes as she gazed out over the room named in her honor.

On busy nights when no book clubs were scheduled, I opened up the Christie room and its neighbor—the Stewart room, named after Mary Stewart—for overflow, but on nights like this one, the Christie room was reserved for the club.

Since the sun had gone down, the autumn chill had returned to the air, and I didn't mind one bit. The cool evening gave me the perfect excuse to use the woodstove, making the Christie room even cozier. By the time I had a cheerful blaze going, it was almost time for the book club to start. As I got up from the hearth and brushed off my knees, a plump woman with long and slightly wild gray hair poked her head into the room.

"Oh, there you are, Sadie."

"Hi, Alma," I greeted. "Come on in."

Alma Potts, one of the Inkwell's regulars and an avid reader of the romance genre, had volunteered to chair the book club.

"So these are our digs for the evening?" she said, entering the room, a hum of conversation from the main room drifting in behind her. When she spotted the fire, her face lit up. "Oh, that's a nice touch. It's chilly outside. The fire makes it nice and cozy in here."

"That's what I was hoping."

Before either of us had a chance to say more,

Shontelle appeared in the doorway, quickly followed by Aunt Gilda and Rhonda. While the other women greeted each other, Shontelle pulled me aside and gave me a quick hug.

"I was so shocked when I got your message. I'd heard from Sofie Talbot earlier that a man had died, but I had no idea it was Eric."

"It's still so hard to believe, but at the same time I can't get rid of the memory of him lying there covered in blood."

"And you still don't know what happened to him?"

I shook my head as a wave of laughter came from the other women. We turned toward them as Alma fished her dog-eared copy of *Caught Looking*, by Jody Holford, out of her large patchwork tote bag. From now on, the members would take turns choosing the book of the month, but for the first meeting I'd done the honors, with input from Alma.

"I'm sure looking forward to discussing this gem." Alma fanned herself with the book. "I do love hunky baseball players, and the one in this story is sizzling hot."

The other women murmured their agreement.

"How about I get drinks for everyone who wants one, and then you can all get started," I suggested.

"I'm trying one of the themed cocktails I haven't tasted yet," Shontelle said, snatching up one of the menus lying on the nearest table.

The other club members picked up their own copies to study, and it didn't take long for the orders to come in.

"I have to try the Happily Ever After," Aunt Gilda decided. "Awfully appropriate for a romance book club meeting, don't you think?" she said to the room at large.

Shontelle and Rhonda agreed enough to order the same cocktail, while Alma requested a Huckleberry Gin, made with gin, soda, and huckleberry syrup. I was about to head back to the bar to mix the drinks when the remaining two club members arrived.

"Oh, good, you're here," Alma said to them. "We can get started in a minute then."

Vera Anderson, owner of a local boutique, was followed into the Christie room by Harriet Jones, the oldest member of the book club. I didn't know her exact age, but I was pretty sure it was north of seventy. She wasn't your typical senior citizen, though, as I'd been quick to learn.

"I'll need a drink first," Harriet said, waving her copy of the book. "I'm going to need something to cool me down when we talk about this steamy hero."

"You've got that right," Shontelle agreed.

A couple of the other ladies giggled as I handed one of the menus to Harriet.

Vera Anderson ran her eyes down another copy

of the menu before dropping it onto the nearest table. "I'll have a glass of pinot gris."

Her nose in the air—where it always seemed to be—Vera claimed one of the armchairs and leaned over to talk quietly to Alma seated in the chair next to her.

"I'm feeling daring," Harriet said, drawing my attention away from Vera. "I'll try the Love-craft."

I beamed at her. "You'll be the first person to do so, aside from the staff here. It's our newest addition to the menu."

"What can I say? I've always been a trail-blazer."

Shontelle took Harriet's arm and led her over to the armchairs.

I'd taken an instant liking to Harriet when I'd met her a few weeks earlier while browsing the selection of novels at Primrose Books. Vera Anderson was another story, however. The few times I'd crossed paths with her, she always seemed condescending and critical of those around her, but so far, I'd managed to shrug off her attitude. I wasn't participating in the book club myself, so I didn't have to spend any real time with her.

After assuring the club that I'd have their drinks shortly, I left them to chat and returned to the bar. Mel's shift had ended earlier, so Damien was the one who helped me mix the drinks. I managed to fit all of them on one tray and returned to the Christie room with them.

"Sadie, you poor thing," Alma said. "I didn't realize the man found dead this morning was someone you knew. I gather he was your ex, but still, it must have been awful for you."

"A terrible shock," Rhonda agreed.

"Unless she was happy to find him dead," a voice whispered, just loud enough for me to hear.

My eyes darted over to Vera as she covered her mouth to unsuccessfully hide her quiet snigger. Alma frowned, but no one else seemed to have heard.

I swallowed hard as I handed a Huckleberry Gin to Alma. "It really was a terrible shock."

"And Grace King at the Creekside Inn said the young man was so hopeful that the two of you would be getting back together," Vera said, loud enough for the whole room to hear this time. "And then boom." She snapped her fingers. "His life is over."

Gilda and Shontelle both frowned in Vera's direction, but she didn't notice.

"He was staying at the Creekside Inn?" I said.

"Didn't you know?" Vera's eyes glittered in an unnerving way.

"I never actually spoke to him," I admitted. "I was at Aunt Gilda's birthday dinner last night, and then this morning . . ." I had to swallow again to keep my emotions in check.

Alma patted my arm. "We shouldn't be digging up all this unpleasantness for you. We just wanted to let you know that we're sorry for your loss."

"Thank you."

"Now," Alma said, taking charge, "time to get down to business."

"Just one more thing before we get started," Harriet said as I handed her the green Lovecraft cocktail, named for horror writer H. P. Lovecraft. Made with Midori liqueur, the drink balanced a sweet melon flavor with a citrus tang.

The other members of the club leaned forward in their seats as she raised the glass to her lips. She closed her eyes as she took a sip. We all waited in suspenseful silence for her judgment, my heart beating harder than normal. I wanted so desperately for every aspect of the pub to be a success, and I knew I'd be upset if the themed cocktails were anything but a hit.

Harriet kept her eyes closed for another second or two, but when she opened them, she grinned. "Horrifically fabulous," she declared.

I exhaled with relief, and Harriet winked at me before I left the room with my empty tray, pulling the door shut behind me. That, at least, had gone well, and I was able to return to the bar with something close to a smile on my face.

Thankfully, by the time I'd closed and cleaned up the pub later that night, I was so tired that I slipped off to sleep as soon as I rested my head against the pillow. I expected to have nightmares, or at the very least unsettled dreams, but I remembered nothing of the sort when I woke up the following morning. It seemed like only a minute or two had passed from the time I closed my eyes to the moment when four little paws padded their way up my side and a furry face nestled against my cheek.

"Mrrgh," I said to Wimsey without opening my eyes.

As usual, he wasn't put off that easily. When his meows failed to get me out of bed, he resorted to pawing at the covers in an attempt to get them off me.

With a sigh of defeat, I forced my eyes open and gave Wimsey a scratch on the head. He purred loudly, enjoying the attention for a moment before deciding that we'd wasted enough time.

With a pointed meow, he jumped down from the bed and trotted to the doorway. He paused there, looking back at me, so I did as expected, throwing back the covers and undertaking the difficult task of getting myself out of bed.

Once His Lordship was fed to his satisfaction, I ate my own breakfast of oatmeal—liberally sprinkled with chocolate chips—and dressed for the morning in jeans and a T-shirt. Despite all that had happened the day before, I didn't have time to wallow in the jumbled emotions that Eric's arrival and subsequent death had triggered. The opening of the Autumn Festival was only two days away now, and I had a long list of things to do before then.

Wimsey followed me out of the apartment and down the stairs, so I went out through the back door, and he settled on the step to watch the birds flitting about at the edge of the forest. I tipped my face up to the sky, hoping to find some warmth, but the sun wasn't yet high enough to reach me between the mill and the forest. The chilly morning air seeped easily through the fabric of my T-shirt, and I considered running back upstairs to grab a sweater, but in the end, I decided to get moving. A bit of physical labor would warm me up in no time.

My first task of the day was to deal with the pumpkins I meant to use as indoor decorations. With the help of a bucket of water and an old cloth, I cleaned off the pumpkins and gourds, wiping them dry with another cloth once they were free of dirt. It took me several trips to get them all inside the pub, and by the time I had each one placed where I wanted it, I was more than warm enough.

Back outdoors, Damien had just arrived on his motorcycle, ready to get back to work on the catapult. I met him at the shed, unlocking the padlock and pulling open the double doors.

"Wow," I said, impressed. "It looks like you've already made good progress."

"I got a fair bit done yesterday." Damien tossed his leather jacket onto the workbench.

"I'll say." He already had the base and part of the frame together. "What do you need me to do?"

"Hold pieces in place while I secure them?"

"Sounds good to me." That was about the only job that would match my construction skills. "How many of these have you made before?" I asked as he collected some screws from a glass jar.

"This will be my fourth."

"Has the pub ever won the competition?"

"Nope. We came in fifth last year. That was our best ever finish." He cast a sidelong glance my way as he attached a bit to his drill. "Have you got your eye on the top prize?"

"Heck, no. I'm just in it to show community spirit." As soon as the words were out of my mouth, I wondered if I'd said the wrong thing. "Are *you* hoping to win?"

"I'm always hoping to win, but I won't be cut up about it if we don't. Like you said, it's really about the community spirit."

For the next while, I simply did whatever Damien instructed me to do, and we soon had a pivoting beam attached to the frame and a sling and pouch affixed to one end of the beam.

"What's left?" I asked when we paused for a break.

"Just the counterweight. This is a trebuchet we're building. In the past, the catapults I've made have been more like giant slingshots. I'm hoping this will be more accurate."

I eyed the plans he had spread out on the workbench, covered with numbers for measurements and angles.

"It's definitely going to be more accurate than anything I could have built on my own." I pulled my phone from the pocket of my jeans and checked the time. The morning was half gone already. "Do you need any more help?"

"No, you go on. I'll attach the counterweight in a couple of days. And I'll get our booth set up on the green tomorrow. For now, I'll get tidied up here and then head off until my shift starts."

"All right. I'll see you later then. Thanks, Damien."

Leaving him in the shed, I wandered outside and turned my eyes to the sky again. Maybe I'd need a sweater after all. Over the past hour or so, clouds had moved in, blotting out the sun. But instead of heading indoors, I decided to nip across the road to see how things were taking shape for the festival.

As soon as I'd crossed the footbridge, the sound of distant hammering reached my ears, a sign that Damien and I weren't the only ones gearing up for the festivities. I followed the sound across the street to the village green, where nearly a dozen people were already hard at work. A handful of people from various local businesses were busy setting up booths where they would display their goods and share information with the festival attendees. At the western end of the green, beyond the bandstand, several other people were in the midst of setting up a large white tent.

I struck off across the grass, heading for the half-raised tent. As I approached, I spotted Rhonda among the workers, and I waved when she glanced my way.

"Morning, Sadie," she said as she left the others to meet me. "I had a great time at the book club last night."

I smiled at that news. "I'm so glad. I'm hoping all the clubs will be a success."

"I'm sure they will be."

"I'm guessing this is for the beer tasting," I said with a nod toward the tent, where two men were hammering metal stakes into the ground.

"Yep. The adults-only area. I think Vera Anderson wants to talk to you about that."

"Oh?"

One of the men helping with the tent called out Rhonda's name.

"Sorry," she said to me, already heading back to the others. "Vera wants this ready within the hour, and we don't want to get on her bad side."

I could understand that. I'd been told Vera was the head organizer for the Autumn Festival and had been for several years running. She was efficient and organized, but I doubted she'd hold back on some rather sharp comments if someone didn't live up to her expectations.

I retraced my steps across the green, a hint of indignation burning at my cheeks as I recalled Vera's whispered comment the night before. The fact that someone could even suggest that I might have wanted Eric dead both shocked and irked me. Vera had never been one of my favorite people in Shady Creek, but I was now on the verge of seriously disliking her.

Not wanting to waste my time thinking about the woman's petty words, I decided instead to focus on my festival preparations. I stopped at the nearest half-assembled booth, where Joel Whitten, owner of the local hardware store, was busily hammering a sign to the front of the booth, the name of his business painted across it in bright red letters.

"Morning, Mr. Whitten. I don't suppose you know where the Inkwell's booth is supposed to go," I said once he'd glanced up from his work.

He had two nails clamped between his lips, but he spat them into his hand before responding. "Nope. Sorry. But Vera will tell you."

He gestured over my shoulder, and when I cast my gaze that way I saw Vera bustling across the grass, clipboard in hand, heading for Rhonda and those helping her with the tent. I thanked Mr. Whitten and set off after her.

At her brisk pace, Vera reached the tent within seconds. She only spent a brief moment talking to Rhonda before noting something on her clipboard and striking off across the grass again, this time heading for Mr. Whitten. I intercepted her before she could reach the hardware store owner.

"Mrs. Anderson, whereabouts should we be setting up the Inkwell's booth? Damien's planning to work on it tomorrow morning."

"In the tent." She jabbed at the air over her shoulder with her pen, not slowing her pace at all.

I hurried to reach her side again. "Isn't that where the Spirit Hill Brewery booth will be?" I asked with some confusion.

"Exactly."

"You mean we'll be sharing the space?" The idea of being stuck in a tent with Grayson Blake for a big chunk of the upcoming week didn't appeal to me in the least.

Vera finally drew to a stop, though not without a huff of irritation. "It's a large space, Ms. Coleman. There's plenty of room for both booths in there."

"Yes, of course," I said quickly. "But I just assumed the Inkwell would have a booth out here with the rest of the businesses."

"Obviously you assumed wrong. The pub's booth needs to be in the tent with the brewery's. Festival attendees interested in one will most likely be interested in the other. Plus, I understand you intend to serve alcohol. That has to take place in the tent so we can check IDs before people go in."

"I guess that makes sense." I couldn't keep a note of disappointment out of my voice.

"Of course it makes sense." Vera took a step toward Mr. Whitten, who was back to hammering away at his booth, but then she stopped and faced me again. "I suppose the police will be interviewing you again, if they haven't already."

"The police?" It took me a second to adjust to the new direction of the conversation. "Why?"

"Because of the change in status of the investigation."

My heart shifted from a normal rate to a galloping one in an instant. "What change in status?"

"You mean you haven't heard?" She smiled, taking obvious pleasure in delivering the news. "The police now consider your ex's death to be a homicide."

CHAPTER 7

"Homicide?" The word came out as little more than a horrified croak. I cleared my throat before speaking again. "Are you sure?"

"Of course, I'm sure." Vera glared down her pointy nose at me. "I'm not one to spread idle gossip. My nephew Eldon is on the police force. This is the first homicide investigation in Shady Creek since he became an officer."

"But who would want to murder Eric? He didn't even know anyone here in Shady Creek."

Vera shrugged her thin shoulders. "Perhaps it was a robbery gone wrong or some such thing. But I'm sure the police will want to rule out the possibility of a targeted killing."

I struggled to find my voice again. "That shouldn't be hard to do. Like I said, Eric didn't know anyone in Shady Creek, except for me."

A smug smile tugged at Vera's rose-pink lips. "And that's why I'm sure the police will want to talk to you again." She tucked her clipboard under one arm. "Now, if you'll excuse me, I have a festival to organize."

She hurried off, and I stared after her, probably doing a good impersonation of a fish, opening and closing my mouth as all the things I wanted to say tumbled around inside my head, never quite managing to make it out into the cool air. Vera didn't look back, her chin up as she strode across the grass, somehow managing to stay completely steady despite the fact that she was traversing uneven ground in high heels.

It took a few moments, but eventually I shut my mouth and turned toward home. I must have walked across the green and back over the footbridge, because I found myself at the Inkwell's large red door, but I didn't remember the journey. Vera's news had left me numb and stunned. My mind seemed incapable of any sort of coherent thought, and for a minute or two, I simply stared at the door, time flowing past me, steadily moving onward while I went nowhere.

When I finally managed to shake myself out of my stupor, I grasped the door handle, the metal cold against my skin. The sensation startled me into greater awareness. I yanked at the door, but when it didn't budge, I realized that it was locked. As I dug around in my pocket for my keys, I heard the tap-tap-tap of high heels on the wooden footbridge.

"I came over as soon as I heard the news," Shontelle said as she hurried toward me. The moment I was within arm's reach, she pulled me into a hug. "It's so terrible. How are you doing?" Before I had a chance to answer, her eyes widened. "You have heard, right? You look shocked enough."

"If you're talking about Eric and the fact that the police are now conducting a homicide investigation, yes, I just found out from Vera Anderson."

Shontelle frowned. "I bet that made her day."

"I think it did." I unlocked the door and yanked at it with greater success than my last attempt. "It must have been a random killing. Nothing else makes sense. Maybe some drunkard was passing through town and tried to rob Eric."

While sharing that theory, I headed for the bar and slipped onto a stool, not trusting my legs to hold me much longer. My numbness was ebbing away, but it hadn't yet left me completely.

Shontelle bypassed the stools and made her way behind the bar. "You look like you need a drink."

"Something strong," I agreed.

She grabbed a bottle of peach brandy and poured some into a snifter before pushing the glass across the bar. I wrapped one hand around the snifter and took a sip. The brandy chased away the remaining vestiges of my shock, and by the time I'd emptied the glass, my tense muscles had relaxed, and I no longer felt quite so off-kilter.

"Are you going to be all right?" Shontelle asked as she came out from behind the bar. "I hate to do this, but I've got to get back to the shop. I closed it and put out a sign saying I'd be back in fifteen minutes."

"I'll be fine," I assured her. "The drink helped. You go on back to your shop before you lose out on any customers."

"We'll have a good talk later." She squeezed my arm as she passed by on her way to the door. "And text me if you need me."

"Thank you," I called out before the door fell shut behind her.

Now that I was alone, silence settled over me like a heavy blanket. I stared into my empty glass, thinking about Eric's family and how this new information would only hurt them further. It was bad enough that Eric had been taken away from them so suddenly, but to know that someone had deliberately ended his life added an extra stroke of cruelty to an already terrible situation.

I probably would have stayed there on the barstool, ruminating on Vera's news until Mel showed up for her shift if a loud knock on the pub's door hadn't interrupted my thoughts. Thinking it might be tourists hoping to get into the pub early, I replaced what was most likely a melancholy expression with something close to a smile. It slipped away half a second later when I discovered Detective Marquez on the other side of the door.

"Ms. Coleman, do you have a moment? I'd like to ask you a few more questions."

I stared at the detective for a couple of seconds before giving myself a swift mental kick. I really needed to stop letting myself get so shocked by everything. Otherwise the whole town would start to think I was a few bricks shy of a full load.

"Of course. Please, come in." I held the door open for her, and she headed straight for the table we'd occupied the day before. "Coffee?" I offered, even though I didn't have any ready.

"That won't be necessary, thank you." She pulled out a chair and nodded at the one across from her.

Obediently, I took a seat, folding my hands in my lap. "I just heard the news. About Eric's death being a murder, I mean. Was it a random attack? It had to be, right?" I clamped my mouth shut, realizing that I was on the verge of rambling, if not already over the edge.

"We don't yet know what happened. It's early days, and we're still waiting on the postmortem."

"But you know enough to believe Eric was murdered."

"We're confident it was a homicide, yes."

"How was he killed?" I asked the question with a good deal of apprehension, wanting to know the answer and not wanting to know it at the same time.

"I'm afraid I can't disclose that at this time."

I twisted one of the silver rings on my right hand. "So what did you want to ask me?"

"Yesterday you said you had no idea that Mr. Jensen was coming to Shady Creek."

"That's right."

"And although you knew he was in town soon after his arrival, you didn't see or speak to him."

"Right," I said again.

"Are you sure about that?"

"Of course, I'm sure." I met Marquez's dark, steady gaze and a thread of anxiety quivered its way along my spine. "I was at Louie Edmonds's place all evening, celebrating my aunt's birthday. She'll confirm that. So will everyone else who was there." I hated that I sounded like I was defending myself. I didn't need to do that.

Did I?

Marquez glanced down at her notebook. "And you left Mr. Edmonds's house at around ten-fifteen?"

"Yes. Just as I told you yesterday." I tried to keep my voice calm, but I could hear that it was becoming strained by anxiety.

"And after that?"

"As I said before, I realized that the antiques shop was on fire. I watched the firefighters for a while, and then I walked home and went to bed."

"You walked home by yourself?"

"Yes."

"After parting ways with Mr. Grayson Blake."

I hadn't mentioned that in our first conversation. Had she spoken to Grayson about that evening, or had someone else filled her in on my movements?

I nodded, and the detective continued.

"Eric Jensen was found on the border between your property and Mr. Blake's. You didn't see or hear anything when you arrived home?"

"No, nothing. Why? Was Eric already dead by then?" My stomach gave an unpleasant squeeze at the thought of Eric lying there all night.

"We don't have a precise time of death at this point," was the detective's non-answer. "So you had no contact with Mr. Jensen while he was in Shady Creek?"

"None." Frustration mingled with my increasing concern. "Why do you keep asking me the same questions?"

"I'm merely trying to get a clear picture of the events surrounding Mr. Jensen's death. How about before he arrived in Shady Creek? When's the last time you had any contact with him?"

"About four months ago, a few days after we broke up."

"What did you talk about on that occasion?"

I wanted to ask how that could possibly be relevant, but the no-nonsense expression on the detective's face kept me on track. "I was retrieving the last of my belongings from the apartment we shared in Boston. Eric asked me to give our relationship another chance, and I told him we were done for good."

"Had you broken up before?"

"Once, about a year before that."

"And what was the problem—or problems—in your relationship?"

This time I couldn't stop my own question from bursting out. "What does any of this have to do with his death?"

"Please answer the question, Ms. Coleman."

"His gambling addiction. His lies. That's what came between us."

"And when you broke up again four months ago, the reasons were the same?"

"Yes. He hadn't been getting help for his problem like he'd promised. He was lying to me again. Still."

"And stealing from you."

I stared at her in astonishment. "How did you find out about that?"

"We've been in touch with his family."

Of course. I didn't know if Eric's parents knew about that particular incident, but his sister did. Natalie and I had been friends since I'd first met her through Eric, and I'd told her about the theft soon after it happened. It was the final straw, the one that drove me to ending my relationship with Eric once and for all. There was no trust left by that point, nothing at all that could sustain a healthy relationship.

"He stole one of my credit cards and used it for online gambling," I told Marquez, though she probably knew all the details already.

"That must have made you angry."

Alarm bells rang in my head.

"Hold on a moment. Am I a suspect?" My astonishment and wariness were evident in my voice.

"I'm just trying to get a picture of Mr. Jensen's life and the circumstances surrounding his death."

Her carefully worded response wasn't fooling me.

My stomach twisted into a tight, bulky knot, and my throat went dry.

"I didn't kill Eric. I didn't even see him here in Shady Creek until he was dead."

"I never said you did."

I felt like I'd been backed into a corner without realizing it. I'd foolishly had my defenses down, and now I had to scramble to protect myself.

"I don't think I should answer any more questions, not without a lawyer present."

Detective Marquez snapped her notebook shut. "If that's your preference."

"It is," I said firmly, despite my almost paralyzing trepidation.

Marquez pushed back her chair and got to her feet. "Thank you for your time, Ms. Coleman."

I didn't move, sitting there stiffly while she left the Inkwell. When the door latched behind her, I realized that my hands were clasped so tightly that my knuckles had turned white. I released them, but then they trembled, so I pressed them flat against the tabletop. As I stared at my splayed hands, my fear and worry slowly morphed into indignation and irritation.

How could anyone think even for a second that I might have killed Eric?

Okay, so the police here in Shady Creek didn't know me. I was an outsider to pretty much everyone here, aside from Aunt Gilda and a couple of friends. Still, the thought that I could be suspected of murder was preposterous. Frightening too, but most assuredly preposterous.

I frowned and let my hands drop down to my lap. First, Eric attempted to disrupt my life here in Shady Creek by showing up unannounced, and now, even though he was dead, he was still causing problems for me.

As soon as that thought formed in my head, guilt poked at my ribs. It was a terrible thing to think, even if there was some truth to it. It wasn't as if Eric had planned to get murdered.

Nevertheless, his death could now be threatening the new life I'd so carefully built over the past few months. I didn't see how the police could possibly find enough evidence to arrest me for a murder I didn't commit, but even if it didn't get to that point, my reputation, my business, and my place in the community could all end up irreparably damaged.

That thought nudged me close to the edge of panic. I jumped up from my seat and paced back and forth between the tables, trying to release some of my anxious energy. My gaze fell upon the books lining the exposed stone walls, the cheerful light holders Rhonda had given me, the pumpkins and gourds. I'd only owned the Inkwell for a matter of weeks, but I loved it with all my heart and soul already.

This place meant so much to me. This *life* meant so much to me. I couldn't stand around worrying, letting it slip through my grasp. I needed to clear my name, to chase away the cloud of suspicion gathering above my head before it overshadowed everything good in my life.

And if I could help get justice for Eric and his family in the process, so much the better.

The question was, where should I start?

CHAPTER 8

I cuddled a reluctant Wimsey and scarfed down a bar of dark chocolate before I decided on a plan of action. I needed information, and I knew where to look for it, but I couldn't leave the mill quite yet. The pub was due to open in half an hour, and I didn't want to leave any customers on the doorstep, contemplating other places to spend their time and money.

Fortified with the delicious dose of chocolate, I changed into a long-sleeved, dark green dress and wove my hair into a side braid. That done, I returned to the lower level, just in time to greet Mel as she arrived for her shift. The first customers of the day were right behind her, so I spent a few minutes chatting with a group of leaf peepers and serving food and drinks. Once everyone had been taken care of for the time being, I asked Mel if she could hold down the fort for a bit.

"Sure thing." She lowered her voice. "I heard about the murder investigation. How are you doing?"

"I'm coping, but it hasn't helped that the police seem to have their sights on me as their number-one suspect."

"No way."

I appreciated the incredulity in her voice.

"That's the message I got from all the questions the detective was asking me this morning."

"You shouldn't answer any questions without a lawyer then."

"That's my plan from here on out." I glanced around the pub, noting that everyone still appeared to be occupied with their food and drinks. "Call my cell if you need me back here. Hopefully I won't be too long."

"I left the scarecrow out front. Take a look on your way, and let me know if you want any changes."

I thanked her and hurried out to see her creation. As soon as I saw the scarecrow, a smile spread across my face. He wasn't the least bit creepy, and to my delight, Mel had decked him out to look like Sherlock Holmes. The scarecrow wore a tweed suit and a deerstalker hat. A pipe stuck out from between his painted-on lips, and he held a magnifying glass in one stuffed hand. He was posed behind the handles of the old wheelbarrow, and it looked like he was inspecting the pumpkins for clues.

I ducked back into the pub and gave Mel two thumbs-up as I mouthed, "I love it!"

When she grinned in my direction, I waved and stepped back outside. Wimsey had appeared in my brief absence and was stalking carefully toward the scarecrow. When he reached it, he leaned forward for a cautious sniff of Sherlock's leg.

"What do you think, Wims?" I asked.

He sniffed the tweed again, and then sat down on the grass, gazing up at the straw-filled detective.

"All good?" I gave Wimsey a pat on the head. "I think so too. See you later, buddy."

I left my cat there with his new companion and set off up the street in the opposite direction from the Spirit Hill Brewery. Beyond the pub's small parking lot, I passed by Rhonda's house and three other houses before reaching the Creekside Inn.

Built in the Queen Anne style when the town was still in its early decades, the Creekside Inn had once been a large and stately private home, but at some point, it had been transformed into accommodations for visitors to Shady Creek. I wasn't sure if that was the doing of the current owner, Grace King, or if it had happened some-time previously. Either way, I'd heard that it was a popular place for tourists to stay, and I'd been hoping for a chance to get a look inside. It was so beautiful and charming from the outside, and I suspected the interior was just as gorgeous. Taking in the architecture and the character wasn't my purpose at the moment, but catching a glimpse of the interior would be a bonus.

I was about to head up the walkway to the front porch when a voice hailed me from down the street. When I spotted Joey Fontana heading my way, I didn't know if I should be wary or glad to see him. Joey was the reporter for Shady Creek's community newspaper. He'd done a story on the Inkwell when I first took over the pub, and I appreciated his help with getting the word out about the changes I'd made to the business. He was in his mid-twenties, energetic, and enthusiastic, but I'd heard that he was also tenacious, and I didn't think he was hurrying this way to ask me about my plans for the Autumn Festival.

"Hey, Sadie." Joey ran a hand through his dark hair, raking it off his forehead. "I was hoping I'd be able to track you down."

"I think I can guess why. In fact, I'm surprised you're only showing up now."

He grinned and shrugged. "It's been an eventful couple of days."

"I'll say."

"So what's the chance you'll give me an interview?"

"Zero."

"Come on. You found the body along with Grayson Blake, *and* the guy was your ex. You're at the heart of the story."

"I know you're just doing your job, Joey, but I don't want people gossiping about Eric any more than they probably are already. He deserves some respect."

Joey held up his hands in surrender. "I can be respectful. The *Shady Creek Tribune* isn't a tabloid, you know."

"I do know that," I said with a sigh. "And I don't mean to be rude, but I really don't want to give an interview right now."

"Right now?" he said, latching onto those words.

I walked toward the inn, leaving him by the road. "Probably never," I called over my shoulder.

"Probably?"

I ignored him.

The hand-painted sign on the inn's front door invited visitors to go right in, so that's what I did. Fortunately, Joey didn't follow me. I hoped that meant he'd given up on the idea of interviewing me, but I doubted it.

When I stepped inside the inn, I found myself in a spacious foyer with beautiful hardwood floors and an elegant staircase curving up toward the second story. To my right was an antique wooden bench, a side table next to it holding a vase of bright flowers. On my left, a large wooden desk sat unoccupied.

I paused for a moment, listening. I couldn't see anyone, but I thought perhaps I heard a murmur of voices somewhere in the distance. A silver bell rested on the desk, so I gave it a tap, the chime sounding loud in the quiet of the foyer.

The bell had the desired effect, footsteps immediately heading my way. A second later, a young woman appeared in the hallway leading toward the back of the house, smiling as she hurried toward me.

"Hello!" she greeted cheerily. "I'm Cordelia King. How can I help you?"

Like me, Cordelia had red hair, though hers was more orange than copper, and while mine was straight, hers was crinkly and formed a soft cloud around her face before reaching all the way down to her waist.

"I'm Sadie Coleman," I said to begin.

Cordelia's blue eyes lit up. "The new owner of the pub!"

"That's right."

"I just love the idea of a literary pub," she enthused. "I heard you're hosting book clubs. Will there be one for mystery readers?"

"Absolutely. That's my favorite genre."

"Mine too!"

I couldn't help but smile at the energy she exuded.

"I'd love to join the club."

"No problem. I'll sign you up. And if you give me your e-mail address, I'll add you to the mailing list so you get all of the meeting reminders and other information."

"Perfect."

She fluttered behind the desk and grabbed a

slip of paper, jotting down an e-mail address. "But that's not why you're here," she said as she handed me the paper. "Sorry about that. My gran's always telling me that getting off track is my superpower. Luckily, she lets me work here anyway."

"The owner is your grandmother?"

"That's right. I just moved back to town recently, and I've been helping her out since . . ." She lowered her voice to a conspiratorial level. "She's not exactly getting any younger." She held up a hand. "But wait. There I go, getting off track again. What can I do for you?"

"I understand Eric Jensen was staying here."

Cordelia's face paled to the point of leaving her looking like a ghost, her freckles standing out like bright specks, although with her skin tone, that didn't take much. She pressed a hand over her heart. "That was the most tragic thing. I'm the one who checked him in. And then the next day the police showed up on the doorstep to tell us he was dead." She glanced down the empty hallway and then up the stairs before lowering her voice once more. "And now they say he was murdered! In Shady Creek! Gran and I were completely shocked."

"It came as a shock to me too."

She inhaled sharply. "Of course! You found his body, didn't you? Along with Mr. Blake from the brewery."

"He was my ex-boyfriend. Eric, not Grayson Blake."

Her eyes widened again, this time to the point where I thought they might pop right out of her head. "Oh, my goodness. I'm so sorry. And here I am gossiping away like an insensitive fool."

"It's all right," I rushed to assure her. "But I'm trying to fill in some blanks. I never actually spoke to him before he died. But I understand he was in town to see me."

"Yes, he was. He told me and Gran how he was here to win back his girlfriend. And he showed us the ring." She gazed heavenward for a second. "So beautiful."

"Ring? What ring?"

"Oh, of course, you wouldn't have had a chance to see it. It was gorgeous. Silver with such a brilliant sapphire. I mean, I'm no expert, so I don't know if it was real or not, but it certainly looked amazing. It's so sad he didn't get a chance to give it to you."

Had Eric meant it as an engagement ring? He had to have been delusional to think I wanted to marry him. Even if it was just meant to be a gift, I never would have accepted the ring. I didn't bother to mention that to Cordelia.

Its purpose aside, how had Eric afforded a ring of any sort, having driven himself into a deep hole of debt?

"Did he say anything else?" I asked. "Did he

mention that he knew anyone else in this town?"

"No, sorry. He only spoke about you. Oh." She smacked herself on the side of her head. "He did mention the job."

"Job?"

"At the brewery. Apparently, he had experience working in that field?"

I nodded. At the time of our breakup, he'd been working for a large chain of breweries, dealing with distribution.

"Well, right after he arrived in the late afternoon, he said he was heading straight over to Spirit Hill to see if he could get a job there so he could be closer to his girlfriend."

I tried not to look as taken aback as I felt. How could he have been so confident that I'd want him here in Shady Creek?

Eric was a smart guy in many ways, but clearly not in others.

A door closed somewhere deep in the house. Cordelia glanced at the still-deserted stairway before continuing. "He didn't look too happy later that day, though he didn't say why. But I heard through the grapevine that things most definitely didn't go well at the brewery."

"How do you mean?"

"Apparently Mr. Blake had your Mr. Jensen escorted from the property." She leaned over the desk toward me. "According to my friend Annalisa—she's a receptionist at the brewery—

Mr. Blake absolutely tore into Mr. Jensen. Annalisa had never seen Mr. Blake get angry like that. Not even close. He's usually as cool as a cucumber. But not that day."

My curiosity was most definitely piqued now. "Any idea why he got so mad at Eric?"

She frowned in disappointment. "Unfortunately, no. Annalisa didn't hear any specific words, just the raised voices."

I shared in her disappointment. I had no idea what Eric might have done to get Grayson mad at him, but it was most definitely an interesting tidbit of information. How mad did Grayson get, exactly? Mad enough to kill?

We'd found Eric at the edge of the brewery property. Had he returned there that evening, his audacity driving Grayson into a murderous rage?

Wasn't the person who found the victim of a homicide often a suspect? I'd met up with Grayson while he was coming down his driveway with his dog. Even if Bowie hadn't raised the alarm, was it Grayson's intention to "accidentally" find Eric's body?

It was definitely something to consider.

"Do you know if the ring's been recovered?" I asked. "If it's missing, that could mean Eric was killed during a robbery."

"I told the police about it when they were here yesterday. They went through all of his belongings but didn't find it. Maybe he took it with him to the brewery, thinking he'd see you before he came back to the inn. But when I told the police about the ring, I got the distinct impression that they didn't know anything about it. That must mean they didn't find anything of the sort on his body, right?"

"That sounds like a safe assumption."

But would Grayson have stolen the ring if he'd killed Eric out of anger?

Maybe, particularly if he'd hoped to throw the police off his scent so they'd look for a violent robber rather than someone with an entirely different motive.

"Did you want to see his belongings?"

The offer took me by surprise, and I found myself torn between wanting to look for clues and not wanting to deal with the emotions that handling Eric's things might bring to the surface.

"The police are done with them, so my gran wants me to pack them up and put his suitcase in the storage closet until someone from his family picks it up or asks us to ship it to them. Being that it's leaf-peeper season, that room is solidly booked, starting tomorrow."

"How did he manage to get a room here at such a busy time?" I asked, putting off my answer to Cordelia's question for the moment.

"Pure luck, really. Good luck for him, and bad luck for someone else. The couple who had that room booked for three nights couldn't make it in the end. The woman ended up with appendicitis and had to have surgery. So their vacation went out the window."

I wasn't so sure that it was good luck for Eric, considering how things turned out. Maybe it would have been better for him if he hadn't found a place to stay in town. Maybe then he would have been elsewhere and wouldn't have ended up dead.

"I can help you pack up Eric's things," I offered, still not sure if that was something I really wanted to do.

I thought Cordelia might fall over with relief. "Would you? That would be so nice of you. To be honest, I've been a bit creeped out by the idea of touching a dead man's things. Having company would make it so much easier."

I glanced at the porcelain mantel clock on the shelf behind the reception desk. "I need to get back to the pub soon, but I'm guessing Eric didn't bring too much with him."

Unless he was so confident that I'd want him in Shady Creek that he'd moved his entire life here.

"Just one suitcase," Cordelia said. "Should we tackle it right now?"

"Please."

She stepped out from behind the desk and headed for the staircase so quickly that her crinkly hair fluffed out behind her on her self-made breeze. "This way."

I rushed to follow her up the stairs, my hand on the smooth, polished banister. Despite our swift pace, I managed to take in the sight of the beautiful stained-glass window above the front door, the crown molding, and the glass knobs on every door, all of which added to the inn's charm and character.

On the second floor, Cordelia led me down a hall with closed doors on either side and then up a second, narrower staircase to two doors on the third floor.

"This is it." She opened the door on the left and allowed me to precede her through it.

The room had a sloped ceiling and was on the small side, but the white paint and a large window made it seem cheery and cozy rather than cramped. The queen bed hadn't been slept in, but an open suitcase sat on the floor, its contents in a jumble. A couple of wrinkled shirts lay haphazardly on the blue-and-white area rug in the middle of the room, and the drawers of the small dresser had all been left open to some degree. The top drawer was empty, but I couldn't see into the lower two.

"The police didn't do the best job of tidying up after themselves," I said while taking in the sight of the mess.

"Oh no. It wasn't the police who left it like this. This was how it looked when I let the officers in."

That was odd. While not exactly a neat freak, Eric had always been a fairly tidy person. In more than two years of living with him, I'd never known him to leave a room in this sort of state.

Cordelia seemed to be waiting for me to make the first move, so I stepped farther into the room.

"It should only take a minute or so to pack this up." I picked up one of the shirts and folded it. Instead of starting in on another shirt, I set the folded one on the end of the bed and wandered toward a closed door at the end of the room. "Is this a washroom?"

"It is. A small one, but with all the necessities."

I stepped inside the tiny blue-and-white room. A small black shaving kit sat on the vanity, its zipper open, a toothbrush and small tube of toothpaste lying next to it. Nothing else of Eric's seemed to be present. I slipped the toothbrush and toothpaste into the black case and zipped it up. Retreating from the washroom, I tucked the shaving kit into the suitcase and got back to folding shirts.

It felt strange to be handling the clothes of the man I'd broken up with months ago, especially knowing that he was now dead. I tried not to think about it too much, instead quickly folding each item and placing it into the suitcase. I kept my eyes open for anything unusual, but only came across the typical items one would pack for a few days away from home. I didn't know what else I might have expected to find. If Eric had died at the hands of a robber, no clues as to the killer's identity would be here at the Creekside Inn.

"Did you know him a long time?" Cordelia asked from the post she'd taken up by the window, her gaze straying back and forth between the view and the suitcase.

"Nearly four years." I folded the last item and set it on top of the rest of the clothes in the suitcase. "We met in Knoxville. We'd been dating about a year and a half when Eric got a job in Boston, and I ended up moving there with him."

"Where's his family?"

"His parents live in Philadelphia, where he grew up. His sister's living in DC." I closed the suitcase and zipped it up. "I think that does it." I checked the nightstand and dresser drawers to be sure I hadn't missed anything, but it didn't appear that I had.

"Thanks so much," Cordelia said, grabbing hold of the suitcase. "I'll put this away in the storage closet for safekeeping."

She led the way back down to the second floor, with me helping her maneuver Eric's suit-case down the narrow staircase. Halfway along the corridor, she opened a door to a walk-in cupboard, tucking the suitcase away just inside the door.

"I'm guessing that guy who's in town isn't related to your ex in any way."

"Sorry?" I said, confused.

"A man came by yesterday, asking if Mr. Jensen was staying here. Maybe I shouldn't have answered the question, since I didn't know who he was, but I said yes. It just popped out, like most things do from my mouth. That was shortly before the police showed up and told us Mr. Jensen was dead."

Unease crept across my shoulders. "Why did the man want to know if Eric was staying here?"

"I didn't get a chance to ask. The phone rang, and I answered it. He took off before I hung up."

"What did this guy look like?"

"Imposing. Even a bit scary. Muscular, and his eyes were a little too close together. He had a Boston accent."

The tension in my shoulders increased. "And you have no idea why he wanted to know where Eric was staying?"

"No, none. Do you know the guy?"

"No, but I know who you mean."

As we headed down the staircase, the inn's front door opened, and a middle-aged couple came inside. Cordelia greeted them cheerily and hurried to the reception desk to assist them. I called out a quick thank-you and waved to her, letting myself out of the inn. On the front porch, I paused and shivered, though not from the cool air.

The man Cordelia had described had to be

the same one who'd been at the Inkwell the day before. Whoever he was, he had an agenda of some sort. I didn't know what that agenda was, but I felt certain that it wasn't a good one.

CHAPTER 9

Back at the Inkwell, more tourists had arrived, and the pub was buzzing. I jumped in to help Mel and didn't have much time to think things over until a couple of hours later when most of the leaf peepers had gone to catch their tour buses. That left a handful of other tourists who were likely staying in Shady Creek for more than a day and a few locals who'd stopped by for an afternoon pint and a chat with their neighbors.

I filled a pint glass with the Spirit Hill Brewery's popular Sweet Adeline—a beer made from sweet potatoes—and set it on a tray along with a glass of the Malt in Our Stars and a Happily Ever After cocktail. I carried the tray of drinks across the pub to a table where Rhonda and Harvey sat chatting with Alma Potts.

"Is it true your ex was killed during a robbery?" Rhonda asked as I set the glass of the Malt in Our Stars in front of her.

"I don't know if anyone knows if that's true or not, but it seems to be a possibility."

"I heard something about a missing ring when I was at Pilates this morning," Alma said before taking a sip of her Happily Ever After cocktail.

"Was the ring meant for you, Sadie?" Harvey asked.

I tucked the empty tray under my arm. "That's the story I heard, but I never saw Eric, and I never saw any ring. But if he did have a ring, it sounds like it's missing now."

"It probably was a robbery gone wrong then." Harvey took a long sip of his beer.

Alma leaned forward and spoke in a hushed voice. "You don't suppose Carl Miller . . ." She shook her head. "No, of course not."

"What about Carl?" Harvey asked.

"You were going to ask if he could be the killer, right?" Rhonda guessed.

"Carl Miller, the guy who always wears that red baseball cap?" I asked.

"That's him," Harvey confirmed before taking another drink.

I stepped closer to the table and kept my voice low. "Why would you think he might have something to do with Eric's death?"

"He's known for having sticky fingers," Rhonda whispered. "He's been to jail a couple of times for stealing."

"And there was that kerfuffle," Alma added.

"What kerfuffle?" the rest of us asked at the same time.

"The one right here at the pub. You know, Sadie, the same night your ex died."

"Oh, right," I said. "Carl was arguing with Eric."

"That doesn't mean Carl killed the guy," Harvey said.

"Doesn't mean he didn't," Alma countered.

Harvey shook his head. "We shouldn't be spreading rumors."

"No, I suppose you're right," Alma said, though she looked disappointed.

Harvey turned the conversation in a new direction, and I excused myself, returning to the bar with the empty tray. I surveyed the pub, but none of the patrons appeared to be in need of immediate assistance. I drummed my fingers against the bar, trying to rein in all of the thoughts that were swirling around in my head.

Eric had brought a ring to Shady Creek, one he'd intended for me. A known thief had argued with Eric within twelve hours of his death, and now the ring was missing and Eric was dead. I needed to find out if there was a connection. It certainly seemed like there could be.

I was also curious about the incident at the brewery that Cordelia had told me about. Grayson had kicked Eric off his property. I wanted to know what had made Grayson so angry and if he could be the killer.

And then there was the beady-eyed mystery man. Where did he fit in all of this?

I wanted to find answers to my questions, but there was something more pressing I needed to do, something I should have done already, though I hadn't been in the right frame of mind before. The pub had quieted down, but I knew it would get busier again soon, so I needed to take my chance and do what needed to be done.

After letting Mel know that I'd be up in my apartment for a while, I left her to take care of the patrons, went upstairs, and settled on my couch with my phone in hand.

"This isn't going to be easy," I said to Wimsey as he hopped up onto the couch next to me.

He sat down and licked his paw before rubbing it against his face.

"I know. It's best to get on with it."

Wimsey spared me the briefest of glances before returning to his grooming.

I stared at the device in my hand, but I knew this call wouldn't get any easier to make as time passed. Scrolling through my contacts, I found Natalie's name and put a call through to her number.

Half an hour after heading upstairs to my apartment, I still hadn't returned to the pub. I'd only spoken to Natalie for about ten minutes or so, and to her parents for five minutes after that, but I needed time to press a cold, damp cloth over my eyes to get rid of the swelling and redness. As soon as Natalie had started crying, I hadn't been able to hold back my own tears. And then Mrs. Jensen had broken down when I called her, setting me off again.

At least Eric's family didn't suspect me of

having anything to do with his death. They were desperate for answers that I didn't have, but they didn't in any way blame me for the loss of their son and brother. That was a relief, but hearing the grief in their voices had been tough, and I hoped they'd get the answers they needed before too long.

I was still lying there on the couch, the damp cloth over my eyes, when I heard footsteps on the stairway beyond my apartment door. Leaving the cloth in the kitchen sink, I reached the door just as somebody knocked on it. I hoped it was either Shontelle or Aunt Gilda on the other side of the door, because those were the only two people I felt up to seeing at the moment.

"I brought dinner," Shontelle announced as soon as I opened the door. She held up a paper bag that had a delicious smell wafting from it.

My stomach gave a loud rumble, and I realized then that I hadn't eaten since breakfast. "I'm not sure if I have time to eat," I said, although I stepped back to let her into the apartment.

She waved off my concern. "I talked to Mel before coming up here. She says she's fine on her own for a while longer. And I can't stay too long myself. Kiandra's at her dance lesson, and I have to pick her up at six."

"Want something to drink?" I asked as I headed for the fridge.

"Just water for me, thanks." She paused by the

couch to give Wimsey a pat. He closed his eyes happily, purring away. "So, you're still hanging in there?"

"Yes," I said as I filled two glasses with ice and water. "Although I'm more confused than ever."

Shontelle unloaded the bag of food onto the kitchen table as I carried over plates and the drinks. The smell of fish tacos grew stronger, and my stomach growled again.

"Get some food into you, and then tell me what's on your mind."

I did as she suggested, and once I'd taken a few delicious bites of my taco, I told her about all the rumors I'd heard that day.

"I talked to Eric's family a little while ago," I said once I'd finished telling her about Carl Miller. "His sister said Eric had recently confided in her that he was being hounded by a couple of thugs."

Shontelle's eyes widened. "Why? Something to do with his gambling?"

"Apparently. He owed money to a loan shark and couldn't pay it back." I shook my head. "He got himself into such a mess. And now I'm wondering if that's what got him killed."

"But he died here in Shady Creek."

"I know, but I think his troubles might have followed him here."

I told her about the beady-eyed man who'd asked after Eric both at the pub and at the

Creekside Inn. "He has a Boston accent, and I thought he looked vaguely familiar. When I was talking to Natalie, I remembered that I'd seen a couple of guys hassling Eric about six months ago. He brushed it off at the time, and I forgot all about it until today. I'm pretty sure the guy who was in the Inkwell yesterday was one of them."

"And you think he's a thug for the loan shark?"

"I think that's a good possibility."

"That's something the police should know."

"Natalie told them about Eric's troubles with the loan shark, and I filled her in about this guy who's in town. She said she'd tell Detective Marquez. She's been in touch with her over the phone a few times already. That was a relief to me. I'm not keen to have another conversation with the police at this point. They seem to think I'm a suspect."

"I thought that was the case."

"You did?" I said with surprise.

"Not because I think you're murder suspect material," Shontelle rushed to assure me. "But that detective came by the store earlier, wanting to know what time we parted company on Tuesday night."

My stomach twisted, and I set my taco on my plate. "They don't know exactly when Eric died, so I could still be in trouble. What if he was killed after I got back to the mill? I don't have anyone to vouch for me after that."

"Try not to worry. Maybe this new information about the loan shark will get the police on the right track and put you in the clear."

"Hopefully." I picked up my taco again. "I want to look into the Grayson angle too, though."

"Please tell me that's because you want an excuse to visit him."

I nearly choked on a bite of fish. "Of course, it's not. I can't stand the guy."

"Sadie, he's gorgeous, successful, and a gentleman."

"He's surly, rude, and unpleasant," I countered.

"I think he must have an evil twin, because we can't be talking about the same man."

I chewed hard on another bite of my taco before swallowing. "It doesn't matter, anyway. Even if he was like you describe, I'm not interested in dating anyone in the near future. No exceptions," I added when I saw that Shontelle was about to speak.

She raised an eyebrow. "None at all?"

"Not unless Shemar Moore moves to Shady Creek."

"You'd have a fight on your hands if that happened."

I smiled a real smile for the first time that day, some of the tension finally easing out of my shoulders. "Thanks for coming by, Shon. I feel a lot better."

"That's probably more the food than me, but you're welcome."

"It's definitely you too," I assured her.

"I'm glad I could help."

She gave me a hug and then hurried off to pick up her daughter. After putting our dishes in the sink, I stepped into the bathroom for a wary glance at myself in the mirror. To my relief, all the puffiness and redness had faded from my eyes. I tidied my braid and headed for the door, pausing only to drop a quick kiss on the top of Wimsey's head. Then I was on my way down the stairs, ready to get back to the pub.

The next day, the clouds had broken up enough to allow the sun to peek through on occasion, its bright light intensifying the beautiful colors of the autumn foliage. The leaf peepers would be getting some great photos, no doubt, and I decided to spend some time of my own enjoying the gorgeous scenery.

My helmet on, I wheeled my bicycle out of the shed and rode it across the footbridge to the street. I set off in the direction of the Creekside Inn, noting that there was already some activity over on the village green. It looked as though most of the booths and their canopies were now set up, a few people hanging around and adding the final touches. Someone—likely as per Vera Anderson's instructions—had decked out the white bandstand in the middle of the green with pumpkins and garlands of autumn leaves.

The sight of the decorations reminded me that I hadn't yet found an autumn wreath for the pub's door. I'd seen some for sale at the general store, but it wasn't quite nine o'clock yet, so I decided I could put off the shopping trip for a little while.

Enjoying the fresh air streaming past me, I cycled at a leisurely pace, passing the Creekside Inn a moment later. From there I turned right onto the picturesque covered bridge that led across the creek to Woodland Road. At that point, I'd left the center of town behind me. Here, the houses were set on acreages, driveways leading off the road now and then through the woods to unseen homes. A couple of cars passed me on their way into town, but otherwise I had the road to myself, birdsong providing the soundtrack to my excursion.

I cycled for a couple of miles or so along the road before turning around near the driveway that led to Hidden Valley Sugarworks. I'd yet to meet the Gibsons, the family that owned the property and business, but I'd purchased some of their maple syrup from a shop in town, and it was the best I'd ever tasted. The Gibsons were going to have a booth at the fair, so maybe I'd have a chance to stop by and see what else they had on offer.

After crossing the covered bridge again, I cycled along Hemlock Street at the western edge of the village green, before turning left onto

Hillview Road and pulling to a stop in front of the general store. It was open now, so I left my bike propped up against the building and hurried inside to look at the selection of fall decorations. Luck was with me that morning as there was still one fall wreath available, a circle of colorful artificial leaves entwined with acorns and dried flowers in autumn hues. It would look perfect on the Inkwell's red door.

With my purchase hanging over one of my handlebars, I walked my bike across the street and onto the green, pushing it along as I circled around the large white tent to the entrance. The flap had been tied back, and I could hear voices coming from inside. Parking my bike with the help of its kickstand, I ducked into the tent. I smiled when I saw Damien to my left, setting up a long folding table, but when I saw who else was present, my smile fizzled away.

Grayson Blake stood at the far end of the tent in conversation with a young and fashionably dressed woman who had her dark hair pulled back into a ponytail. Without interrupting his conversation, Grayson glanced my way, his gaze as cool as mine must have been. He quickly shifted his attention back to the woman with the ponytail.

Deciding not to let his presence deter me, I stepped farther into the tent, joining Damien over by the table.

"I figured we'd make do with a table, rather than hauling over the booth that's been used in past years," Damien said to me. "Are you all right with that?"

From the way he asked the question, I got the sense he wasn't sure that my answer would be positive.

"Of course," I said. "Maybe we can spruce it up with a tablecloth. I've got a nice red-and-white-checked one at home that I can bring over later."

Damien gave no indication of what he thought about that idea. He nodded at a couple of folding chairs set up behind the table. "I brought those over as well, but I didn't know what else you wanted."

"That's good for now. I'll bring the tablecloth and the dry-erase boards over later. And I'll make sure we've got plenty of ice for the coolers tomorrow."

I was planning to have samples of some of our literary-themed cocktails available during the festival. I knew Grayson's brewery was planning on offering beer tastings and pints for sale, and I wasn't about to compete with him directly by offering any beer. Besides, the literary cocktails were the Inkwell's trademark, one of the things that made it unique, so that's what I wanted to showcase during the festival. Hopefully those who enjoyed the samples would cross the road at some point to drop in at the pub to buy a full-sized cocktail or to enjoy one of the other drinks we had on offer.

Having a booth at the festival was going to cost me some extra money in wages since both Mel and Damien would be working extra hours, but I hoped it would be worth it. The goal was for the pub's presence at the festival to pique the interest of tourists and locals who hadn't yet stopped by the Inkwell.

"If you don't need me to transport anything more, I'll be on my way," Damien said.

"Of course. Thanks for your help, Damien. See you tonight."

He raised a hand in acknowledgment, already heading out of the tent.

I stared after him for a moment, trying for the umpteenth time since I'd met him to figure him out. He wasn't an easy guy to read, and I often wasn't sure what he was thinking. I couldn't tell if he was annoyed at having to help out here, or if he was simply anxious to get somewhere else.

In the end, I decided not to worry about it. Wondering wasn't going to make the answer any more obvious. I stepped back and studied the table. It definitely needed something more. A quick glance across the tent showed me that Grayson already had a large chalkboard propped up next to his table, the names of the three beers he'd be selling printed in colorful block letters. I could also see a stack of shiny pamphlets set on the brewery's table, which was covered with a white cloth. Other than that, there wasn't much going on over there either, and I was glad it didn't appear that the brewery would make the Inkwell's table look shabby, at least not once I'd touched it up.

As I was about to leave the tent, the woman with the ponytail said a final few words to Grayson and strode past me out into the open, not even glancing my way, her strides brisk and full of purpose. Grayson was on his way out of the tent now too, so I fell into step with him.

"Good morning," I said, trying my best to sound cordial. "Are your festival preparations going well?"

"They are."

I waited for a moment, but he clearly wasn't going to do any work to keep the conversation going.

"I guess you heard the police don't think Eric's death was accidental."

He paused his steps and glanced at his cell phone. "I'm sure the whole town knows that by now."

I scowled at him, although he was too busy tapping away at his phone to notice. "Have the police questioned you again?"

He finally looked my way, but his blue eyes were as cool as ever. "They did. They asked me several questions about you, actually."

"Me?" Maybe that shouldn't have surprised me, but it definitely irked me. "What did you say about me?"

His eyes strayed back to his phone. "I'm not sure I should talk about that."

I glared at him. "Well, I'm sure the questions weren't just about me. Why did you have Eric thrown off your property the other day?"

He froze—just for a split second—before shoving his phone into the pocket of his jeans.

"Because I knew what he was up to." He struck off across the grass.

I scurried to keep up with him. "Up to? What do you mean? I heard he was looking for a job."

A humorless smile showed on his face for a brief moment before dropping away. "We both know why he was really there."

I had to half run to keep up with his long strides, and that only irked me further. "Um, actually, I have no idea what you're talking about."

He didn't even glance my way. "You might want to take some acting classes."

I stopped in my tracks and gaped at him, my anger building. "Are you accusing me of lying?" The words sputtered out of me, but Grayson hadn't slowed his strides and was already out of earshot. "Why you . . . Ugh!"

I was tempted to shake my fist at his retreating back but managed to reel in my emotions, not wanting to put on a show for the gaggle of tourists who'd just disembarked from a bus that had stopped at the edge of the green. Furious, but trying not to let it show, I marched back to the tent, where I'd left my bike. Grabbing the handlebars, I gave the kickstand a swift wallop with my foot and set off again.

As my emotions slowly simmered down, I thought back over what Grayson had said. What the Charles Dickens had he meant about Eric being up to something other than looking for a job? Despite his accusations, I really had no clue.

As I paused at the edge of Creekside Road to let a car drive past, I glanced back over my shoulder. When Grayson had walked away from me, he was heading in the opposite direction from the brewery, and now he was out of sight. I waited at the edge of the road a little longer than necessary, thinking.

By the time I pushed my bike across the street to the old mill a moment later, I'd already decided on my next course of action.

CHAPTER 10

Fortunately, there was already a small hook on the pub's front door, so I had the wreath up in no time. I spotted Wimsey crouched in the grass near the edge of the forest, his tail twitching, but I didn't call out to him. He was probably looking for a mouse or other critter to pounce on. Hopefully he wouldn't catch anything, but he'd left gifts of a dubious nature for me on only a couple of occasions over the two years since I'd adopted him from an animal shelter.

Leaving him to his entertainment, I returned my helmet to my head and hopped back on my bike. When I reached the road, I paused and looked around. Grayson was still nowhere in sight. Satisfied, I pedaled my way down the road to the spot where I'd confronted Grayson shortly before we'd discovered Eric's body. I zoomed past the sign welcoming visitors to the Spirit Hill Brewery and headed up the driveway.

My pace dropped as I pedaled up the hill, working hard to keep moving. Two-thirds of the way to the top, I almost gave up. A few years ago, cycling up a hill like this one wouldn't have given me any trouble at all, but I hadn't been as active over the past couple of years, and especially since I'd moved to Shady Creek. I'd been too caught up in learning the ropes of running a business and generally not making a disaster out of my new life. But as I puffed and gasped my way up to the crest of the hill, I vowed to get out on my bicycle more often.

I drifted to a stop at a junction where the driveway branched out in a V. The left-hand arm led to a parking lot near the brewery buildings. The right-hand arm disappeared through the woods, a sign marking that branch of the driveway as private. I figured it was safe to assume that it led to Grayson's house, so I set off to the left, and another couple pushes of my pedals sent me coasting along a flat stretch of ground to a one-story building with a sign that read OFFICE outside the door. I leaned my bike up against the building and removed my helmet, running a hand through my hair and taking another moment to catch my breath. I didn't need anyone getting the full effect of my disheveled and out-of-shape self.

About a dozen vehicles of various sizes occupied spots in the parking lot, and I noticed a couple of men in coveralls walking between two of the other buildings, but otherwise the place seemed quiet. All the visitors were probably off having a tour or tasting Grayson's beers. I was hoping that meant the person I'd come to see would be free to talk to me.

My breathing back to normal, I combed my

fingers through my hair one last time and opened the door to the office, walking into the building like I had no reason not to be there. For a brief second, I worried that Grayson had returned while I was hanging the wreath on the Inkwell's door, that he might be the one I found in the office, but that concern quickly dissolved. The only person in the outer office was a young woman seated behind the curved reception desk, her blond hair pulled back into a sleek French braid, not a single strand out of place.

"Good morning and welcome to the Spirit Hill Brewery. How can I help you?"

Her voice and smile were both so chipper that I wondered how much caffeine she'd had. That thought led me to wishing I'd had more than just a single cup of coffee that morning.

Pushing my sudden coffee craving aside, I smiled back at the woman and glanced at her nameplate, my smile growing brighter as I read it. "Annalisa. You must be Cordelia King's friend."

"That's right." She beamed at me. "How do you know Cordelia?"

"Actually, I just met her for the first time yesterday when I was visiting the Creekside Inn."

"Isn't that place gorgeous?"

"It really is. Anyway, I've been living in town for a few months now, but I hadn't yet made it up here for a tour of the brewery."

"Oh, I can help you out with that, no problem."

She snatched up a glossy brochure from her desk and handed it over to me. "We have daily tours at this time of year, several in the morning and a couple each afternoon. Was there anything you were particularly interested in, or were you just looking for a general introduction to the place?"

"A general introduction," I said, glancing over the brochure without taking in the contents.

Annalisa checked her computer screen. "There's a tour scheduled to start in fifteen minutes, if you want to join that one."

"Oh . . . I'm afraid I can't hang around very long today, but I'll take a good look at this." I waved the brochure. "And I'll come back some other time."

"Whenever is best for you," Annalisa said with a nod.

I glanced at a door to my left that stood ajar. It looked as though it led to an inner office, but the lights were out in that room, so I figured we were most likely alone.

"Cordelia mentioned the kerfuffle that took place here the other day." I said as casually as possible, hoping Cordelia's friend liked to chat as much as she did.

Annalisa's forehead furrowed, but then it smoothed out, and her eyes lit up with understanding. "You mean the scene with that man who supposedly wanted a job?"

"That's the one."

"I heard they found him dead the next day," she whispered. "My boss, Mr. Blake, was one of the people who found his body."

"You don't say." I tried to act as though that were news to me. "What did the guy do? I heard he got thrown off the property."

"He sure did," Annalisa said, nodding. "After that incident a few months back, Mr. Blake wasn't going to put up with any more spying."

"Spying?" I latched onto her last word. "What do you mean?"

"About eight months ago, Mr. Blake discovered one of the guys he had working here was actually planted by a large brewery chain. He was a mole," she said, her gray eyes wide. "Can you believe it?"

The news certainly took me by surprise. "Why would a large brewery chain plant a mole here?"

"They want Mr. Blake's recipes. He's got the knack. Sure, any brewer can make beer, but Mr. Blake creates the most amazing recipes. He's won tons of awards, including a whole bunch of gold medals at a recent world championship. A lot of the big brewery chains are trying to get in on the craft brewery scene now. I guess they figured the easiest way would be to lift some recipes they already knew would be successful."

"That sounds awfully sneaky."

"You're telling me."

"But what does that have to do with the guy

who was here the other day?" I asked, steering the conversation back to Eric.

"He wanted a job—so he said—but Mr. Blake's been on alert since the last incident, and it didn't take much looking to find out that the guy worked for the same brewery chain that planted the mole last time. They were at it again!"

"I can see how that would have made your boss angry."

"I've never seen him get mad before, but that day . . . whoa. He had security get the guy off the property right away." The phone jangled on her desk. "Sorry," she said, her hand going to the receiver. "Is there anything else I can help you with today?"

"No, that's everything, thanks," I said quickly, backing toward the door. "It was nice chatting with you."

I left the building as she answered the phone with her chipper voice. About a dozen or so tourists were on their way out of one of the other buildings, heading for the parking lot, their indistinct voices floating through the morning air. Before anyone had a chance to drive my way, I jumped on my bike and pedaled back to the branch in the driveway. After a quick check over my shoulder to make sure no one had their eyes on me, I veered off along the private arm of the drive.

My conversation with Annalisa had been even

more illuminating than I could have hoped. I didn't know if Eric had requested a job at his employer's behest, but I doubted it. He wasn't the type to allow himself to get roped into something like that. Unless there'd been extra compensation involved. With his gambling debts, that might have tempted him.

Either way, though, Grayson clearly believed that Eric had sought a job at the Spirit Hill Brewery for less than honest reasons, and from what Annalisa had said, the situation wasn't one the brewer took lightly.

Maybe the theory I'd considered the day before was a good one. Had Eric returned to the brewery for some reason, perhaps after he'd had too much to drink and wasn't thinking clearly? If Grayson had found him on his property again, no doubt that would have reignited his anger, maybe even more intensely than the time before.

It was a scenario I couldn't discount. Grayson had a motive, and I didn't yet know if he had an alibi, so he joined Carl Miller and the muscular stranger on my suspect list. And since I was so conveniently close to Grayson's home, I decided to try to find out more about him.

What, exactly, I hoped to find at his house, I didn't know. Most likely I wouldn't find anything, but with my reputation at stake, I wasn't about to leave any stone unturned, no matter what gross, slimy things might slither out from beneath them.

The driveway curved to the left and then to the right before the house came into view. The blue-and-gray two-story structure was far more modern than most of the homes around Shady Creek, and the main level had several floor-to-ceiling windows. While the forest provided a backdrop to the house, off to my right I could see the town below, not too far away. To my left, gentle green hills rolled off into the distance, probably meeting up with the brewery buildings beyond.

It was definitely a private setting, a good home for someone with secrets to keep hidden. There was no sign that anyone was around, and no cars were parked in the driveway, although there was an attached double garage off to the right, its doors shut. I coasted my way over to the garage and braked as I left the driveway for the grass at the side of the building. Dismounting, I leaned my bike against the garage and peered into the side window, cupping my hands around my eyes so I could see more than reflected daylight.

The murky interior slowly took shape. Tools hung on a pegboard on the opposite wall, and a motorcycle was parked close to the window. Next to it was a sporty black car, one I'd seen Grayson driving on more than one occasion. The presence of the car sent an uneasy flutter through my stomach, but I quickly reassured myself. There was a good chance that Grayson had walked down to the village green earlier. After all, he couldn't park on any of the streets directly around the green, and it probably took less than ten minutes to walk from his house down to the center of town.

Nevertheless, I made sure to tread carefully and quietly as I crept around the back of the garage and toward the main part of the house. When I reached the first back window, I raised myself up on tiptoes and shaded my eyes again. There were no lights on in the kitchen I was peering into, but I could still make out the sleek design with granite countertops, a large island, dark cupboards, and stainless-steel appliances.

I eyed the six-burner gas stove and the double-wall ovens with skepticism, wondering if Grayson ever made use of them or if they were there mostly for show. I didn't know if the house had come with the property or if he'd had it built. Either way, he clearly wasn't hurting for money. Nothing in that kitchen looked anywhere close to cheap.

Moving on, I hurried across a slate patio, dashing past a set of French doors, before pausing next to one of the house's many floor-to-ceiling windows. This time, I was looking in at a large living room decorated in classy tones of gray and white. I caught sight of a glint of metal in a display case along the wall to my left and leaned closer to the window for a better look.

"Can I help you with something?"

I tipped forward, and my nose squashed up against the glass. Pushing myself away from the house, I stumbled backward, my arms flailing until I regained my balance.

Grayson stood a few feet away, arms crossed over his chest, his face impassive except for the cool intensity in his blue eyes.

"I was just having a look at your house," I sputtered.

One of his dark eyebrows arched. "Planning a robbery?"

"Of course not!" I silently cursed my cheeks as they heated up.

"I could have you arrested for trespassing."

"That wouldn't be very neighborly," I said.

"Neither is peering in somebody's windows."

I clamped my teeth together, annoyed that he was right about that.

Aside from his eyebrow, he hadn't moved an inch. "I'd like you to leave now."

"Not a problem. I was about to leave anyway." I strode past him, not looking back, but I heard him follow me.

"If I see you sneaking around here again, I'll call the police," he warned.

I jerked my bike away from the side of the garage and turned to glare at him. Instead I got the full force of his blue gaze—only two feet away this time—and my insides suddenly went all squishy. Probably because I knew I could be looking into the eyes of a murderer. Coming here on my own wasn't the smartest idea I'd ever had.

"I can assure you that I have no intention of setting foot on your property ever again," I told him.

"Glad to hear it."

I walked my bike to the driveway, but then stopped and turned around again. "By the way, up until today I didn't know anything about the whole mole-at-your-brewery thing. I highly doubt Eric was involved in any corporate espionage, but even if he was, I had absolutely nothing to do with it."

"Right. So it's just a coincidence that you bought the pub out from under my nose?"

"I didn't buy it out from under anybody's nose. I saw that it was up for sale, I made an offer, and it was accepted. If you wanted to buy the place, you shouldn't have waited around. I heard it had been on the market for over a month before I ever arrived in Shady Creek."

"I was in the midst of negotiating with the owner."

"Clearly you didn't negotiate fast enough."

He didn't look like he believed a word I'd said, and that only irked me all the more.

"Don't believe me if you don't want to," I said as I climbed onto my bike. "But you might not want to be so eager to call the police up here, whether I return or not."

"Why's that?"

"You might make their job too easy for them."

He narrowed his eyes at me. "Are you suggesting that *I* had something to do with Eric Jensen's death?"

"You're awfully quick to jump to that conclusion."

"What other conclusion was I supposed to jump to?"

As tempted as I was to stay there and argue with him, I knew that ticking off one of my murder suspects wasn't the best move, especially in such an isolated spot. I was already dancing too close to the edge and decided I should make a hasty retreat.

I pushed off from the ground and cycled off along the driveway. Unable to stop myself, I called over my shoulder as I went, "A guilty conscience needs no accuser!"

I pedaled hard, not slowing down until I'd reached the safety of Creekside Road.

CHAPTER 11

The next morning, I was up at what I considered a ridiculous hour, two hours earlier than Wimsey usually prodded me out of bed. Downstairs, I flicked on the lights over the bar and set to work. The plan was to offer samples of three different literary-themed cocktails on each day of the festival. Today I was going to offer the Happily Ever After cocktail, the Malt in Our Stars, and the Yellow Brick Road, a cocktail made with limoncello, yellow lemonade, and lemon-lime soda.

The festivalgoers would only get a small sample of each drink, but I'd been warned that thousands of tourists would attend throughout the week, along with most of the locals. Luckily, the green was just across the street from the pub, so I wouldn't have far to go if I needed to replenish my supply of samples, but I still hoped to have enough to keep the attendees happy for a few hours.

I was used to mixing up small batches of cocktails, but I'd planned ahead and worked out the amounts of each ingredient I'd need for the larger recipes. I started with the Happily Ever After cocktail, mixing together coconut rum, pineapple juice, and lemon-lime soda. I'd given this one a tropical twist, because I couldn't think of a better happily ever after than riding off into a tropical sunset with a devastatingly handsome hero. Not that I'd ever experienced that myself, but my imagination assured me it would be absolutely perfect.

Once the drink was prepared, I funneled it into swing-top glass bottles that I'd ordered online for the occasion. They looked nice and would fit easily into the coolers of ice they'd be stored in. With the first set of bottles filled, I moved on to the Yellow Brick Road cocktail.

I'd be looking after the Inkwell's festival booth for the morning, switching out with Mel shortly before noon, after which I'd look after the customers at the pub. It would be a long day for me—a long week, really—but I was looking forward to it. This was the first town activity I'd be taking part in, and I was excited to be involved in what I'd heard was the best and most anticipated event of the year in Shady Creek.

By the time I was ready to go, I had two coolers packed full of ice and bottles, and a plastic bin holding the brochures I'd had printed to promote the Inkwell. I added the book I was reading, just in case there were any slow spells during the festival. On top of the book and brochures, I stacked several packets of small plastic cups to serve the samples in. I'd use the plastic bin as a receptacle for the used cups so I could recycle them later.

I propped open the Inkwell's front door with a doorstop and took the coolers outside one at a time. I returned inside once more for the plastic bin and set it on top of one of the coolers.

Perhaps I should have thought things through more carefully, I realized. There was no way I'd be able to carry both heavy coolers and the bin at the same time. I'd have to make at least two trips.

I stood there with my hands on my hips, preparing myself for the trek ahead, when I heard Mel call my name. She jogged across the footbridge, her bright blue and bleached-blond hair standing straight up, hardly wavering as she hurried toward me.

"I thought you might need some help getting everything over to the tent."

"You're a lifesaver," I said with a rush of gratitude. "I was just thinking how I'd have to make two or three trips."

"Not anymore." She grabbed the bin with one hand and a cooler with the other.

"Are you sure you can manage both of those?" I asked.

"Sure, no problem."

I should have known. Mel was an amateur boxer as well as an artist, and her arms were probably twice as strong as mine. I got a secure grip on the handle of the remaining cooler, and we headed off across the footbridge together. The festival wasn't set to open officially for another half hour or so, but most of the booths on the green were already manned, ready for visitors. A few early arrivals milled about by the bandstand, where the opening ceremony would take place.

With Mel's help, I was set up at my table in the tent in no time. Across the tent, a man I didn't recognize was at work behind the brewery's table, tapping kegs of beer in preparation for the samples they'd be offering as well as the full-sized pints they'd have for sale. I was relieved that Grayson wasn't there. After our encounter the day before, any interaction was bound to be awkward at best.

I'd experienced more than one twinge of remorse since my visit to the brewery. I'd come to accept that I didn't really want to believe Grayson was Eric's killer. Why, I wasn't entirely sure. The guy was irritating, but maybe it was because I knew that the business side of things could get complicated if he were arrested for murder. Would I still be able to sell his beers? Would the brewery shut down, forcing me to find a new supplier?

Plus, as much as Grayson annoyed me, I didn't like to think that my neighbor was a killer. I didn't want to believe that *anyone* from my newly adopted town was a cold-blooded murderer. That took my thoughts back to the stranger in town, the one I suspected of working for a loan shark. I didn't know if he was still in Shady Creek or if he'd gone back to Boston, but I figured there was a good chance he was already gone, whether or not he was the murderer.

After Mel had left and I'd exchanged a few words with the man at the brewery's table, I sat back in my folding chair to think while awaiting the arrival of the tent's first visitors. My thoughts returned immediately to the muscular stranger. If he was a loan shark's enforcer, he could easily be the one who'd killed Eric, using him as an example to the loan shark's other debtors. Sure, that wiped out any chance of getting payment from Eric, but if they figured that wasn't going to happen anyway, maybe the loan shark would have instructed his thug to make Eric pay in a much deadlier way. In fact, Mr. Beady Eyes probably belonged at the top of my suspect list. I thought that over for a moment, ultimately deciding that all three suspects could share the top spot for the time being. After all, I still didn't know if Grayson had an alibi or not, and the same was true for Carl.

I could hear Alec McCafferty, the town moderator, speaking into a microphone out by the bandstand, welcoming everyone to the Autumn Festival and officially opening the event. Within minutes, several people had entered the tent, seeking out samples of beer and cocktails. Only a few people seemed interested in purchasing actual pints of beer from Grayson's employee, but I knew that would change as the day wore on. As for my offerings, they generated good interest, and I enjoyed the next few hours as I poured samples, handed out brochures, and chatted with visitors about the Inkwell and the inspiration behind the drinks being sampled.

The response from everyone was positive throughout the morning, and by the time Mel showed up to take over, my cheeks were beginning to ache from having a genuine smile on my face for hours.

"How did things go?" Mel asked during a brief lull at our table.

"It's been amazing," I said. "Everyone seems to be enjoying the cocktails and hearing the stories behind them."

"And our supplies?"

I checked the coolers. "I'll go get a couple more bottles of Happily Ever After, and maybe one each of the Malt in Our Stars and Yellow Brick Road. That should be enough to get us through the day, but give me a call if you need more."

"No problem. Will you be okay with the cooler?"

"It's just the one, so yes. Thanks."

With the remaining drinks packed into the cooler I was leaving behind, I took the other with me and crossed the green toward the pub.

The town was abuzz with activity, more people on the green than I'd ever seen there before. A small band—from the local high school, from the looks of it—played live music, and all the booths seemed to be getting plenty of interest.

As I crossed Creekside Road, I noticed a few people snapping photos of the mill, and I couldn't stop myself from beaming with pride as I took in the sight of the beautiful old building myself. Aside from a few puffy clouds, the sky was clear today, and I could have sworn that the autumn foliage was brighter than ever, providing a picture-perfect backdrop for the mill.

When the tourists had finished snapping photos, I hurried into the pub and fetched the spare bottles of cocktails I'd left in the fridge. I packed them into the cooler with fresh ice and hauled everything over to the tent. Then I was back at the pub again, getting ready to open for the day.

I was pleased by the number of tourists who stopped in at the pub for a drink and a bite to eat before heading back out to enjoy more of the festivities. I was disappointed that I didn't have my literary-themed food menu available yet, but there wasn't anything I could do about that now. Finding a chef needed to be a priority, though, and I made a mental note to get to work on that as soon as possible.

In the middle of the afternoon, two men I'd seen

at the Inkwell on a few previous occasions claimed stools at the bar. I supplied them with pints of lager before returning to the other end of the bar where Rhonda sat, enjoying a glass of red wine.

"Where's Harvey today?" I asked her.

"Helping out with the festival. Speaking of which, if you need help with your booth anytime this weekend, just let me know. I'll be happy to lend a hand."

"Thank you. I'll keep that in mind." I nodded discreetly at the two men at the opposite end of the bar. "The guy in the red baseball cap—is that Carl Miller?"

"Yep. And that's his buddy Greg with him."

A short time later, after Rhonda had left, I served Carl and his friend Greg another round of drinks.

"It's Sadie, right?" Greg asked. He was taller than Carl, and rounder.

"That's right."

"I heard about what happened to your ex. I just wanted to say I'm sorry for your loss. Even if he was your ex, it still can't be easy to know someone who got murdered."

Carl nodded his agreement.

"Thank you."

I was surprised by their kindness. This was the first time I'd spoken to them, but the reports I'd heard recently hadn't given me a particularly positive impression of either man.

"I heard you two had a disagreement with Eric here at the pub," I said after a moment, deciding to try to get some information out of them.

Greg look embarrassed, but Carl just frowned into his lager.

"We shouldn't have let it go that far," Greg said.

"He started it," Carl muttered.

"Started what, exactly?" I asked. "Eric wasn't the type to start brawls."

"It never went that far," Greg assured me. "We just argued, and he got in a shove or two. He kept going on and on about how he was going to woo you back, how he'd bought you this expensive ring. It all got a bit pompous, if you know what I mean. When we tried to shut him down, he took exception."

"He'd had a few drinks by then," Carl put in.

"Trying to settle his nerves, I think," Greg said. "When he first came in, he looked real nervous. I don't think he was as confident about winning you back as he wanted everyone to think."

"So Damien kicked all three of you out?"

"He asked us to leave, and we did, on our own. It was your ex he had to escort out the door."

"What happened then?"

"What do you mean?" Carl asked. "That was the end of it."

I had to wonder if that was really the case, especially since Carl had a history of theft and clearly knew about the ring. "Did you see where Eric went? Did you see anyone else hanging around outside?"

"Nah," Carl said before taking a long drink.

"We didn't actually see the guy go anywhere," Greg said. "He was still talking to Damien when we left. We cut across the green and went over to the pool hall on Mulberry Street."

"So you have no idea what happened to him after that?"

"Nope. Sorry. I wish I could finger the killer for the cops, but like I said, we went straight to the pool hall."

Disappointed, I thanked the men for the information and headed down to the other end of the bar to serve a couple who'd just arrived.

Later on, after Damien had arrived, Aunt Gilda showed up with her friend Betty. They claimed a small table near one of the windows, and once I'd served them their drinks—a Huckleberry Gin for Aunt Gilda and a glass of white wine for Betty—I hung around to chat.

"How was your day at the salon?" I asked both of them.

"Busy but good," Gilda replied as Betty nodded her agreement. "You'd think people would be too busy enjoying the festival to be wanting their hair cut or their nails done, but that doesn't seem to be the case. We hardly had a spare minute between us."

"Which is why we're treating ourselves to drinks and dinner out," Betty said.

"We reserved a table at Lumière," Gilda added.

"Sounds lovely," I remarked.

Lumière was the nicest restaurant in town. Despite that, reservations usually weren't necessary, but with all the tourists in town for the Autumn Festival, reservations would probably be required all week for anyone who didn't want to stand in line waiting for a table.

"You should come join us, if you can get away," Aunt Gilda said. "Between the pub and the festival, you must have had a busy day too."

"I did." I glanced over at the bar where Damien was busy working the taps. "What time are you heading over to Lumière?"

"Seven."

That was nearly an hour away. "I'll see how things go here, but I'd love to join you."

"Be sure to if you can," Aunt Gilda said.

I was about to leave them to their drinks when Betty spoke up. "Did you hear the news, Sadie?"

"What news?" I asked, wondering if there'd been progress with the murder investigation.

Aunt Gilda was the one to reply. "About the fire."

"Do they know what caused it?"

Betty raised her wineglass to her lips. "What, but not who." She took a sip of her drink.

"Who?" I said with surprise. "You mean the fire was deliberately set?"

"Seems there's no doubt about it," Aunt Gilda said. "The fire was the work of an arsonist."

CHAPTER 12

"How did you find out?" I asked, still surprised by the news. I'd just assumed the fire was accidental.

"April O'Hare told us when she was in to get her hair permed this morning," Aunt Gilda said. "Her husband's a volunteer firefighter."

"Someone used gasoline to start the fire," Betty picked up the story. "Too bad there aren't any security cameras in the area. That might have helped identify the arsonist."

As much as I wanted to stay and chat some more about the fire, I could see that Damien had his hands full, so I excused myself and returned to the bar to help him out. While I mixed drinks and pulled pints, my thoughts kept straying back to the fire. It was hard to think about anything else, especially since I overheard a couple of patrons discussing the news.

"Arson and a murder in less than twenty-four hours," one woman said with a shake of her head before she took a long drink of her India pale ale. "Must be because of all the tourists in town. You never know what kind of riffraff's gonna show up for the festival."

I winced, hoping none of the tourists had overheard, but it didn't appear as though they had. I didn't wait around to see what the woman's companion had to say about the matter. I had my own opinions. If a random tourist had killed Eric, the murderer was either deranged and killed for no reason or they'd botched a robbery. As for the fire, why the heck would a tourist want to burn down the antiques shop? I supposed it was possible that the arsonist had had an unpleasant encounter with the shop's proprietor earlier that day, or it could have been the work of a pyromaniac, unable to resist starting a fire even while on vacation.

Those were possibilities, but unlikely ones, in my opinion. The murder suspects on my list were far more viable candidates. But the woman I'd overheard had been right about one thing—it was surprising that the murder and arson had both happened in such a short time frame in a town that rarely saw much in the way of crime. The timing made me wonder—not for the first time—if the two incidents were somehow related, but as I turned that over in my mind, I discounted the theory. As I'd thought the day after the fire, the timing of the two crimes had to be a coincidence.

After all, Grayson and I had found Eric's body on this side of Creekside Road. The antiques shop was diagonally all the way across the green and down Hemlock Street. If the arsonist had killed Eric because he'd witnessed the firebug at work, his body most likely would have been closer to the antiques shop. Maybe the arsonist would have tossed his body into the fire in an attempt to destroy evidence of the murder.

I shuddered at that horrible thought, but quickly recovered, knowing that wasn't what had happened.

Shortly before seven o'clock, Aunt Gilda and Betty vacated their table, and I glanced around the pub. It was only moderately busy at the moment, so I figured I could slip out for a short break.

"Are you coming with us, hon?" Aunt Gilda asked, stopping by the bar before heading for the door.

"I think so. I should at least be able to join you for appetizers. You go on ahead, though. I'll be a few more minutes."

"We'll order those crispy fried shrimp that you love," Aunt Gilda said over her shoulder as she followed Betty to the door.

My stomach grumbled in anticipation.

"If you're all right here on your own, I'll take a dinner break," I said to Damien as he slid a pint of beer across the bar to a waiting patron.

"I'm sure I can handle things," he said, his voice and expression deadpan so I couldn't tell if he was being sarcastic.

I decided not to worry about it. "I've been meaning to ask you about Tuesday night. I heard you were talking to Eric outside after Carl and Greg went on their way."

"I was."

"Did you notice anyone else around?"

"No. It was quiet out there at the time."

"What did you guys talk about?"

"I told him getting drunk and causing a scene wasn't the best way to win you back." He shot me a sidelong look as he filled a pint glass with Autumn Nights, a beer that combined vanilla with spices like nutmeg and cinnamon. "I figured that was a safe assumption."

"It was," I confirmed. "Although nothing he did or didn't do was going to win me back."

Damien slid the pint glass over to its waiting recipient and accepted cash in return. "By that time, he'd settled down a bit, and he agreed with me. He seemed embarrassed."

"What time was that? And did he say where he was going or what he was going to do next?"

"It was shortly after nine. He said he'd take a walk. He thought the fresh air would help clear his head."

"Which way did he go?"

"West along Creekside Road."

In the direction of the Creekside Inn, where he was staying. Perhaps more importantly, if he'd taken a left at Hemlock Street, that would have taken him in the direction of the antiques shop. Still, it didn't make sense for his body to be so far away from the shop if his death had anything to do with the fire.

"Aren't you heading out?" Damien's voice prodded me out of my thoughts.

"Right. I won't be too long."

I grabbed my purse from upstairs and locked the cat door so Wimsey—currently lounging on the back of the couch—couldn't leave the apartment. I didn't like him being out after dark.

"I'll see you later," I called to him as I headed out the door again.

He cracked his eyes open as I blew him a kiss, but he'd already closed them again before I had the door shut. I set off on foot, noting that the green was mostly deserted now that darkness was settling over the town, the festivities done for the day.

Lumière was two doors down from Aunt Gilda's salon and within a two-minute walk from the Inkwell. When I arrived at the restaurant, it was as busy as I expected it to be, all of the tables occupied and about half a dozen people waiting to be seated. I spotted Gilda and Betty near the back of the dining area, so I bypassed the hostess and wound my way around the other tables to join them. As I passed a table occupied by three women, I noticed one of them glaring at me. My automatic reaction was to turn my head away as heat rushed to my cheeks, but I looked back her way only a second later. By then she was focused on her food and companions.

I wondered briefly if I'd been mistaken about her giving me the evil eye, but I knew that wasn't the case. Although I'd never met her, I knew her name was Eleanor Grimes. She was in charge of Shady Creek's museum, a place I'd yet to visit.

Shrugging off the incident, I approached my aunt's table and saw that she and Betty weren't alone. Harriet Jones was seated at the table with them.

"Oh, good, you made it," Aunt Gilda said when she saw me. "The appetizers should be here soon."

"Great," I said as my stomach gave another anticipatory rumble. I pulled out the remaining vacant chair and sat down. "How are you today, Harriet?"

"Just peachy, now that I've got my martini." She saluted me with her glass. "And I'm looking forward to the next book club meeting."

"I'm glad to hear that. It seems like everyone enjoyed themselves."

"Even Vera Anderson seemed to relax for a few minutes," Harriet said after taking a healthy sip of her martini. "Although she still managed to sound hoity-toity whenever she had something to say about the book."

"That's Vera for you," Betty said.

"Hoo-yeah. That's one who will never change."

A waitress arrived at our table, bearing platters of crispy fried shrimp and chicken wings. The delicious smells wafted toward me, and my mouth watered. I requested a glass of ice water from the waitress, and as soon as she was gone, we started in on the appetizers.

"So how were things at the festival today?" Aunt Gilda asked me as I devoured a shrimp.

"Good," I said once I'd swallowed.

"You're in the tent with the brewery, right?" Betty asked.

"That's right."

"Then I need to pay you a visit tomorrow, and maybe every day during the festival," Harriet said. "I'll take any chance I can get to drink in the sight of that hunk of a brewer, Mr. Blake."

I nearly choked on a bite of my second shrimp. Fortunately, the waitress had just set a glass of water in front of me. I grabbed it and took a quick drink, sending the shrimp safely down my esophagus.

"Of course, I'll sample your wares too, Sadie." Harriet clapped me on the back, almost making me choke again. "Two birds with one stone, if you know what I mean."

"You're incorrigible, Harriet," Betty said as I gulped down more water.

"I might be old, but that doesn't mean I can't enjoy the scenery."

"Stopping by the tent won't guarantee that

you'll see that particular scenery," I said. "I was there for a few hours today, and Mr. Blake didn't make an appearance." Thank goodness, I wanted to add, but didn't.

"That's a shame," Aunt Gilda said with a pointed look in my direction. "He's single, isn't he?"

"I wouldn't know," I replied, trying my best to sound disinterested. "Although Shontelle seems to think he is."

"Has she got her eye on him?" Betty asked. "She's a stunner."

"She is," I agreed. "But no, she's in a long-distance relationship with a man in Savannah."

"A proper southern gentleman, I hope," Aunt Gilda said.

"I hope so too."

Harriet jabbed my ribs with her bony elbow. "You should find out for sure if Mr. Blake is single. You'd make a good-looking couple."

I focused on the shrimp I'd just taken from the platter. "I'm really not interested."

"Bad boys not your type? They always were mine. Still are, really." She let out a cackle of laughter.

"Bad boy?" I said, forgetting my pretense of disinterest. "Why do you say that?"

Harriet lowered her voice, although that just took it down to a regular volume. "I heard he has some sort of criminal past."

"Really?"

"I heard that too," Betty said.

"But it was Gretchen Dingle who said that," Gilda reminded her. "You never know if what's coming out of her mouth is truth or fiction, or some combination of the two."

"What kind of criminal past?" I pressed, hoping for more information. If the brewer had a history of violence, that would make him an even more likely suspect for Eric's murder.

Harriet polished off her martini. "I have no idea, but if you find out, be sure to let me know. I always love a juicy bit of gossip."

I looked to Aunt Gilda and Betty, but they had no details either. By then we'd polished off the appetizers, so I pushed back my chair and told the ladies I'd have to be on my way. I tried to contribute some money for the food, but Aunt Gilda wouldn't hear of it.

"You go on back to work, and maybe I'll pop by the tent for a quick visit tomorrow," she told me.

"That would be nice." I kissed her on the cheek and waved good-bye to Betty and Harriet.

On my way to the door, I noticed that Eleanor Grimes and her companions were no longer present, their table now occupied by a young couple. I didn't know what I'd done to deserve the death glare Eleanor had sent my way, but maybe I was a target simply because I was an outsider, not born and raised in Shady Creek. That seemed to be enough for some people to find fault with.

When I stepped outside, I shivered and wished I'd thought to bring a coat. I'd need to get into the habit of wearing more layers whenever I headed outdoors. As soon as the sun disappeared these days, I could feel the promise of the approaching winter in the air.

Fortunately, I didn't have far to walk, and I set off at a brisk pace, hoping that would help to keep me warm. When I neared Creekside Road, however, my steps slowed. A police car was pulled up against the curb, its flashing lights illuminating the silver sedan parked in front of it. I could see three figures standing near the cars, two in uniform, the third in jeans and a short sleeve T-shirt that exposed the man's bulging muscles.

I picked up my pace, hurrying their way. I reached the scene in time to see the male police officer snap handcuffs onto the wrists of the muscular man I'd last seen at the Inkwell.

"Reggie Stone, you're under arrest . . ."

I strained to hear the officer's next words but couldn't catch them. When I stepped closer, I realized the officer was reading Stone his rights. His female partner stood a few feet away, saying something into her radio. According to her name tag, she was Officer Rogers. I marched past her and stopped in front of Reggie Stone and the other officer.

"Did you kill Eric?" My voice wavered as I glared into Stone's dark eyes.

All he did was smirk at me.

Anger coiled its way around me. I was about to ask the question again when Officer Rogers put a hand on my arm.

"Ma'am, please leave this to us."

"He works for the loan shark who was hounding Eric Jensen before his death, right?"

Rogers appeared surprised for a moment, but then she nodded in recognition. "You're the victim's ex. You found his body along with Mr. Blake from the brewery."

"Yes," I said without ever taking my eyes off Stone. "Are you arresting him for murder?"

"No, on an outstanding warrant for assault."

"But he works for the loan shark in Boston, right?" I pressed.

"I really shouldn't be discussing that with you."

Maybe not, but I could tell I was right.

I wanted to say more to Stone, but I was too choked up. The male officer turned him toward the vehicle and patted him down. He paused at one of the pockets of Stone's jeans and reached into it with a gloved hand, pulling out a small velvet box. When he cracked it open, a sapphire ring glinted in the flashing lights of the patrol car.

"Thinking of proposing to someone, were you?" the male officer asked in a wry voice.

Stone said nothing.

The officer handed the box to his partner and continued on with the search.

"Are you able to identify this ring as belonging to your ex?" Rogers asked me.

I shook my head as I tried to compose myself. "I never saw it, but it fits the description I heard from someone who did see it."

"Do you remember who that was?"

"Cordelia King. Her grandmother owns the Creekside Inn."

Officer Rogers nodded. "I know Cordelia and Grace."

The male officer had Stone in the back of the patrol car now.

"Do you have enough evidence to charge him with Eric's murder?" I asked.

"You should talk to Detective Marquez if you have questions about that," Rogers said. "Excuse me, but we'll need to be on our way now."

I stood and watched as a tow truck pulled up to the scene. Officer Rogers had a quick word with the driver through his window, and he pulled up in front of the silver sedan. Rogers got into the passenger side of the patrol car, and seconds later the officers and their prisoner were gone, leaving the tow truck driver to his work.

I forced myself to get moving again, but my

pace was slow as I crossed the street toward the old mill. It seemed as though my theory about the loan shark's enforcer was the right one. Stone must have killed Eric to make an example of him, and he took the ring as payment—or partial payment—for Eric's debts.

A rush of anger and sadness coursed through me as I thought of Reggie Stone taking Eric's life for such a stupid reason. But the police knew about his connection to Eric and would likely have the case wrapped up before long.

At least, I hoped they would.

CHAPTER 13

I thought I'd sleep soundly that night, knowing Reggie Stone was off the streets and in police custody, but that wasn't how it turned out. Every time I drifted off to sleep, I'd wake up again, my mind racing. As much as I wanted to believe the police would arrest Stone for Eric's murder once he'd been questioned about the ring and why he was in Shady Creek, I was becoming less hopeful by the hour.

Having the ring in his possession was definitely a strike against Stone, but if he'd killed Eric, why was he still in town? Wouldn't he have hightailed it back to Boston instead of hanging around, making people suspicious with all his questions?

Okay, so a loan shark's thug probably wasn't the sharpest tool in the shed, but surely he'd have more sense than that. Then again, maybe he really was that dumb.

Trying not to think any more about it, I rolled over for the umpteenth time that night. Wimsey, snuggled up by my feet, got annoyed and shifted away from me before settling down again. I fluffed up my pillow and did my best to relax and clear my mind. It felt as though I'd just managed to slip off to sleep when my eyes flew open.

I was on my back now, and I stared up at the

ceiling. Had I heard something? I strained to detect any further noises, but all seemed quiet. I glanced at my clock. It was just after six o'clock. I'd slept longer than I'd thought, but I still didn't want to be awake so early. I shut my eyes, but they flew open again a second later.

This time, I was sure I'd heard something. I raised my head and noticed that Wimsey was wide awake and listening too. He tensed, then got up and hopped down to the floor, trotting out of the bedroom.

Fear pushed aside any of my remaining sleepiness. I threw back the covers and swung my legs over the side of the bed. I stuffed my feet into my fuzzy slippers and grabbed my fluffy white robe, pulling it on as I hurried out of the room after Wimsey. I found him perched on the windowsill in the living room, peering out through the glass. I joined him over there, looking out at the forest. Although the sky was pale, the sun wasn't yet up, and there were still plenty of murky shadows to make it difficult to see clearly. One shadow flickered right below the window, and I leaned closer, almost pressing my face against the glass.

It was no good. I couldn't see straight down.

"You stay here, Wimsey," I said, running my hand over his fur.

His ears and tail twitched, but he remained on the windowsill.

"I'll go take a quick look."

I tried to sound unconcerned, more to convince myself that I wasn't scared than to reassure my cat, but I wasn't particularly successful.

After slipping out my apartment door, I hurried down the interior steps, moving as quietly as possible, skipping the third step from the bottom since it had a tendency to creak loudly. When I reached the back door, I rested my hand on the knob, my heart booming away in my chest. I hesitated for only a second, and then turned the lock and yanked the door open.

I had my mouth half open, ready to scream, but there was no one on the other side of the door. I was about to step outside, hoping for a better view of the expanse of grass between the mill and the forest, but a dark shape caught my eye near my feet. My eyes widened as I realized that it was a gas can sitting next to the door.

My heart had calmed down, but it was back to booming in an instant. I ran through the dewy grass to the western end of the building, where the pub's main entrance was located. Aside from a couple of birds flying into one of the maple trees, nothing stirred. I ran back the way I'd come, passing the open door and heading for the opposite end of the building. At first, I thought there was no one in sight again, but then I spotted two figures on Creekside Road, one two-legged and one four-legged.

Peering through the murky dawn, I knew I wasn't mistaken. It was Grayson, jogging along the road with Bowie, the white German shepherd, trotting by his side.

My anger, fueled by my recent fear, ignited in a quick burst. I nearly charged out to the road, until I remembered that there was a creek between us; the footbridge was at the other end of the building. As my initial flare of anger dwindled to a flicker, Grayson turned up his driveway, disappearing behind the trees. There was no way I could catch up to him.

Maybe that was for the best, I realized as I stormed back to the open door. He probably wouldn't take me seriously if I confronted him in my robe and fuzzy slippers, and he was going to need to take me seriously.

The sight of the gas can reignited my anger. Was this Grayson's sick idea of a joke? Or was it more sinister than that?

An arsonist had burned down the antiques store. Was that what Grayson had intended to do to the mill? Burn it down with me and Wimsey inside?

My anger drained out of me in a rush, leaving me weak and shaky. I sank down on the doorstep, my eyes on the gas can, clearly red now that the sky was growing lighter.

Had I scared Grayson off just in time?

I sniffed the air, but the only smell of gasoline

seemed to come from the can. I almost grabbed it to check how full it was, but I stopped myself at the last second. I didn't want to mess up any fingerprint evidence.

I got up slowly, one hand on the door frame. My legs were steadier now, so I quickly shut and locked the door and hurried up the stairs to my apartment. As reluctant as I was to have another conversation with the police, I had to call them. I definitely wasn't going to let this incident slide.

After I'd made my report to the dispatcher, I hurriedly changed into jeans, a T-shirt, and my long cardigan. I ran a brush through my hair and glanced out the bedroom window in time to see a patrol car pull up to the curb across the creek.

Wimsey tapped at my leg with his paw, but I rushed out of the bedroom and straight to the door.

"Sorry, Wims. I'll feed you later."

I closed the door on his meow of protest, feeling bad about disappointing him, but not wanting to leave the police waiting. I heard a firm knock on the front door, so I flicked on the lights in the pub and rushed to answer it.

"Officer Rogers," I said when I saw who was on the doorstep.

"Sadie Coleman, right?" When I confirmed that, she continued. "You reported a prowler?"

"One who left an unnerving present behind."

I led her around the corner of the building and

to the other door, explaining what had happened as we went. For a second, I feared that Grayson might have returned in my absence and taken away the evidence, but then I spotted the gas can and felt a rush of relief. At the same time, some of my anger bubbled back to the surface.

"After hearing that the fire at the antiques shop was arson, this really worried me," I told Officer Rogers once I'd pointed out the can.

"Understandable." She looked around and walked to the other end of the building, checking around the corner before returning to my side. "And you say the only person you saw out and about was Grayson Blake?"

"Yes. He was running with his dog."

"As in running away, or out for an early morning jog?"

I hesitated. "He could have been doing either, I guess. He was going at a relaxed pace, but maybe he just wanted to look like he was out for an innocent jog."

Officer Rogers gave no indication of what she thought of that. She stood back and examined the building. "No security cameras?"

"No," I said. "It never occurred to me that I'd need them here in Shady Creek."

"Crime can happen anywhere, even in a nice town like this. You might want to think about at least getting some motion sensitive lights out here."

"I'll definitely consider it."

She pulled on a pair of gloves and picked up the gas can. Liquid sloshed around inside. "I'll take this and see if we can get any prints off of it."

"What about Grayson Blake? Will you question him?"

"I'll have a word with him."

I couldn't tell how seriously she was taking the matter. I pulled my sweater around me, shivering in the cold morning air.

"Think carefully about getting some better security," Officer Rogers said. "And if you notice any other suspicious activity, don't hesitate to call 911."

"I won't," I assured her.

I walked with her to the footbridge, but then returned to my apartment. Wimsey was waiting impatiently for me, so I dished out his breakfast, but I couldn't bring myself to eat anything. I considered making some coffee, but I was already so jittery that I nixed that idea. Instead, I took a long shower, letting the hot water ease some of the tension out of my muscles. Once I was dry and dressed again, I felt more settled, though I couldn't quite ignore my lingering fear and anger.

If Grayson had planned to burn down the mill, there was a good chance he'd burned down the antiques shop as well. Why, I didn't know, but maybe he was a pyromaniac.

I remembered what Harriet had said the night before. Grayson was rumored to have a criminal past of some sort. Maybe this wasn't the first town where he'd started fires.

Grabbing my laptop from the coffee table, I settled on the couch and opened the Internet browser. I typed Grayson's full name into the search bar and quickly scanned through the results. There were numerous links to social media profiles for people named Grayson Blake, but it only took a few clicks to figure out that they weren't for the Grayson Blake currently living in Shady Creek.

I tried a new search, including the name of Grayson's brewery. This time the top result was a link to the Spirit Hill Brewery's website, and below that I found several articles about the brewery's successes at national and international beer competitions. I skimmed through the information on the company's website, but to my disappointment, it didn't provide much in the way of personal background information on the man behind the company.

Returning to the search results, I scrolled down the page until I found a link near the bottom that led me to the *Shady Creek Tribune*'s site and an article written by Joe Fontana. The piece dated back nearly four years, when the brewing company was in its first months of operation. I skimmed through the text until I finally found what I'd been looking for—some biographical information on Grayson.

According to the article, Grayson was born in Chicago but had spent time living in Syracuse and Boston. I'd hoped the article would tell me what Grayson was up to before he opened the brewery, but it only mentioned that he'd spent several months in Chicago and in Germany, learning the craft of brewing beer. What he'd done before that, the article didn't say. I didn't know Grayson's exact age, but I guessed he was a few years older than me. If he'd delved into the craft beer scene about six years ago, that left several years of adulthood unaccounted for.

I tried a few more searches, looking for information on people named Grayson Blake in Syracuse and Boston. I even tried adding search terms like "arson," "arrest," and "criminal record." To my annoyance, I came up empty. Nothing I found pertained to the right Grayson.

Maybe Joey knew more than he'd written in the article. He'd interviewed Grayson at the time, as was evident from quotes included in the news piece, so it was possible he'd learned more than he'd shared in the *Tribune*.

Maybe I'd ask Joey, although I wasn't keen on getting hounded to provide him with an interview about Eric. Still, it might be worth the risk. The rumors about Grayson's past had piqued my curiosity, and I'd never been good at snuffing out my curiosity once something sparked it.

Speaking to Joey—if I decided to do so—would have to wait, however. At the moment, I needed to get started on the day's to-do list.

As I wandered down to the pub and got to work mixing up cocktails to take over to the festival later, an annoying thought niggled at my mind. What if Grayson really had been out for a jog? I realized I wanted that to be the case, but I quickly gave myself a mental kick for thinking that way. It was ridiculous to want him to be innocent because he was attractive. Besides, I didn't even like the guy, so what did I care if he was good-looking? And why did I care if he was innocent or not?

Someone had been up to no good recently. Maybe more than one person. Even if it turned out that Reggie Stone was the one who'd killed Eric, Grayson still could have been responsible for the fire at the antiques shop and leaving the gas can outside my door.

No, I wouldn't be swayed by a handsome face. I'd practically caught him in the act this morning. I'd do my best to give the police a chance to check the gas can for fingerprints and to talk to Grayson, but if I ran into him at the festival, I knew I wouldn't be able to help myself. A good idea or not, if I came face-to-face with the brewer, he'd be getting a piece of my mind.

For the day's offerings at the festival, I decided to keep one cocktail the same—the Happily Ever After—but I replaced the other two with the Count Dracula and the Evil Stepmother. The first was a deep red drink made from blood orange juice, cranberry juice, cinnamon syrup, and coconut rum. It was a great cocktail to enjoy before a crackling fire on a chilly evening. As for the Evil Stepmother, I figured such characters tended to have sour dispositions, so the drink was made with sour mix, white grape juice, vodka, and ginger ale.

Since I was up and working earlier than I'd planned, I stored the bottles of cocktails in the commercial-sized refrigerator in the pub's kitchen. Both my stomach and my nerves had settled, and I was missing the breakfast and coffee I'd skipped first thing. I made sure I had both cat doors unlocked so Wimsey could come and go as he pleased, and then I set off, cutting across the northeast corner of the green to the Village Bean, situated at the end of Sycamore Street, four doors down from Aunt Gilda's salon.

I knew I should tell my aunt about the prowler and gas can before she heard the news through the grapevine, but I wasn't up to talking to anyone at the moment. All I could think about was getting some food and caffeine into me.

A handful of people sat scattered at tables in the coffee shop. I smiled and said hello to a woman I'd seen around town a few times, but she didn't respond in kind. Instead, she leaned toward her companion and whispered to her, both sets of eyes following me as I continued on my way to the counter. My heart sank, though I tried not to let my smile falter. Did they think I was a killer? Were rumors of that kind flying around town? So far, the murder investigation hadn't slowed business at the Inkwell. At this point, people were still showing up as usual, curious and wanting to hear the latest news. But what if that changed?

I decided it was best not to dwell on that thought.

After exchanging greetings with Nettie Jo, the owner of the coffee shop, I ordered a carrot muffin—my favorite of all the food items at the Village Bean—and a large mocha latte to go. I sat down at a table near the back of the coffee shop, staying just long enough to finish off my scrumptious muffin. Then, with my latte in hand, I walked down the road toward Aunt Gilda's salon.

Out on the green, some of the merchants were already busy getting their booths ready for another day. Most of the festival's activities would get underway at ten o'clock, but the tent wouldn't open until noon—the same time as the pub—so I still had plenty of time.

When I reached the salon, I peered in through the large front window, but the lights were off, and there was no sign of Aunt Gilda. I continued on to the private door at the side of the salon and pressed the buzzer. I tried twice but received no response. My aunt was either sound asleep, in the shower, or already out somewhere.

I crossed the street to the green and sat down on a bench while I finished my latte, enjoying a few minutes of peace and quiet before the crowds appeared. I wished I could relax completely, but my mind didn't want to stop racing, and there was still some residual tension in my muscles that probably wouldn't disappear until all the recent crimes in Shady Creek had been solved.

"Just the woman I've been looking for."

I glanced up to see Joey approaching. "If you're here to ask for an interview again, my answer is still the same," I said as he plunked himself down on the bench beside me.

"Even if it's an interview about something else?"

I eyed him warily. "Like what?"

"This morning. The cops responded to a call from the mill. Word is you had a prowler."

"If you already know the story, why do you need me?"

"It's always better to have a quote or two from someone directly involved."

The truth was that I didn't mind talking to him

about that incident, but I wanted to make sure I got something from him in exchange.

"I'll talk to you about what happened this morning if you'll talk to me about Grayson Blake."

"Bartering for information now?" he said with a grin. "I hope you haven't got your sights on my job."

"No need to worry about that. I've got my hands full with the pub."

"Good to hear." He fished his phone out of his pocket. "So you've got a thing for our local brewer, huh?"

"No," I said quickly.

Joey's eyebrows rose.

"I just want to know more about him," I hurried to add. "I like to know who I'm doing business with."

"Right," he said, drawing out the word.

I let out a huff of air. "Do we have a deal?"

"Sure. What is it you want to know about Blake?"

"What did he do before he decided to take up brewing beer?"

"No idea. But that's a good question. If he'll ever agree to an interview, I'll ask him."

"He hasn't given you an interview about finding Eric either?"

"He provided a one-line statement. That's it. He said he thought it would be insensitive to you and the deceased's family for him to say more."

"Really?" My opinion of Grayson improved slightly until I remembered I suspected him of two crimes. I focused on what else Joey had said. "How can you have no idea? Didn't you ask about his background when you wrote the story about the brewery's opening?"

"I didn't write a story about the brewery's opening. I've done a couple short pieces about awards he's won at beer competitions, but that's pretty much it."

"I just read the article this morning. It was from about four years ago."

"Ah, but I only moved back here two years ago when my dad's eyesight started failing. He must have written the article."

"It said it was written by Joe Fontana."

"Yep. That's my dad. He's Joe, I'm Joey. I can see how that confused you, though."

"Would your dad know about Grayson's past?"

"Maybe? He's not doing so well these days. He's got problems with his lungs, and he's almost blind now. Plus, his memory cuts in and out."

"I'm sorry to hear that," I said, my words sincere.

"Thanks. Was there anything else you wanted to know?"

"I've heard that he might have some sort of criminal past. Do you know anything about that?"

"Huh. Nope, but I'd like to. Where'd you hear that?"

"From Harriet Jones."

"Hmm. It might just be a rumor. You'd be surprised by some of the stories that fly around town. Still, it's interesting."

"You haven't given me any information," I said, disappointed.

"Does that mean you're backing out of the deal?"

I let out a sigh. "No. I'll talk about this morning."

I described the events, starting with the noises that had woken both me and Wimsey. It didn't take long, since there wasn't a whole lot to tell. Joey recorded my monologue on his phone, asking a few questions at the end, which I answered as best I could.

"See?" He tucked his phone back in his pocket. "That was painless, wasn't it?"

I drank down the last of my latte instead of responding.

He grinned as he got up from the bench. "Thanks, Sadie. See you around."

He set off across the green, leaving me alone with my thoughts. Joey probably wasn't the only one who knew the police had visited the mill that morning. I didn't want Aunt Gilda or Shontelle hearing about the incident from anyone but me, so before leaving my spot on the bench, I filled them in via text messages, assuring them that I was spooked, but otherwise fine. By then, the first tourists had appeared on the green, some with kids in tow, so I headed back toward the Inkwell.

As with the night before, I didn't make it past Creekside Road without stopping. Two patrol cars and an unmarked vehicle had just turned up the driveway to the brewery. They didn't have their lights flashing or their sirens blaring, but they most definitely weren't out for a Sunday drive.

Once the road was clear, I jogged across it, heading for the brewery instead of the pub. I tried to run the whole way up the hill, but my latte sloshed around in my stomach, and I had to slow to a walk to fend off a stitch in my side. When I reached the V in the driveway, I paused for a moment. There were a couple of cars in the brewery's parking lot, but no police vehicles, so I set off along the other branch of the driveway, heading for Grayson's house.

Before I rounded the last bend, I spotted one of the patrol cars through the gaps in the trees. The stitch in my side had faded, so I picked up my pace again, jogging until I reached the three vehicles parked in front of the gray-and-blue house. The front door stood wide open, and I caught sight of officers moving about inside through the floor-to-ceiling windows.

Grayson was out front of the garage, pacing as he spoke into his cell phone. Another man, dressed in black pants and a black T-shirt, stood outside the front door, his muscular brown arms crossed over his broad chest.

I stood near one of the patrol cars, watching as a uniformed officer exited the house, carrying what looked like two swords wrapped in plastic. Grayson ended his call and shoved his phone into his pocket, clearly unhappy. He scowled at the officer, who was now stashing the plastic-wrapped swords in the trunk of one of the patrol cars.

As another officer came out of the house carrying a similar load as his colleague, Grayson's gaze fell on me. Despite the fact that his scowl was now directed my way, I dodged around the police car and hurried over to him.

"Did you instigate this?" he asked, his blue eyes as cold as ice.

"Me? Why would you think that?"

Grayson jabbed a finger in the direction of the two officers by the patrol car. "They're seizing my sword collection."

"I didn't even know you had a sword collection."

"I caught you peering in the window at it just yesterday."

"I never saw any swords!" Even as I said that, I realized the weapons were probably in the display case I'd caught a glimpse of. "Besides, why would I tell the police about your sword collection anyway?"

"Because," Grayson said, the muscles of his jaw tense, "Eric Jensen was killed with a sword."

CHAPTER 14

My recently consumed breakfast churned in my stomach.

"Someone killed Eric with a sword?" I said, my voice fading with the last word.

Grayson grabbed my elbow. "Maybe you should sit down."

I stared at him, still shocked by the news, and surprised as well by the concern that had replaced the ice in his eyes.

Pulling myself together, I shook my arm free of his grasp. "I'm not going to faint. Why do you always think that?" I pulled my cardigan close around me and focused on staying as steady as possible. There was no way I'd admit to Grayson that I really was a bit shaky. "Did you do it?" I asked him. "Did you kill Eric?" I hated the faint tremble beneath my words.

Grayson's eyes iced over again. Without answering, he shifted his attention to the muscular man in dark clothes standing by the front door. "Jason!"

The man uncrossed his arms and strode over to us. Judging by the way he towered over me, he had to be at least six-foot-four. He spared me only a flick of a glance before focusing on Grayson.

"Problem?" he asked in a deep voice.

Grayson nodded my way without looking at me. "Please escort Ms. Parker from the property."

"My name is Sadie *Coleman,* as you know perfectly well," I said through clenched teeth.

Grayson walked off, not even acknowledging that I'd spoken, disappearing into the house a second later. I glared after him.

"Ma'am?" Jason said, the single word somehow incredibly intimidating.

I shifted my glare to him but couldn't keep it up in the face of his imposing figure.

Not wanting to get tossed from the property, I started off along the driveway, although not without a huff of annoyance. I walked quickly, but Jason easily kept pace with me, each of his strides almost twice as long as my own.

"He did that on purpose, didn't he?" I said. "He knows my name."

"Yes, ma'am."

I eyed Jason as we walked around the bend in the driveway. "That's a bit immature, don't you think?"

"He did find you sneaking around his house yesterday," Jason said, his expression remaining impassive.

Warmth rushed to my cheeks. "He told you about that?"

"I'm in charge of security here."

I stopped short as something clicked in my

head. Jason paused one stride ahead of me, his dark eyes never shifting away from me.

"*Nosey* Parker? Is that what he meant? Because I don't think he meant Dorothy!"

One corner of Jason's mouth gave the slightest twitch. It was enough to tell me I was right.

"That . . ." I couldn't think of a word sufficient to sum up what I thought of Grayson Blake in that moment. "Oh, for Poe's sake!"

Jason cleared his throat, and I got the message, resuming my trek along the driveway.

Although I was tempted to rant about Grayson the whole way down to Creekside Road, something stopped me. Maybe it was the fact that I was at least somewhat deserving of the name Grayson had called me, not that I would have admitted that to anybody.

I thought about asking Jason if he knew anything about Grayson's involvement in the murder, but I figured that probably wasn't the best move. The guy could easily snap me in two with his bare hands, and if his loyalty to his employer ran deep, he might be in on the crime.

He drew to a stop at the foot of the driveway, and I continued on along the road, casting a sidelong glance toward the green, hoping no one had seen me getting escorted by the brewery's head of security. Fortunately, it seemed like everyone out on the green was focused on other things. The festivities had started up for the day, and I caught the delicious scent of pumpkin waffles on the air. One of the booths closest to Creekside Road was cooking them up and selling them to hungry customers. If I hadn't already eaten, and if Grayson's news hadn't unsettled my stomach, I might have been tempted to buy some for myself.

I'd known for a while now that Eric had been murdered, and he'd clearly bled a lot from whatever had happened to him, but somehow I found the thought of him getting stabbed with a sword particularly gruesome. And strange. Who the Holly Golightly wandered around a town like Shady Creek with a sword?

Obviously, the police thought Grayson was a strong suspect. I was glad they were thinking along the same lines as I was. Of course, the fact that they were pursuing Grayson as a suspect meant they weren't fixed on Reggie Stone as the killer. I wondered why that was, but without knowing what the police knew, I couldn't come up with an answer.

Back at the Inkwell, I kept myself busy by accepting delivery of the day's vat of soup from the deli and packing the swing-top bottles filled with cocktails into the coolers along with plenty of ice. When Mel arrived, she helped me haul everything over to the tent before leaving me there to get set up for the day. She'd be looking after the Inkwell for the next few hours, so I'd be the one doling out samples to festivalgoers. I was looking forward to chatting with everyone who came through the tent, but I was also preoccupied by thoughts about Eric's murder.

Grayson and Reggie Stone were both suspects, in my mind, but the police force's interest in Grayson's sword collection bumped him up to the top of my suspect list. My thoughts didn't get beyond that point as I plunked myself down in one of the folding chairs behind the table. Across the tent, the brunette with the ponytail was looking after things at the brewery's table again. Her name was Juliana, I'd learned since I saw her on the first day of the festival. Knowing what I did, I wasn't surprised that Grayson wasn't there himself. I doubted he'd show up at all during the day. Most likely he'd be too busy making phone calls to his lawyer or things of that sort. If he had a lawyer.

I wondered if his dodgy past included a criminal record. If it did, no doubt that would make him an even stronger suspect in the minds of the cops. I drummed my fingers against the tabletop for several minutes, but my mind kept going back to the image of Eric's blood-covered body lying by the creek, and I didn't want to think about that. When the tent opened a few minutes later, I relaxed, relieved to have something to distract me.

The tourists started trickling in almost right

away, and I gladly got caught up in chatting with them and serving samples of cocktails. A couple of hours later, Aunt Gilda stopped by for a visit.

"I got your text message," she said after slipping behind the table." Are you sure you're all right?"

"I'm sure," I said, smiling at three women approaching the table.

I wanted to tell her about the police seizing Grayson's swords, but I wasn't about to talk about that in front of the tourists.

"Maybe we can chat later?" I suggested once I'd handed out cocktail samples.

Before Aunt Gilda could reply, Rhonda appeared in the tent.

"Looks like your samples have been popular," she said with a nod at the three empty bottles sitting atop one of the coolers next to my chair.

"They seem to be," I said. "I'll have to head back to the pub soon to get more. I've only got a quarter of a bottle left of each cocktail."

"I can watch over things here if you want to pop over there now," Rhonda offered.

"There's a good idea." Aunt Gilda patted my shoulder. "You should take a break. I can help Rhonda here while you're gone."

"Thanks, both of you."

A group of French-speaking tourists filed out of the tent, leaving it free of visitors for the first time in more than an hour. Juliana set out a sign on the brewery's table saying she'd return shortly, and then she too left the tent.

"Now that we're alone, how about a quick chat before you go?" Aunt Gilda said, and I nodded my agreement. "Did you tell the police what happened at the mill this morning?"

"I did."

"The police?" Rhonda's eyes widened. "What did I miss?"

I told the story about the noises that had woken me, and the gas can I'd found sitting outside my door.

"That's awful," Rhonda said. "Do you really think someone meant to burn down the pub?"

"Either that, or they wanted to rattle me. But after the fire at the antiques shop, there's a good chance they had worse intentions."

"Whoever it was, I'd like to wring their neck. How could anyone put you in danger like that? And who would want to burn down that beautiful building? My dad spent nearly a year of his life renovating it."

"I know it means a lot to you," I said. "It does to me too. I'm going to look into adding some security."

"Maybe you should stay with me for a while," Aunt Gilda suggested, her face pale. "Just until the police find out who's behind this. What did they have to say?"

"Not much, and they seem to have their hands

full lately. Even if there are fingerprints on the gas can, I don't know how long it'll take for the police to find that out."

"Do you know if they're any closer to finding your ex's killer?" Rhonda asked.

"They're certainly working on it. As far as I know, they've got at least a couple of suspects."

"Who?"

"Anyone we know?" Aunt Gilda chimed in.

"One of them, yes. The other is from Boston. He works for a loan shark who wanted to collect a debt from Eric. The police took him into custody on an outstanding warrant and found a ring in his pocket. It looked like the ring Eric had planned to give to me."

"If a thug followed Eric from Boston and stole the ring, that sounds to me like the murder investigation should be wrapped up," Rhonda said.

"But then there's Grayson Blake."

"Surely you don't mean he's a suspect?" Aunt Gilda protested.

"I definitely do." I explained how Grayson thought Eric was planning to steal his recipes and how he'd thrown Eric off his property. "Apparently he was really mad, and it turns out Eric was killed with a sword. Grayson has a whole collection of swords. The police seized it this morning, so they obviously think he's a good suspect."

Aunt Gilda shook her head. "I can't believe that nice man is involved in any way."

"Nice man?" I said with disbelief. "He's aggravating and rude. He basically accused me of being in cahoots with Eric in some corporate espionage scheme. And don't forget about his criminal past."

Gilda shook her head again. "I'm sure that's just a rumor. He came in to get his hair trimmed a week or so ago, and I thought he was just delightful. He was raised right, if you ask me."

"I don't know . . . ," Rhonda said. "I'm with Sadie. It does seem like there's an awful lot of evidence pointing his way."

"Exactly," I said. "What else would explain the fact that Eric was killed with a sword? Grayson collects them, and Eric was found at the edge of his property. It must have been him. I mean, really, who goes around Shady Creek carrying a sword?"

"Everyone who goes to those sword-fighting classes at the community center," Aunt Gilda said.

"The community center holds sword-fighting classes?" That was the first I'd heard of it.

"Oh, sure. I don't think they had any during the summer, but the rest of the year they do. Louie talked about signing up, but he hasn't got around to it so far."

Rhonda nodded. "Harvey goes. I'm thinking of

signing up myself this winter. It seems like a lot of fun. And good exercise."

I could feel the foundation of my case against Grayson trembling. "So you're saying there are plenty of people in Shady Creek who own swords?"

"I think there must be close to a dozen," Aunt Gilda said, and Rhonda agreed with her. "Maybe even more."

I slumped down in my chair. So the type of murder weapon wasn't as big a clue as I'd originally thought. That didn't let Grayson off the hook completely, though. He still had a motive for killing Eric, and so what if other people owned swords? That didn't mean Grayson hadn't used one of his to commit murder.

Not wanting to talk about Grayson anymore, I decided to steer the conversation in a slightly different direction. "What about the arsonist? Do either of you know if the police are making any progress on that front? I'll feel a whole lot safer once the arsonist and killer are behind bars, whether they're the same person or two different people."

"You really think the two crimes could be related?" Rhonda said.

"I don't know about that," Aunt Gilda said. "I was touching up Giselle Hampton's roots yesterday afternoon. She lives next door to Barry and Doris Lanik. Barry's the proprietor of the antiques shop," she added for my benefit. "Anyway, according to Giselle, Barry's business was on the brink of failure. Apparently it's just one in a long line of failed business ventures for him, and Doris is actually relieved that the business is a goner, although Barry's pretty upset about it."

"Hmm." I tucked that information away at the back of my mind.

"But enough of that for now. You go on and take your break, honey. Rhonda and I will be fine here."

I thanked them both and left with one of the coolers—the empty bottles inside—just as a cluster of tourists arrived at the tent, Juliana right behind them. As I walked over to the Inkwell, I mulled over everything Gilda and Rhonda had said. Maybe Barry Lanik wasn't as upset about his ruined business as everyone thought. Maybe he'd decided to give up on the venture and burn down his shop so he could collect insurance on the contents. That was definitely something to consider.

As for the murder, I'd thought the choice of weapon had narrowed the field of potential suspects significantly, but apparently that wasn't the case. Still, if one of Grayson's swords turned out to be the murder weapon, that would pretty much wrap up the case, in my mind at least.

How long it would take the police to determine

if a sword from Grayson's collection was a match for Eric's fatal wound, I didn't know. It wouldn't surprise me in the least if the local force had to ship the evidence off to a bigger center for testing.

In the meantime, I'd have to keep my eyes and ears open for any potential clues and for any further signs that I might be in danger. I didn't want to have to take Aunt Gilda up on her offer to stay with her. I loved spending time with her, but I didn't want to get scared out of my own home. Installing security lights would be a good idea, but would they be enough to keep me safe?

Maybe, maybe not.

I had to wonder if the person who had left the gas can outside the mill was the same individual who'd slashed my tires. If Grayson wasn't behind that incident, then I had no idea who was.

I shook my head, trying to clear it. Everything was such a jumble in my mind. I decided to focus only on the festival for the rest of the day, but as soon as I stepped inside the pub, I knew that wouldn't be possible.

Seated at a table in the middle of the room, a cup of coffee and a bowl of soup in front of her, was Detective Marquez.

CHAPTER 15

I dropped into the seat across from the detective. "Do I need to call a lawyer?"

Marquez paused with a spoonful of soup halfway to her mouth. "Not on my account."

"So you're not here to grill me?"

She swallowed her spoonful of soup before responding. "No."

My stomach flip-flopped with alarm. "To arrest me?"

"Should I be?"

"Of course not!"

Was that a humorous twinkle I detected in her dark eyes as she spooned more soup into her mouth? I couldn't be sure.

"Several people confirmed your alibi," she said.

"But does my alibi cover the window of death?" I asked, hoping that was the case.

"It does."

"So I'm officially off the suspect list?"

"You are."

Relief rushed through me. "I'm glad you're focusing on more viable suspects now. Reggie Stone and Grayson Blake are both good possibilities."

"Is that so?"

This time I was certain my words had amused her.

I continued on, undeterred. "What was likely Eric's ring was found in Stone's possession, and Grayson certainly had access to swords."

Detective Marquez finished off the last of her soup and pushed the bowl aside. "We're looking at the case from every possible angle."

"That's good to hear," I said. "So which one is the most likely culprit?"

"I can't discuss an ongoing investigation."

"You can't tell me anything at all?"

"I can say that Reggie Stone has been charged with theft."

"But not murder."

"No."

"What's the chance that he will be?"

She hesitated, and I worried she wouldn't answer the question, but a second later she did. "Very slim."

"But he followed Eric all the way from Boston, and not so they could go leaf-peeping together."

"I'm aware of that, but Mr. Stone didn't arrive in Shady Creek until very early on Wednesday morning. We have receipts and gas station security footage to confirm that he was still in Boston when Mr. Jensen was killed."

"So you know exactly when Eric died?"

"Not exactly, but we've narrowed down the window."

I waited, hoping she'd share it with me, but she didn't. "What about the ring?" I asked.

"We believe Mr. Stone stole it from Mr. Jensen's room at the Creekside Inn, after the murder took place."

That made sense, especially considering the uncharacteristic mess I'd found when Cordelia showed me Eric's room.

Another question popped into my head. "But why did Stone stick around? Once Eric was dead and he'd stolen the ring, why not go back to Boston?"

"Apparently he met a woman while having a drink at the local pool hall. He decided to extend his stay here so he could . . . spend some time with her."

"Ah," I said.

While the detective sipped her coffee, I stared at the books on the shelf behind her, turning everything over in my mind. With Reggie Stone out of the picture, that left Grayson all alone at the top of my suspect list. But I still had another question about the thug.

"How did Reggie Stone know Eric was coming to Shady Creek? If he didn't arrive until Wednesday, he didn't literally follow behind Eric's car."

"Mr. Jensen posted about his intentions on his Facebook page, which wasn't private, as so many aren't."

That explained it.

Detective Marquez set down her empty coffee cup. "Now, if *you're* done grilling *me,* I need to get back to work."

She paid for her meal and went on her way. Once she was out of the pub, I could finally breathe more easily. Even though she'd said she wasn't there to question me, I hadn't completely trusted her. I was relieved now, though, knowing for certain that I was no longer a suspect.

"Everything okay?" Mel asked a moment later when I joined her behind the bar.

"You mean because of the detective being here?"

She nodded as she filled a pint glass with Sweet Adeline.

"It seems to be. They haven't caught the killer yet, but I'm not a suspect anymore."

"That's an improvement."

"I'll say."

Mel delivered a tray of full pint glasses to a table of customers while I carried the cooler into the kitchen and restocked it with ice and cocktails.

"Who do *you* think killed Eric?" Mel asked when she joined me in the kitchen to fill two bowls with soup.

"Grayson Blake had a motive. Plus, Eric was killed with a sword . . ."

"And the police seized Grayson's swords this morning," she finished.

"You heard about that?"

"It's been the talk of the town for the past hour or two."

That didn't surprise me. News traveled fast around here.

"But he's not the only person with access to swords in Shady Creek," Mel said.

"So I've been told. Apparently there's a whole class of sword fighters at the community center."

"Yep. Stage combat, I think. I've seen them there when I've gone to use the gym. It looks like a lot of fun. I might join them the next time a class starts up."

A plan took shape in my mind. "When are the classes?"

"Wednesdays and Sundays, I think."

"Sunday. That's today."

"The class starts at six and runs for an hour and a half. Are you thinking of checking it out?"

"Maybe."

Actually, it was highly likely that I would, but not because I was eager to learn stage combat.

Mel left the kitchen to deliver the bowls of soup to hungry customers, and I followed after her, heading out the door with the cooler. When I returned to the tent, Aunt Gilda and Rhonda lingered for a few more minutes, but then they set off to enjoy the rest of what the festival had to offer.

By the time the tent shut down at six-thirty, I was almost twitching with impatience. As much as I enjoyed being at the festival, the community center was where I really wanted to be.

I packed up the coolers in record time and hauled them both back to the pub. Mel had already left for the day, and Damien was at work, manning the taps. Fortunately—in light of my immediate plans, at least—the Inkwell was only moderately busy, probably because many locals and tourists were staking out prime spectator spots at the elementary school's playing field, where the Autumn Festival's fireworks display would be taking place that night.

The sun had already set behind the hills, so I grabbed a coat from upstairs before telling Damien that I needed to go out for a while. Then I hurried off toward the community center, located a couple of blocks beyond the far side of the green, within sight of Shady Creek Elementary.

I walked quickly, chilled by the evening air despite my coat. The activities on the green had shut down for the night, but there were still several clusters of people out and about, many heading in the direction of the school. When I reached the community center, I jogged up the front steps and entered the brightly lit reception area. A young man sat behind the desk to my right, talking on the telephone, but I bypassed him, heading straight for the hallway that led to the main floor's activity rooms.

I'd been to the center only a couple of times

since I'd moved to town, once for a Chamber of Commerce meeting and more recently to watch one of Kiandra's dance classes at her request. Although I didn't know for sure where to find the sword-fighting class, I figured it wouldn't be difficult to track down.

I was right. As soon as I entered the hallway, I could hear the clash of blade upon blade. The door to the third room on the left stood open, and when I poked my head in, I saw that I'd found the right place.

Five men and three women stood in two lines, facing each other. They all wielded swords, going through what appeared to be choreographed movements. Some of the students moved cautiously, as if afraid of hurting their partner, while others went through the moves with gusto.

I remained in the doorway, watching. I noticed Rhonda's boyfriend, Harvey, dressed in sweats and a black T-shirt, swinging his blade around. His movements looked a bit wild, but he appeared to be enjoying himself.

Moments later, a deep voice called the class to a halt. The students lowered their swords and turned their attention to one end of the room. I leaned farther through the doorway to see the instructor. My eyes widened when I recognized Jason, head of security at the Spirit Hill Brewery, wielding a sword and demonstrating movements for his students.

Ducking back out into the hallway, I leaned against the wall, thinking. Maybe Grayson wasn't the only person from the brewery to deserve a spot on my suspect list. After all, when Grayson had wanted me removed from his property, Jason had carried out the task. What if he'd done the same with Eric?

I'd wondered before if Jason knew about his boss's involvement, but what if he himself was the guilty party? Just how loyal was he to Grayson and the brewery? If he believed, as his boss did, that Eric was there to steal recipes, might he have killed Eric to eliminate the threat to the brewery?

That was a definite possibility.

Jason and Harvey weren't the only people in the room I'd recognized, though. Carl Miller was also there. He was partnered with Harvey, and from what little I'd seen of the class so far, he appeared to be one of the more confident sword-wielders in the room.

Since finding out that Reggie Stone was the one who'd stolen the ring Eric had bought for me, I hadn't given any thought to Carl as a suspect. I'd always assumed that his motive to attack Eric would have been robbery.

I shouldn't have discounted him so easily, I realized now, even though he'd told me he'd gone straight from the Inkwell to the pool hall with his friend Greg. I didn't know exactly when Eric had died, but if my alibi cleared me, the murder had happened between a few minutes past nine o'clock—when Eric left the Inkwell—and a little before eleven.

Just how long had Carl stayed at the pool hall?

Even though Stone was the one who'd ended up with the ring, that didn't mean Carl couldn't have made an attempt to get it from Eric. Maybe he'd only meant to use his sword to frighten Eric into handing over the jewelry, but if Eric resisted, or if Carl realized that Eric didn't have the ring on him, he might have become agitated, leading to an unplanned attack.

I returned to the doorway, watching the class for several more minutes. It actually did look quite fun. If Rhonda ended up attending the classes, maybe I'd give it a shot too. The class schedule wasn't great for me, though. I slipped away from the pub now and again for short spells, but I wasn't sure I could manage a couple of hours away on a regular basis.

Oh well. I still had my bicycle to help keep me in shape.

Harvey spotted me watching and waved. I smiled and waved back, deciding it was time for me to be on my way. I needed to return to the Inkwell to help Damien.

As I left the community center, I paused on the front steps, wondering if I could spare a few more minutes away from the pub to do more investigating. I didn't want to ask Carl what time he'd left the pool hall, because I couldn't guarantee that he'd tell me the truth, and if he was Eric's killer, I didn't want him thinking I was on to him. I hadn't exercised that type of caution with Grayson, but I should have. Somehow the brewer got under my skin and made me act in ways I wasn't entirely proud of.

The best way to get the information I needed was to go to the pool hall and ask people there about Carl. I only had a vague idea of where the pool hall was located, but surely it couldn't be too hard to find any place in a small town like Shady Creek.

Deciding to give it a shot, I resumed my path down the stairs and turned left onto the sidewalk, away from the elementary school. When I reached the end of the street, I turned left again. I had my eyes on the clearing sky, where bright stars were beginning to show through the thinning clouds, which was probably why I walked right into someone.

"I'm so sorry!" I said as I took a quick step backward.

In the light of a nearby streetlamp, I got my first look at the person I'd collided with. My second apology died away on my tongue.

"Not going to the fireworks?" Grayson asked.

I cleared my throat, buying myself a second or

two since my tongue seemed oddly tied up. "No," I managed to say. "You?"

"I thought I'd go check them out."

Neither of us moved. We stood there looking at each other, only a foot of space between us. He was clean-shaven tonight, and I noticed—not for the first time—that he had thick, dark eyelashes that I would have liked to have as my own. I also noticed that he wasn't scowling at me, which made a change from earlier in the day.

"Clearly you haven't been arrested yet," I said before I could stop myself.

Maybe it was a trick of the light from the streetlamp, but his blue eyes seemed to darken.

"Clearly."

I took another step back, adjusting my purse strap over my shoulder and clearing my throat again. "I'll let you go on your way, then. Do you happen to know where I can find the pool hall?"

His forehead furrowed. I told myself it wasn't a good look for him at all, but my treacherous heart disagreed and did a little flip-flop in my chest.

"Why would you want to go there?"

"That's not really any of your business, is it?"

He stared at me for a moment, sending my heart into another somersault. Probably because I was alone with a potential killer, I decided. Definitely *not* because of the intensity in his eyes.

His forehead smoothed out, and he half-turned away from me. "I'll go with you."

"I asked for directions, not company," I pointed out.

My mother would have been horrified to hear me being so rude, but I couldn't help myself.

"I'm still going with you."

"You'll miss the fireworks."

"I'll live."

I wanted to growl with annoyance, but I could tell I wasn't going to get rid of him, so I resumed walking.

He fell into step beside me. "Shouldn't you be at the pub?"

"Shouldn't you be at the brewery?" I shot back.

"We closed to visitors at five."

I didn't have a good response to that, so I answered his original question instead. "Damien's looking after things at the Inkwell, and I don't plan to be gone much longer."

"Not planning on playing a round of pool, then?"

"I'm going in search of information, not recreation."

"That's what I figured."

I shot a glance his way. "Because you think I'm a nosey Parker?"

I could tell he tried to stifle his smile, but he wasn't successful. I was about to say something scathing when he surprised me into silence with his next words.

"I owe you an apology. I talked to a friend in Boston who has his finger on the pulse of the brewing industry there. He's the one who alerted me to the fact that I had a mole among my staff eight months ago. According to him, your ex wasn't another mole. He'd recently lost his job in Boston and was genuinely looking for one here so he could be closer to you."

I'd figured as much, but in a way, it was still nice to have it confirmed. "So what is it you're apologizing for?"

"I also got in touch with Mr. Hogarth and asked him straight up why he'd sold the pub to you instead of me. He said he was in a hurry to retire to Arizona with his wife. Your offer was close to mine dollar-wise, but you were able to close the deal sooner. He wanted it done and over with, so he went with your offer instead of countering mine."

I remained silent as we continued walking along the street, still waiting for the actual apology.

"So I've been wrong to take out my frustrations on you and to suspect you of anything sneaky," he continued. "And I'm sorry for that."

Some of the defenses I automatically put up when I was around him melted away. "I appreciate the apology. Maybe we can start fresh, on a better foot this time."

We drew to a stop outside the pool hall, the

establishment's pink and green neon signs glowing brightly.

"I'd like that," he said, his eyes meeting mine.

I temporarily lost the ability to speak as I got distracted by the reflection of the neon lights in his eyes. I cleared my throat and forced myself to look away. That seemed to prod him into motion. He grabbed the door and opened it for me. I thanked him and stepped through it, thinking that maybe Shontelle—and much of the rest of Shady Creek—had been right about him after all.

CHAPTER 16

"I appreciate you showing me the way here, but don't let me keep you any longer," I said as Grayson followed me into the pool hall.

"I don't mind missing the fireworks." His gaze scanned the room with its four billiards tables. "The people who hang out here aren't always the politest. I'll stick around."

My first instinct was to tell him that I didn't need him to protect me, but then I remembered we were starting fresh and kept quiet. Besides, he was being a gentleman, and I couldn't fault him for that.

To the right of the room was a scuffed and scratched bar, a pudgy man with thinning brown hair perched on a stool behind it. Only one of the pool tables was currently in use, two men in grubby jeans and T-shirts in the midst of a game. A woman with lots of frizzy blond hair and wearing a short skirt sat on a sagging couch next to the pool table, all her attention focused on her smartphone.

The gazes of the two pool players slid our way, not quite hostile, yet also not welcoming, but they returned to their game after a second or two. The man behind the bar had his attention focused on a television set bolted to the wall near the ceiling.

A sportscaster yammered away on the set while game results slid across the bottom of the screen.

Although I felt uneasy and completely out of place, I walked over to the bar with what I hoped was an air of purpose about me. The man behind the bar didn't pay me any attention, though, his eyes remaining fixed on the TV screen.

"Excuse me," I said loudly enough to be heard over the voice of the sportscaster and the obnoxious music playing in the background of the broadcast.

Slowly, the man shifted his gaze from the screen to me. He appeared half-asleep, his eyes dull.

"I'm hoping you can answer a couple of questions for me."

After a stretch of simply staring at me, the man picked up the remote and turned down the TV's volume, his every movement unhurried. I was beginning to wonder if he was a human-sloth hybrid.

When I no longer had to compete with the sportscaster, I tried my first question. "Do you know Carl Miller?"

His dull expression didn't change. "Who's asking?"

"I'm Sadie Coleman, owner of the Inkwell pub."

"I should've figured." His gaze shifted to a spot over my shoulder.

I glanced that way as Grayson came up beside me.

"Getting a woman to do your negotiating now, are we, Blake?" the man behind the bar said, acrimony sneaking into his previously flat voice.

"I'm not here to negotiate anything," I said, trying to draw the man's attention back to me. "I just want to know how long Carl Miller was here on Tuesday night."

The man jutted his chin at Grayson. "He wants me to sell his fancy-pants beer here."

"Not anymore, I don't, Maury," Grayson said. "I've come to accept that you don't have the right clientele."

"Damn straight I don't," Maury said, apparently not realizing that Grayson's statement was most definitely not a compliment. "We get real men in here. Real men who drink real beer."

A muscle in Grayson's jaw twitched, and I had to struggle to keep myself from making a face.

"Carl Miller?" I said, trying to steer the conversation back on track. "What time did he arrive here on Tuesday night, and how long did he stay?"

"I'm not sure I like you barging in here, asking me all these questions." Maury's eyes took on a belligerent light, the first sign of any real life in them.

"It's about the murder," Grayson cut in before I had a chance to say anything more. "You don't want the police knocking on your door, do you?"

"The police have already been here, asking the same questions."

"Then it should be easy for you to answer them again," I said.

He focused the full force of his belligerent gaze on me, but I stared right back at him.

"If it'll get rid of you," he muttered when I didn't blink, "Carl and Greg showed up around nine, like they usually do on Tuesday nights. Greg stayed and played a few games with some of the other guys. He was here until nearly midnight, but Carl only stayed about ten minutes."

So much for his alibi.

"Now that you've got your answers," Maury went on, "how about you get out of here and let me get back to running my business?"

I struggled to remain polite. "I appreciate your time."

Not wanting to linger, I got myself out of there and back onto the sidewalk.

"So Carl Miller doesn't have an alibi," Grayson said once we were outside, the door to the pool hall shut behind us. "But why would he kill your ex?"

"I have a theory."

"One you're not going to share with me?" he guessed when I said nothing more.

I stepped around him and set off along the

sidewalk, heading in the direction of the pub.

"Are you hoping to find a stronger suspect than yourself?" I asked when he fell into step beside me.

"Of course I am. Isn't that what you want to do? My understanding is that you're a suspect too."

"Was," I corrected. "I have an alibi. Do you?"

"Unfortunately, no. I was alone most of the evening."

I could feel his eyes on me as we walked, but I refused to look his way.

"You think I might have done it, don't you?" he said after a time.

It was more of a statement than a question. I couldn't tell if he was disappointed.

"The police seem to think it's a possibility."

"And as soon as they've done their tests, they'll find out that none of my swords was the murder weapon."

"Until then, you had a motive—at the time you still thought Eric was a mole. You also had opportunity, and possibly the means to commit the murder."

He let out a deep breath, a puffy cloud forming in front of his face before dissipating. "Which is why the police questioned me for three hours earlier today."

If they hadn't arrested him, they must not have had enough evidence against him without knowing if one of his swords was the murder weapon.

"I'm sure your past was of interest to them too," I said, my curiosity prompting the comment.

"My past?" He seemed genuinely confused.

"I heard it mentioned that you have a criminal history."

I could tell he was staring at me, even though I kept my eyes straight ahead. But when he let out a sudden burst of laughter, it was my turn to stare at him.

"Is that what people are saying about me?" He'd stopped laughing, but he was grinning, and his eyes practically danced with mirth.

Amusement only made him all the more handsome, and when his bright gaze locked with mine, my heart tripped over itself, and a hint of warmth touched my previously chilled cheeks.

"So it's not true?" I asked.

He stopped on the street corner we'd just arrived at. The first firework of the evening blasted up into the night air, exploding with a bang and a shower of green sparks.

Grayson was still grinning as he watched the sky. "This is where I leave you. Good night, Ms. Coleman."

"Is it true or not?" I called after him, my curiosity almost ready to make me explode like the firework.

He shoved his hands into the pockets of his

black wool coat and didn't look back. I heard him chuckle as he strode away from me. I tried to be infuriated with him as I stood there watching him go, but as another firework shot into the air and burst into colorful sparks high over his retreating form, somehow I couldn't quite manage it.

The next day was Monday, the only day of the week when the Inkwell wasn't open. I took full advantage of my day off by sleeping as long as Wimsey would let me. Then I enjoyed a leisurely bike ride along quiet country roads and followed it up with a shower before heading over to the village green to check out the festival.

I wandered past the various booths, stopping now and then to chat with someone or to check out the goods on display. When I got to the Hidden Valley Sugarworks booth, I wasted no time purchasing a glass bottle filled with delicious maple syrup. I also indulged in a small packet of maple sugar candies, letting one melt in my mouth as soon as I'd made the purchase.

I returned to the Inkwell after that to get the cocktail samples ready for the tent's noon opening. This time I went with the Huckleberry Gin, the Count Dracula, and the Lovecraft. Since Mel and Damien both had the day off, I had to lug the coolers over to the green on my own. I only wanted to make one trip, so I grabbed one in each hand and set off, wishing with every step that I had stronger arms.

Once I'd crossed both the footbridge and Creekside Road, I paused for a rest, setting the coolers down on the grass. As I shook out my arms, I caught sight of two familiar figures over by the bandstand.

Grayson Blake and Carl Miller.

My curiosity overrode my need to rest my arms, so I grabbed the coolers again and made my way awkwardly across the grass toward the two men. I'd hoped to overhear at least a snippet of their conversation, but my heavy load slowed me down too much. Before I could get within earshot, Carl stalked off, his face stormy.

"What was that about?" I asked Grayson, setting the coolers down again.

He'd been watching Carl's retreat, but when I spoke he shifted his attention to me. "Are you taking those to the tent?" he said with a nod at the coolers.

"Yes."

"Let me give you a hand." He picked up both coolers as easily as if they weighed next to nothing.

"What were you talking to Carl about?" I tried again.

Grayson struck off toward the tent without responding.

I jogged to catch up with him. "Were you talking about his alibi?"

"I mentioned that I knew he hadn't stayed at the pool hall for more than a few minutes."

"And? What did he say?"

"That he was tired so he went straight home from there."

A small crowd of tourists barreled toward us, and I had to dart around them before returning to Grayson's side. "Did he say if anyone could confirm that?"

"He lives alone, and it was dark out. Nobody saw him after he left the pool hall. He wasn't happy about having holes poked in his alibi."

"So I noticed. But if the police asked Maury the same questions as I did, they already know his alibi doesn't stand up to scrutiny."

"They talked to Carl again this morning. I guess that put him in a bad mood. He wasn't very friendly right from the start of our conversation."

We'd reached the tent, so I untied the flap and held it open for him while he carried in the coolers. He set them on the Inkwell's table, and I thanked him for the help.

"Carl Miller's in the sword-fighting class at the community center," I said, returning to our previous subject. "He's a good suspect."

"I'm glad I'm not the only one."

I didn't say anything in response to that. For some reason I was having trouble remembering to be careful around him. Although I found myself wanting to believe he was innocent, I couldn't be sure that he was.

"The students in that class aren't the only ones aside from me who own or have access to swords," he said.

"You're right. The teacher does too. Jason, your head of security."

He looked at me like I'd suddenly sprouted a second head. "Why would Jason kill your ex?"

"Maybe he did it on your behalf, to protect the brewery, or to protect his job."

"Jason isn't the killer any more than I am. And if he were to kill someone—which he wouldn't—he's too smart to leave the body lying around to be found."

"Maybe he panicked or got spooked by a passing car and took off."

"Jason doesn't panic, and he doesn't get spooked. He would have hidden the body."

"In the woods?" I guessed.

"There or in the brewery's old cellar. No one would find it there. Plus it's damp down there since it tends to flood when it rains. Good conditions to move along the decomposition process."

I made a face. "Sounds like you've given it a lot of thought."

"This is the first time I've considered it."

I let the matter drop and opened a new package

of plastic cups while Grayson tidied up the stack of glossy pamphlets over on the brewery's table.

"What did you mean about others having access to swords?" I asked after several seconds, realizing he'd never said.

"Barry Lanik."

"The owner of the antiques shop?"

"The owner of the business, but not the building."

"Right." I recalled that Rhonda's boss, Frank Fournier, was the landlord.

"Did you ever go in the shop?"

"No. Why?"

"Barry had some antique swords available for sale. I bought one of the nicer ones he had, but he still had a few more."

"Interesting," I said, deciding that my theory about Barry burning down the shop to collect insurance on his stock was a pretty good one. Although, even if he killed Eric for witnessing him set the fire, that didn't explain the location of Eric's body. "Do you know anything else related to the case?"

Grayson opened his own package of plastic cups and set a stack on the brewery's table. "Do you?"

"I have a few theories. We could share information. They always say two heads are better than one."

"I'm not so sure you should be playing detective."

I frowned across the tent at him. "And what were you doing when you were questioning Carl earlier? Are you saying it's okay for you to play detective because you're a man?"

"No."

"Then what's the problem? We could be a crime-solving duo. Like Holmes and Watson, or Poirot and Hastings." I smiled at the thought.

Grayson crumpled up the plastic packaging from the cups and tossed it into a cardboard box behind his table. "I don't need a sidekick."

My jaw nearly dropped to the ground. "*Sidekick?* Who says *I'd* be the sidekick?"

"I'm nobody's sidekick."

"Neither am I!"

"Then I guess that's settled."

He pushed aside the tent flap and stepped out of sight. I thought I caught a hint of a grin on his face before he disappeared, and that only made me fume all the more. For the life of me, I couldn't remember why I'd ever started to like the man.

CHAPTER 17

By the middle of the afternoon, my stomach was rumbling with hunger, and I was getting desperate for a bathroom break. Despite the fact that it was a weekday, a steady stream of people passed through the tent each hour. I didn't want to leave my table unattended while I slipped away for a few minutes, worried that I'd miss out on the chance to interest potential future patrons in the Inkwell and its unique characteristics. At the same time, I knew I'd likely have to at some point. Several tour buses were scheduled to arrive in Shady Creek that day, as they would all week long, so the stream of tourists probably wouldn't let up.

As I poured the last of the Huckleberry Gin into a plastic cup and passed the sample to an eagerly waiting tourist, I realized I'd have to leave the tent sooner rather than later. I'd made up a double batch of the cocktails that morning, but I'd left a bottle of each back in the Inkwell's fridge, and the ice in the coolers had completely melted now. I was about to ask Juliana if I could borrow her BACK SOON sign when I spotted a head of bleached blond and electric blue hair among the latest crowd of people entering the tent.

"I thought you might be in need of a break,"

Mel said when she reached the Inkwell's table.

"But it's your day off," I reminded her as I passed out samples of the Lovecraft.

"I don't mind hanging out here for an hour or two."

"Really? Because that would be fantastic."

She shooed me out of the folding chair. "You go on. I'll take care of things here."

"I'll nip over to the pub and get the backup bottles before I do anything else," I said. "We're all out of Huckleberry Gin and running low on the others."

Mel eyed the two nearly empty bottles sitting on the table. "Looks like they've been as popular as ever."

"Thankfully."

A group of four tourists approached the table, so I told Mel I'd be back soon and ducked out of the tent, one of the empty coolers in hand. When I reached the Inkwell, I only hung around long enough to use the facilities and restock the cooler.

"I'm going to go find something to eat," I told Mel upon my return to the tent.

"Take your time," she said as she served more tourists.

Once outside the tent again, I headed straight for the line of food trucks that had been allowed to park along Hemlock Street during the festival. A myriad of delicious smells wafted through the air, making my stomach grumble more loudly than ever. It wasn't easy to decide what to eat— there was Greek food, Mexican food, burgers, and several other choices. In the end, I settled on quesadillas and black cherry lemonade.

Picnic tables had been set up nearby for the duration of the festival, and I plunked myself down at one end of the only vacant one. My mouth watering, I dug into my meal, enjoying every bite and every sip. I was about halfway through my quesadillas when I became aware of the people at the table next to mine. Four women sat there, eating salads and burgers as they chatted. I didn't know any of their names, but I recognized a couple of faces, so I figured they were locals rather than tourists. As I took a long sip of my lemonade, Vera Anderson joined them, carrying a salad from one of the food trucks.

"Any word on the arson investigation, Doris?" she asked once she was settled at the table and had greeted the other women.

Those words caught my attention. Although I kept eating, I cast surreptitious glances their way and zeroed in on their conversation.

A woman with short dark hair sprinkled with gray replied to the question. "Not yet." She let out a heavy sigh. "And the insurance company is giving us a hard time."

"Why's that?" one of the other women asked.

"They insinuated that Barry might have been the one to burn down the shop."

One of her companions gasped.

"It's ridiculous," Doris said firmly. "Barry had nothing to do with it, of course."

"I suppose it doesn't help that he didn't respond to phone calls right away," Vera said.

"You mean on the night of the fire?" a blond woman asked.

Vera gave a prim nod as she speared half a cherry tomato with her plastic fork. "Greg Wilmer tried to phone him from the scene of the fire, but it took a few tries before he answered."

"He was sound asleep," Doris said defensively. "And so was I. Plus, Greg called Barry's cell phone first, and he'd left it in the kitchen."

"I'm sure he did," Vera said, though her tone suggested otherwise. "I just mean that from the investigators' point of view, it might seem like he didn't answer because he was out of the house, returning from the shop after lighting the fire."

I pretended to only be interested in my quesadillas, but when I shot another sneaky glance their way, I saw that Doris's face was flushed.

"That's ridiculous," she said.

"I'm not saying that's what happened, only that it might look that way to some people."

"Well, those people would be wrong. Barry loved that shop. And you couldn't pay him a million bucks to start a fire. His family's house burned down when he was ten, and he's been terrified of fire ever since. He won't even light a match."

"Hopefully the investigators will believe that." Vera sounded like she didn't particularly believe it herself.

Doris excused herself and left the table, a frown on her face.

"It's true," one of the other women said when she was gone. "I've known Barry and Doris since before they moved to town. He really is terrified of even the smallest flame."

They didn't say much more on the subject, soon chatting instead about the festival and the next day's pumpkin pie baking contest. That reminded me of my upcoming judging duties. Despite Shontelle's wary view of the contest, I was looking forward to it. I loved pumpkin pie.

I finished up my meal and tossed the garbage and recyclables into their respective bins. I'd been away from the tent for well under an hour, so I decided to take a little more time to do a bit of my own investigating. From the conversation I'd overheard, I figured it was safe to assume that Doris was Barry's wife. If he really was too terrified to so much as light a match, then he didn't belong on my suspect list. But *someone* had burned down the antiques shop. Who else would have had reason to?

Doris, possibly. With or without her husband's knowledge, she might have decided to put an end to his business before it lost them any more money. She didn't look like an arsonist, but what did an arsonist look like anyway?

There was also the landlord, Frank Fournier, to consider. But why would he want to burn down the building? It had housed two units, one occupied by Barry's business. The other one had stood empty the whole time I'd lived in Shady Creek. That struck me as odd, now that I thought about it. The building was just a stone's throw away from the village green, so it should have been a prime location for any business geared toward tourists.

I wondered if Rhonda could shed some light on that. She worked as a secretary for Mr. Fournier, so there was a good chance she'd know at least something about the various properties he owned around town. I could afford to make a quick visit to the offices of Fournier Real Estate and Developments and still get back to the tent before Mel had been there too long. Deciding on that course of action, I crossed the grass and followed Maple Street a block away from the green before turning left. I'd never been inside Mr. Fournier's office, but I'd walked past it on several occasions, so I knew where to find it.

It took me less than five minutes to reach my destination. When I stepped into the reception area, I was relieved to see Rhonda behind her desk. I quickly realized she wasn't alone, however. A tall, balding man in a gray business suit stood next to her desk, speaking to her.

"So please set up a meeting with O'Reilly for early next week," he said to Rhonda before sending a brilliant smile my way. "Good afternoon. Frank Fournier." He offered me his hand and gave mine a good shake when I took it. "How can I help you today?"

"Sadie Coleman," I said once I had my hand back. "I'm a friend of Rhonda's. I was passing by, so I thought I'd pop in to say hi to her. But I don't want to interrupt if you're both busy."

Mr. Fournier waved off my comment. "I'm on my way out to a meeting, but I'm in no hurry. And I'm sure Rhonda can spare a minute or two. You didn't take much of a lunch break today, did you, Rhonda?"

"Just fifteen minutes," she said.

"Then you're due for another one." He returned his attention to me. "You're the new owner of the pub, aren't you?"

"That's right," I replied.

He gave a satisfied nod. "I knew I recognized your name. I always keep tabs on all the real estate goings-on in this town."

"Speaking of real estate," I said, jumping at the chance to segue into a possibly enlightening conversation, "I'm sorry about the building you lost to the fire."

"Thank you," Mr. Fournier said, his face growing serious. "It's quite a loss, but we must move forward in the face of adversity." His flashy smile returned.

"Do you have any plans for rebuilding?" I asked.

His smile faltered before he fixed it back in place. "Not as of yet. All in due time." He checked his silver wristwatch. "I'm afraid I must be on my way now. It was a pleasure to meet you, Ms. Coleman."

"You too," I said, but he was already on his way out the door.

Rhonda watched him disappear from sight before leaning toward me across her desk. "He wasn't telling the truth," she said in a hushed voice, although I couldn't see or hear any sign of anyone else nearby.

"About his plans for rebuilding?" I asked.

She nodded. "Hold on a moment." She pushed back her chair and got up from behind the desk, hurrying through a door to an inner office. I heard the sound of rustling papers before she reappeared a moment later, shutting the door behind her. She set a large sheet of paper out on the desk and smoothed it out. "See?"

I stepped closer for a better look. The paper appeared to be part of a set of blueprints for a building, I realized as I studied the design. "What's this for? A hotel?"

"A boutique hotel," Rhonda confirmed. "He's been planning to put one on that site for weeks now, maybe even for months."

"But why lie about that unless . . ."

"Unless he didn't want to look like he had a reason to burn down his own building," Rhonda finished, her eyes wide. "That's what I'm afraid of."

"Hold on a second. So what if he wants to build a hotel? Why not just tear down what was there and get on with the project?"

"He's been losing money on the place. There was a lot of water damage in the second unit from a pipe that burst last winter, and there's also been a bit of a . . . rodent problem."

I made a face. "That's why the second unit has been empty for so long?"

Rhonda nodded. "And Barry Lanik's lease had another year on it, and he wasn't interested in making any sort of deal to cut it short. That's one of the reasons Mr. Fournier and Barry haven't been getting along."

My ears perked up at that. "They don't get along?"

"They haven't for more than a year. Barry tried to get Mr. Fournier to lower his rent, but of course he didn't agree. Ever since, they've squabbled over every little thing."

"So maybe Mr. Fournier saw arson as the best way to get rid of Barry and his business quickly so he could get on with building his boutique hotel?"

Rhonda's eyes were still wide. "I'm crazy for thinking that, right?"

"I'm not so sure."

Her face fell. "I should tell the police about all of this, shouldn't I?"

"That might be a good idea."

"But if I'm wrong and he's innocent, I could lose my job if he finds out I talked to the police about him."

"Maybe he won't find out. And if he is an arsonist, he shouldn't get away with it. Besides, there's a possibility that the arsonist could also be Eric's murderer."

Rhonda's already wide eyes looked about ready to pop out of her head. "Really?"

"The two crimes aren't necessarily connected, but now I'm thinking it's something to consider."

She closed her eyes for a moment. "I've been so worried about all of this. I've wanted to tell someone, but I wasn't sure if I should."

"I'm glad you told me, and I really do think you should tell the police."

She sighed. "I will, but I hope I'm wrong to suspect Mr. Fournier."

She glanced past me toward the front window. I followed her line of sight and saw Harvey peering through the glass at us. He waved, and I waved back as Rhonda hurriedly rolled up the blueprints. As Harvey entered the office, she dashed through the inner door with the rolled-up paper. I heard what sounded like a metal drawer shutting, and then she was back.

"Afternoon, ladies," Harvey greeted us. He kissed Rhonda on the cheek. "I just stopped by to say hi and to bring you this." He handed Rhonda a takeout coffee cup.

"It's been good to see you both, but I need to get back to the festival," I said, already heading for the door. "Talk to you again soon."

I pushed my way out the door with a wave and hurried back to the village green, not wanting to impose on Mel any longer. I spent the rest of the afternoon serving more samples and handing out brochures about the Inkwell, but the entire time, my mind was spinning with all the information Rhonda had shared with me.

CHAPTER 18

When I returned to the mill after the tent had closed down for the day, I ate a peanut butter sandwich for dinner—sharing some of the peanut butter with Wimsey—and then flopped down on the couch. It had been five days since Grayson and I had found Eric's body by the creek, and the police had yet to charge anyone with his murder. I hoped the cops were closer to fingering the culprit than I was. I had plenty of suspects, some stronger than others, but I didn't think I was on the verge of proving that any one of them was the killer.

I couldn't help but think of Eric's family and how tough it must be for them to know his murderer was still on the loose, not paying for taking their son and brother away from them. That thought tugged my spirits down toward the floor. I stared up at the ceiling, unable to muster the energy required to move. Wimsey hopped up on the couch near my legs and walked across my stomach to settle on my left shoulder.

"Hey, buddy." I stroked his fur, and he closed his eyes, purring. "I wish my life were as simple as yours."

His purring subsided as he drifted off to sleep. I was tempted to do the same, even though it was early in the evening. Deciding that didn't matter, I shut my eyes, allowing myself to relax. My attempted nap didn't last long. Within a minute or two of closing my eyes, my cell phone rang on the coffee table.

I reached out to grab it, trying not to disturb Wimsey in the process. He cracked open his eyes but otherwise didn't move. I checked the screen of my phone. It was my younger brother, Taylor, calling.

"To what do I owe this honor?" I asked by way of greeting. "I don't remember the last time the King of Texts actually phoned me."

"Dire situations call for dire measures," Taylor said, his tone good-natured, as it usually was.

"I think I've had enough dire situations to last me the rest of the month, thank you. Actually, make that the rest of the year."

"Sorry, Sis. This one's not of my making."

"So what's wrong?" I wasn't too worried, since he didn't sound concerned.

"I saw the news about Eric's death on Facebook. Natalie wrote a post about it."

I winced. "I'm sorry that's how you found out. I should have let you know."

"I'm sure you've had a lot on your mind. I can't believe someone killed him! It's hard to wrap my head around it. But what I really called to say is that somebody saw Natalie's post and told their mom, who then told our mother."

I groaned, slapping my free hand to my forehead. "Don't tell me . . ."

"Yep. I can pretty much guarantee you're going to get a phone call from her in the immediate future."

I sighed, deciding to deal with the inevitable head-on. "I'll call her first."

"Good idea. But before you go, how are you holding up?"

"I'm all right. But I'll feel better once Eric's killer is caught and put behind bars."

"I bet. It's crazy. I can't believe someone killed him. I mean, I kind of wanted to wring his neck after all those times he lied to you, but why would anyone else want to hurt him?"

"That's the question." And I had several answers to it. I just wished I knew which one was the right one.

We chatted for another minute or so about his job as a tattoo artist, then wrapped up our conversation.

"Thanks for the warning," I said.

"No problem. Good luck."

I was probably going to need it.

After I'd ended the call with Taylor, I logged onto Facebook and found the post he'd mentioned. I had to fight tears as I read Natalie's tribute to her brother. She wrapped it up by stating that her family was planning a funeral that would take place soon in Philadelphia. For a second, I wondered if I should make plans to go to the funeral, but I quickly decided against that idea. I needed to stay at the Inkwell, and I didn't want to make things awkward for anyone.

I got off the Internet and simply stared at my phone for a full minute before selecting my mom's number.

"Here we go, Wimsey," I said to my cat.

He continued snoozing away.

My mom picked up after the first ring.

"Sadie Elizabeth Coleman," she said to start, and I knew that wasn't a good sign. "Why on earth didn't you call me sooner?"

"Sorry, Mom. I've had a lot going on."

"A lot going on? Sadie, I had to hear about Eric's death from Mary Beth Robinson in the middle of the grocery store. What do you think that was like?"

"I'm sorry," I said again, sincerely this time. "I should have called."

"Yes, you should have." She let out a sigh on the other end of the line, and I hoped she was releasing some of her disappointment in me along with it. "Have they caught the killer?"

"Not yet."

"Then you need to pack up and come home."

I sat up, dislodging a perturbed Wimsey from my shoulder. "Mom! I can't pack up and go anywhere. I've got a business to run."

"You won't be running anything if you get murdered in your sleep."

"That's not going to happen."

"There's a killer on the loose," she reminded me unnecessarily. "What kind of town is it you're living in, anyway?"

"Mom, there are murders in Knoxville every year. Far more than here in Shady Creek."

"Honestly," she went on as if she hadn't heard me, "I don't know what Gilda was thinking encouraging you to stay there."

"Aunt Gilda didn't try to sway me either way," I said with a roll of my eyes. We'd been through this many times before. "It was my decision to move here, my decision to buy the pub. And now it's also my decision to stay here in Shady Creek."

"Sometimes, Sadie, I really don't know what to do with you."

"I know, Mom," I said with a sigh.

"I guess I'll just have to hope that you come to your senses soon."

By that she meant leaving Shady Creek and getting a "normal job" like the one I'd had in the human resources department of a Boston company before my former life fell apart. She would have preferred that I'd gone to dental or law school, but in her mind almost anything— except working at a tattoo parlor—would be better than owning a pub.

At least this time she didn't go on about how my older brother, Michael, never caused her this much stress. She was always lamenting how Taylor and I weren't more like her oldest child.

"But life would be so boring if we were all dull like Michael," Taylor liked to say to her, which always got a reaction, though never a good one.

I usually kept quiet and let her rant, though secretly I did agree with Taylor. Michael was a tax lawyer with his own firm. I could see how that made her proud, but I didn't understand why she wanted so badly for me and Taylor to follow a similar path. It wasn't like we'd turned out badly. I didn't think we had, anyway.

I apologized to her again for not calling sooner and told her I had some things to attend to. I was making excuses, but at least they got me off the phone. The aftermath of the call left me feeling gloomier than ever, and I sat there staring at the coffee table for several minutes. The only thing that nudged me out of my melancholy trance was my phone chiming to indicate that I'd received a new text.

The message was from Shontelle, asking if I wanted to hang out at her place for a bit. I took her up on the offer, not particularly eager to be alone with my low spirits.

"I'll see you later, Wims," I said, giving him a good-bye scratch on the head as I pulled on my coat.

I passed through the pub on my way out, making a stop in the Mary Stewart room. I headed directly for the shelf running along the exposed stone wall and the row of yellow spines lined up next to a collection of blue ones. There was a small gap where one book had been removed. I pulled out the volume next to the gap and slipped it into my purse before setting off to Shontelle's apartment located over her gift shop.

Shontelle buzzed me in through the street-level door, and I climbed the steps to her apartment. As soon as it opened, eight-year-old Kiandra jumped up and down and threw her arms around my waist.

"Sadie! Guess what! Guess what!"

"Umm . . . you're turning into a pumpkin?"

Kiandra released me and clapped her hands over her mouth as she giggled. "No!"

"Really?" I said, eyeing her cloud of curly hair. "I could have sworn I saw a stem growing out of your head."

She giggled harder. "I'm not turning into a pumpkin. I'm going to dance a solo at my next dance recital."

"That's fantastic! I can't wait to see it."

"So you'll come watch?"

"I wouldn't miss it for the world," I assured her.

She told me all about the upcoming recital and showed off a snippet of her solo before Shontelle told her it was time to get into her pajamas and brush her teeth.

"Awww, Mom."

"If you go without complaint, you can read for ten minutes before the lights go out."

"But I finished my Nancy Drew," Kiandra said, sounding forlorn.

I opened my purse. "Then I guess it's a good thing I brought this along." I held up the yellow book.

"Yes!" Kiandra bounced up and down. "Thank you, Sadie!" She took the book from me and hugged it to her chest. "One second."

She disappeared into her bedroom and returned a moment later with *The Secret of Red Gate Farm*, the previous book in the series. I'd been loaning them to her one at a time. She'd been a reluctant reader until I'd introduced her to Nancy Drew a few weeks earlier. Since then she'd been reading the series hungrily. Shontelle had even caught her reading under her blankets with a flashlight on more than one occasion. That was something I'd done many a time when I was young, and as stern as Shontelle acted in front of her daughter when that happened, she'd confessed to me that she was pleased Kiandra now loved reading so much that she was sneaking in more time for it.

With *The Clue in the Diary* to look forward to, Kiandra obediently got ready for bed. After the promised ten minutes of reading had stretched to twenty, we both said good night to Kiandra, and Shontelle switched off the light and shut her bedroom door.

"I can't thank you enough for introducing her to Nancy Drew," Shontelle said once we were in the kitchen. "If only I'd known that's all it would take to get her hooked on reading."

"It's my pleasure. I couldn't get enough of Nancy Drew when I was her age."

Shontelle poured each of us a small glass of red wine, and I curled up in one of her arm chairs while she settled on the couch.

"Any more news about your prowler?" she asked once we were seated.

"No." I swirled my wine in the glass.

"Please be careful until the police catch whoever's responsible."

"I will be."

Shontelle took a sip of her drink before speaking again. "So, what's this I hear about you and Grayson?"

I stopped with my wineglass halfway to my lips. "Um, there is no me and Grayson."

She arched an eyebrow. "Really? Because you were seen walking around together last night. Word is you went on a date to the pool hall. To be honest, I would have expected the two of you to pick a classier joint, but I suppose billiards and romance aren't necessarily mutually exclusive."

"Whoa, hold on," I said. "We were not on a date."

Her eyebrow quirked upward again.

"Not. On. A. Date." I repeated, emphasizing each word. "I asked for directions to the pool hall so I could ask the owner some questions, and Grayson decided to show me the way."

"How very chivalrous of him."

"Hardly," I muttered into my wine, still annoyed with him after our conversation that morning.

"So you're saying there aren't any sparks between the two of you?"

"There are sparks, all right. Just not of the romantic variety."

"Mmm-hmm." Shontelle eyed me over the rim of her wineglass as she took a sip.

"I did find out that Carl Miller doesn't have an alibi for Tuesday night like he claimed." I hoped that would be enough to encourage Shontelle to steer the subject away from Grayson.

From the way her eyebrow arched yet again, I knew she saw through my attempt to switch topics, but to my relief she didn't pursue the matter further.

"Carl isn't exactly a rocket scientist," she said. "If he is the murderer, he won't get away with it for long. He probably would have panicked once the deed was done. If the murder weapon wasn't found at the scene—"

"Which it wasn't. Otherwise, the police wouldn't be looking for it," I interjected.

"Exactly. And the police didn't find any swords when they searched his place."

"What? When did they do that?"

"This afternoon."

"And I'm not hearing about it until now?"

"You spent too much time cooped up in that tent today."

"I must have."

"Of course, being cooped up in the tent wouldn't be so bad if a certain handsome brewer were there with you."

"One of his employees looks after the brewery's table," I said.

I wasn't about to mention the fact that Grayson had carried my coolers for me that morning. No doubt she'd read far too much into that.

"So," I said, deciding to get us back on track, "maybe Carl stashed the weapon somewhere between the scene of the crime and his house."

"Sounds like a possibility."

"Do you know where he lives?"

"Somewhere south of the green, I think, but I don't know exactly where."

"I'm sure someone will be able to tell me."

"I don't doubt it." Shontelle regarded me from her seat on the couch. "Are you planning to look for the weapon yourself?"

"It couldn't hurt."

"The police have probably beat you to it."

"Probably," I agreed.

Shontelle swirled the last of her wine in her glass. "Maybe you should leave it to them. Judging by the things that have happened to you lately, the killer might already be annoyed that you're nosing around."

"Except my tires were slashed before I even knew Eric was dead," I pointed out. "So if the same person is responsible for slashing my tires and leaving the gas can outside the mill, how can those things be related to the murder?"

"I don't know," Shontelle admitted. "But we also don't know that the same person was behind both of the incidents directed at you. Maybe it was a delinquent teenager who slashed your tires."

"Maybe," I said, although I was having trouble believing it. "Have you heard anything around town about me?"

She tipped her head to the side as she considered the question. "There's that rumor about you and Grayson . . ."

I rolled my eyes. "I meant anything along the lines of people not wanting me here."

"Is that what you think the pranks are about?"

"That's what it *feels* like."

Shontelle finished off her wine and set her glass on the coffee table. "No, I haven't heard anything of the kind. And why would anyone not want you here? Okay, so some people here aren't entirely welcoming of people who weren't born and raised in Shady Creek, but most people are nice."

I stared into the depths of my almost-empty glass. "At first, I thought it was Grayson since he didn't seem to like me, but now I'm not so sure."

"What was that all about, anyway? Between you and Grayson, I mean."

I filled her in on how Grayson had thought I was mixed up in the brewery chain's plan to steal his recipes. "Plus, he wanted to buy the pub, and he thought I'd sneaked in and bought it out from under his nose as part of the nefarious plan."

"But that's all sorted out now?"

"I think so." When Shontelle smiled, I hurried to add, "But don't think that means there's going to be anything between us. He's still a jerk."

Shontelle shook her head. "I haven't seen what you've seen, apparently. Maybe you bring out the worst in him."

"Hey!"

"Just kidding," she said. "Sort of."

I tried to glare at her but failed.

After finishing the last of my wine, I pushed myself up from the armchair—not an easy task since I was getting sleepy and didn't much want to move.

"Thanks for the wine. I'd better get home and get some sleep."

"Good luck with the pumpkin pie judging tomorrow," Shontelle said as she walked me to the door. "You might need it."

"I refuse to worry about that," I told her.

"For your sake, I hope there's no reason to."

"Either way, it'll be done with soon enough." I pulled on my coat and gave her a quick hug. "Good night, Shon."

"Good night."

I descended the stairs and stepped out into the cold night air, shivering as I buttoned up my coat. I walked quickly, trying to keep warm, my hands deep in my coat pockets. It was a good thing I didn't have to walk far. I hadn't brought a hat with me, and my ears were already going numb from the chilly breeze that was lifting my hair from my shoulders.

Most of the businesses around the green had closed hours earlier. Lumière was the only establishment with lights still blazing. The sidewalks were deserted, and the only sound I could hear was that of my own footsteps on the sidewalk. As I crossed from Hillview Road to Sycamore Street, I thought I saw a shadow move next to the building on the corner, but then everything went still.

Just your imagination, I told myself.

I maintained my pace, turning my thoughts

to my plans for the next day. As I stepped up onto the sidewalk on Sycamore Street, I heard a scuffling sound close by.

I didn't have a chance to look in the direction of the noise before someone grabbed me from behind.

CHAPTER 19

I tried to scream, but a gloved hand clapped over my mouth, muffling the sound. Panic shot through me. I squirmed and tried to yell through the hand over my mouth. My assailant's arm only tightened around me, pinning my own arm to my side. I tried to pry the hand off my mouth with my free arm, but without success. I opened my mouth and chomped down on one of the gloved fingers, stomping on my assailant's foot at the same time.

I heard a grunt of pain near my left ear. My attacker released me, but then shoved me hard from behind. I fell forward, my hands and knees smacking into the sidewalk. I scrambled over to the nearest streetlamp and grabbed it, using it to pull myself upright. A figure in dark clothing disappeared around the corner, moving quickly. No one else was in sight.

My breaths coming in frightened gasps, I clung to the streetlamp. Laughter and chatting voices erupted into the night air. I whipped my head in the direction of the noise. A group of five people had exited Lumière. Unaware of my distress, they crossed the road and headed off over the green.

As I leaned against the lamppost, I became aware of stinging scrapes on my hands and knees.

My legs trembled beneath me, but I managed to let go of the streetlamp and stay upright. I wiped my shaky hands on my jeans and walked as quickly as I could along the street. I kept glancing over my shoulder, but there was no more sign of my attacker. Even so, my heart didn't want to slow down.

It occurred to me that I should call the police, but all I wanted right then was to not be alone. I stumbled over to the door to Aunt Gilda's apartment and hit the buzzer. I hit it again when I received no response, but it was no use. Aunt Gilda wasn't home.

I was tempted to cry but refused to let myself. Instead, I headed for the restaurant and the light it was spilling out onto the sidewalk. I'd almost reached Lumière when the front door opened again. This time someone familiar stepped out onto the sidewalk, a paper takeout bag in one hand.

"Sadie?" Grayson's forehead furrowed as he took in the sight of me. "Are you all right?"

"Someone grabbed me while I was walking down the street," I said in a rush. "I broke free, and they ran off."

Grayson's whole demeanor changed. "When and where?"

I pointed down the street. "Near the corner. Maybe a minute ago."

He shoved the takeout bag into my arms

and took off down the street at a run. When he disappeared around the corner, I stared down at the bag he'd left with me. Warmth from the food inside seeped through the paper to my hands. That made me realize how cold I was.

Shivering, I considered going inside the restaurant, but I couldn't bring myself to move. My gaze went back to the street corner, waiting for Grayson to reappear, wondering what— or whom—he'd find. A minute or two later, he jogged back around the corner.

"I couldn't see anyone," he said when he came to stop in front of me. He rested a hand on my shoulder. "Are you hurt?"

I shook my head. "Just some scrapes. Whoever it was, they pushed me to the ground."

He relieved me of the takeout bag and set it on the sidewalk. He took my hands in his and turned them palm up so he could see the scrapes. They were only minor abrasions, barely even stinging anymore.

"I'll call the police." He released my hands and reached into his pocket for his phone.

Immediately, I missed the delicious warmth from his touch.

"You're shivering," he said. "Why don't we go inside?"

I shook my head, stepping away from the restaurant. "I don't want to make a scene."

Before he could argue with me, I moved to

the curb, sitting there with my back against a lamppost. Now that I had company, I wanted to stay away from the crowd inside the restaurant. Getting stared at would only make me feel worse than I already did. I heard Grayson talking on his phone behind me, but his words blurred to meaningless noise. Now that my initial shock had worn off, my head was spinning. Who had grabbed me and why?

I didn't think it was a random attack. Too much had happened lately for that to be the case.

Was it Eric's killer? Had the murderer had me in his or her grasp?

I shuddered at that thought and hugged my knees. I knew my attacker wasn't Grayson, but he was the only person from my suspect list I could rule out. All I'd seen of my assailant was a dark blur disappearing in the distance. I wouldn't be able to provide the police with a description.

Taller than me? Shorter than me? Man? Woman?

I didn't know.

I rested my forehead against my knees. A wave of chattering voices and clinking cutlery washed over me before the peace and quiet of the night returned.

"Sadie? What are you doing sitting over there?"

I jumped to my feet at the sound of Aunt Gilda's voice. She'd just stepped out of the restaurant, Louie behind her.

Grayson ended his call and addressed me. "The police will be here soon."

"The police? Sadie, what's going on?" A note of alarm had entered Aunt Gilda's voice.

I hurried to explain. "Someone grabbed me from behind when I was walking home from Shontelle's. They ran away, and I'm okay. Grayson called the police for me."

Aunt Gilda pulled me into a fierce hug. "What in God's name is going on these days? You're sure you're all right?"

I nodded against her shoulder. "I'm fine. It shook me up a bit, that's all."

She held me at arm's length, looking me over before finally deciding for herself that I was okay. "Thank heavens you weren't hurt."

"We'll stay with you until the police get here," Louie said.

"Of course we will," Gilda agreed. "And you'll stay at my place tonight."

My first instinct was to protest, but before I got any words out I realized that I didn't want to argue with her. "Can I bring Wimsey over too?" I asked. "I don't want to leave him alone at the mill after everything that's happened lately."

"We'll go get him after you've spoken to the police," Aunt Gilda said.

She put an arm around me, and I rested my head on her shoulder, grateful for her presence. I was still shaken, although with every minute that passed I felt a bit better. The cogs in my brain continued to turn, trying to figure out who my attacker was, but I came up empty. When a patrol car pulled up to the curb a minute later, I still had no real clues to share.

The responding officer turned out to be Vera Anderson's nephew, Officer Eldon Howes. I told him what had happened in as much detail as I could—which was hardly any—and Grayson gave his brief account as well.

"We'll do some extra patrols of the area throughout the night," Officer Howes assured us.

Despite that promise, I didn't have high hopes that the police would catch my attacker. He or she was long gone by now, and with basically no description to go on, my assailant would likely never be identified. Unless Eric's killer was found and my attacker turned out to be the same person.

As Officer Howes drove off in his patrol car, Aunt Gilda returned her arm to my shoulders. "Let's go pick up Wimsey so we can get you settled at my place."

I glanced at Grayson, who was standing next to Louie. "I'll just be a moment," I said to Aunt Gilda.

As Louie moved to join Aunt Gilda by the streetlamp, I approached Grayson, rubbing my arms to keep warm. "Thank you for calling the police and for looking for the attacker."

"You're welcome," he said. "I'm glad nothing worse happened to you."

I was about to turn away when Grayson touched a hand to my arm. "Sadie."

I raised my eyes to meet his.

"It really would be safer for you to leave the investigating to the police."

If exhaustion hadn't been seeping into my bones, his words would have annoyed me. As it was, all I wanted to do was snuggle up into bed with Wimsey, so I simply nodded and returned to Aunt Gilda's side. She tucked her arm through mine, and Louie accompanied us as we set off toward the mill. When I glanced over my shoulder, I saw Grayson still standing out front of the restaurant, watching us. I focused on the mill ahead of me, too tired to sort out the conflicting emotions that the sight of him stirred up inside of me.

Less than an hour later, I was under the covers in Aunt Gilda's guest room, Wimsey curled up on the pillow next to me. He'd stayed with me at Aunt Gilda's apartment when I'd first arrived in Shady Creek, so he'd settled into our temporary accommodations easily, and now he was completely relaxed, his front paws tucked beneath him and his eyes closed.

If only I could have relaxed with such little effort. I kept closing my eyes, only to realize that I was once again staring up at the ceiling a few minutes later. I wished I'd brought a book with me, but I'd left my Kathy Reichs novel at home on my bedside table.

A couple of times during the night, I got up from the bed and tiptoed toward the window, opening it and shivering as I stuck my head out to peer down the street toward the darkened mill. When I saw that it wasn't on fire or otherwise in jeopardy, I was able to return to bed and shut my eyes, but only for a short while. My worries wouldn't leave me completely, and the scary moments from earlier in the night kept replaying in my mind.

Eventually, I managed to sink into a restless sleep, waking up around seven in the morning when I heard Aunt Gilda moving about in the kitchen. I'd left the bedroom door partially open during the night, and Wimsey was nowhere to be seen. I slowly disentangled myself from the sheets and headed out into the living area in my pajamas, yawning widely. Wimsey was in the kitchen, happily eating breakfast from a dish on the floor while Aunt Gilda stirred a pot on the stove.

"Did you manage to get any sleep?" she asked when I entered the kitchen and leaned against the counter.

I made a so-so gesture with my hand and tucked my messy hair behind my ear. "Thanks for letting me stay here."

She left the stove to come over and kiss me on the top of my head. "You're welcome here anytime. You know that."

I smiled at her, and she patted my cheek before returning to the stove.

"I'm making you some oatmeal."

I'd already suspected that from the smell I'd detected as soon as I'd entered the kitchen. "Yum."

"It'll be ready in a minute. Grab yourself a bowl. There's a bag of chocolate chips in the pantry."

A few minutes later, I was settled at the kitchen table, eating the delicious oatmeal topped with chocolate chips. Aunt Gilda assured me that she'd already eaten some toast for breakfast, but she joined me at the table with a cup of coffee.

"You should take some time to relax today," she said. "You've been through a lot lately, and you should try to enjoy the festival."

"I've got to be back at the tent by noon. And before that, I need to mix up the cocktails for the day's samples."

"I'll leave that last part to you, but why don't you let me look after the tent for a while?"

"You already helped out yesterday," I reminded her. "And won't you be busy at the salon?"

"Not today or tomorrow. I made sure to keep a couple of days free this week so I could check out the festival."

"Then that's what you should do," I said. "Don't worry about me and the Inkwell."

She set down her coffee cup. "Honey, of course I'm going to worry after all that's happened lately. I had a walk around the festival yesterday, and I've got tomorrow off too. You mix up the cocktails. Then I'll hand out the samples, at least for a few hours. No arguments."

I set down my spoon in my empty bowl and reached across the table to squeeze her hand. "Thank you, Aunt Gilda. You're the best."

Once I was dressed, I gathered up my overnight bag and put Wimsey into his carrier. After hugging Aunt Gilda, I headed for home, the cool morning air working together with the coffee Gilda had served me to bring me fully awake.

As soon as I was out on the street, my gaze zeroed in on the mill. With relief, I saw that it was still standing. I didn't know if I had reason to fear for my home and business, but I was concerned nonetheless. Before, I'd been able to comfort myself with the thought that the slashed tires and the ominous placement of the gas can might have been nothing more than mean-spirited pranks, but now that someone had tried to attack me directly, I didn't have a single scrap of peace of mind left to grab on to.

I tried to remain calm as I walked, breathing in the crisp morning air scented with a hint of wood smoke, but I couldn't keep myself from looking this way and that, checking to make sure no one was following me or showing too much interest in me. Everyone seemed to be absorbed in their own business, most of which related to the festival on the village green, but I still couldn't relax completely.

I checked that Creekside Road was free of oncoming traffic and then stepped out onto the street. Three strides later, I came to an abrupt stop, staring at the mill. The building was still standing, but all of the windows were streaked with a gooey substance.

"Oh, Sweet Sherlock. What now?" I muttered as my heart broke into a fretful gallop.

I took a step closer to the mill and stopped again, realizing that all of the windows had been egged.

Anger bubbled its way up through my initial wash of anxiety.

My unknown enemy had struck again.

CHAPTER 20

A car honked at me, and I realized I was still standing in the middle of the road.

I strode quickly to the other side of the street and across the footbridge, setting down my bag and Wimsey's carrier on the grass. I marched along the side of the mill, noting that fragments of eggshell littered the ground and had stuck to the stone walls. I wouldn't have been surprised if steam had poured out of my ears. I was tempted to release my frustration by yelling at the top of my lungs, but the first tour bus of the day had just unloaded its passengers onto the green, and I didn't want people avoiding the Inkwell because they thought I was a crazy lady. So instead, I muttered a few choice words under my breath and rested my hands on my hips.

What a mess. It would take ages to clean up.

If I hadn't been so angry, I probably would have sat down on the ground, ready for a good cry. Since I was too irate for that, I stormed around the entire building, checking each of the windows. Not one had been spared.

When I returned to the front of the mill, I heard a plaintive meow come from Wimsey's cat carrier. Some of my anger drained away at the sound, and I hurried over to my cat.

"I'm sorry, buddy," I said, leaning down to talk to him through the door. "Let's get you inside."

Under other circumstances, I would have opened the door right there, but I was too uneasy to let him run free at the moment. Who knew what else the culprit would be willing to do to cause trouble in my life? I didn't want to give them the opportunity to harm Wimsey in any way.

Once up in my apartment, I set Wimsey free, although I kept the cat doors shut tight. Then I grabbed a bucket from the storeroom on the first floor and filled it with soapy water. I plopped a sponge into the water and grabbed a squeegee before heading outdoors. Since I wanted as few tourists as possible to see the condition of the mill, I started with the windows visible from the green—the ones on the creek side of the mill.

I was still fuming when I got to work scrubbing down the glass with the soapy sponge, so I channeled that energy into the task of cleaning. By the time I finished the ground floor windows near the waterwheel and the ones on either side of the pub's front door, my anger had reduced to a simmer. That allowed my mind to clear, and I realized that I should have reported the incident to the police. I wiped my hands on my jeans and dug my phone out of my pocket, deciding to get that over with. Lately I'd made far too many reports to the police for my liking, and I hoped that would soon change.

There must not have been much else going on crime-wise in Shady Creek that morning, because a patrol car showed up within five minutes, Officer Delaney at the wheel. I told her what had happened and showed her the upper windows that were all still streaked with egg. She promised to make a report and went on her way within minutes of arriving.

Leaving the bucket and squeegee on the footpath, I crossed the grass to the shed and unlocked the double doors, pulling them both open so the daylight would allow me to see into the small building's dim interior. I had to move two sawhorses and a rake to get at the extension ladder stored on one wall, but I was soon hauling it out onto the grass.

When I stepped out into the sunlight, Damien was crossing the footbridge toward me.

"What's going on?" he said when he saw me. "I thought I'd find you mixing cocktails, not wrestling with a ladder."

I tried to brush a clump of cobwebs out of my hair, but only succeeded in dropping the ladder to the ground with a clatter.

"Let me," Damien grabbed the ladder. "Where do you want this?"

I pointed toward the mill. "I'm trying to get at the second-floor windows."

I could tell that he was about to ask me why, but then he took in the sight of the windows and swore instead. "When did that happen?"

"Sometime during the night."

As he carried the ladder over to the mill, I explained to him what had happened on my way home from Shontelle's the night before. "And when I came home this morning, every single one of the windows had been egged."

Damien set the ladder up against the mill, the top of it resting under the sill of a second-floor window. "Did you tell the police?"

"An officer just left a few minutes ago." I rested my hands on my hips and glared up at the dirty window above me.

"This is getting serious," Damien said. "You need to be careful."

"I plan to be."

"I'll look after the windows. You go get ready for the festival."

"Your shift doesn't start until this evening," I reminded him. "Don't you have other things you want to do?"

"I was coming by to have a last look at the catapult, but that'll keep. I'm doing the windows, so there's no point in wasting your breath arguing with me."

I gave him a grateful smile. "Thanks, Damien. I seriously don't know what I'd do without you and Mel."

He shrugged out of his leather jacket and draped it over one of the straw bales decorating the lawn. "Let me know if you need a hand with the cocktails."

I thanked him again and headed inside. It didn't take me long to prepare the drinks, so I grabbed a second sponge before heading back outside. All the windows that would be visible to anyone coming to the pub were now spotless. When I headed around to the forest side of the mill, I found Damien up the ladder, working on the last of the upper-story windows.

"That looks great," I said as he gave the pane one last swipe with the squeegee.

He descended the ladder, the bucket in one hand. "It shouldn't take long to finish the last of them. Then there's just the shells to pick up."

"The cocktails are done, so I can take over now."

"I'll stay until the job is done." He started in on one of the ground-floor windows.

I dunked my sponge in the water and got to work on the next window. We worked in silence for a few minutes before the urge to ask questions distracted me from the task at hand. I glanced Damien's way, but he didn't seem to notice. He finished up the window he was working on, grabbed the bucket, and moved past me to work on a different window.

"Do you think I'm a terrible boss?" The

question burst out of me despite my efforts to keep it tucked away.

Damien paused with his sponge against a pane of glass. He sent a sidelong glance my way before resuming his scrubbing.

My stomach flipped over, and I wondered if I was about to get an answer I didn't want to hear.

"Is that the impression I give you?" he asked.

The fact that he hadn't answered my question only intensified my anxiety.

"I'm not sure." I returned to cleaning the window in front of me. "I guess I have trouble reading you. I'm not sure if you don't like me or if you're just reserved."

Another stretch of silence—punctuated only by the squeak of my sponge running across the glass—sent my stomach into another somersault.

"It's not that I don't like you," he said at last.

"But?" I prodded, sensing he'd left something unsaid.

He dipped his sponge in the bucket and set to work on another pane. "I suppose I've been wary."

"Of me? Why?"

"I want to send my girls to college," he said, referring to his two teenage daughters, whom he was raising on his own. "To do that, I need both my carpentry work and this job."

I stopped cleaning, holding my sponge away from me so the excess water would drip on the ground instead of my clothes. I thought I understood what he was getting at. "And you weren't sure if I'd be able to keep the business going."

A slight tip of his head indicated that I was right.

I stared at the egg-streaked window in front of me as I sifted through my thoughts and emotions. As soon as I'd taken on the pub, I'd felt a weight of responsibility toward my employees. I didn't want to let them down and leave them without work, so I understood his point of view. In his shoes, I probably would have been wary too.

Even so, I couldn't help but want the confidence of everyone around me. I'd never had that, though. I wasn't blind to the fact that there were some people in town who thought a city girl who'd never owned a business would drive their favorite pub into the ground. On top of that, my own mother and older brother thought I was foolish for buying the pub and bound to fail within the first year. As much as I wanted to prove all of those people wrong, there were times when I wondered if they were right.

"I like you as a person, Sadie," Damien said, as if to reassure me.

"But not as a boss?" I tried not to sound hurt.

"I've got no complaints there either."

"But as a business owner?"

A hint of a smile showed on his face. "Let's just

say that I'm less wary than I was three months ago."

That wasn't quite what I'd hoped for, but it could have been worse, and it would have to do. Maybe one day I'd earn his full confidence.

We finished off the remaining windows without much further conversation, and Damien took off on his motorcycle not long after. I emptied the bucket and walked around the mill, picking up bits of eggshell and dropping them into the pail. I didn't get every little piece, but by the time I'd made my way around the building, the worst of the mess was cleaned up.

My spirits weren't particularly high as I dumped the eggshells into the pub's compost bin and washed my hands. Knowing that someone had targeted me once again wasn't at all comforting. Would they ever stop, or would they keep causing trouble for me? I wasn't sure I wanted to know the answer to that question.

When I checked my phone, I had a message from the local mechanic, letting me know that my car was ready to be picked up. I wasn't sure if I wanted to go get it right away. All I really felt like doing was lounging on my couch and cuddling with Wimsey, but at the same time I didn't want the gloomy cloud hanging over my head to envelop me completely. Maybe if I did as Aunt Gilda suggested and tried to enjoy the Autumn Festival, my mood would improve.

First, though, I decided to go get my car. It only took me twenty minutes to walk to the garage, and once I'd paid my bill, I drove back to the Inkwell, parking in the empty lot at the edge of the property. It wasn't quite time to haul the coolers over to the tent, so I stood beneath one of the maple trees, thinking about what to do next.

A colorful leaf fell to the ground at my feet as I stood there. I picked it up and twirled the stem between my fingers. Shady Creek really was a beautiful town, and I loved my new life here, despite all the bad things that had happened over the past several days.

I didn't know why someone was targeting me and the mill, especially since my tires had been slashed before I'd known of Eric's death. That timing suggested that the incident wasn't meant to scare me off from asking questions about the murder. Maybe someone wanted me out of town for some other reason. But the only person I could think of who felt that way was Grayson, and he seemed to have changed his view in that regard. So even if the slashed tires and egged windows weren't connected to the attempted attack on me the night before, I didn't think Grayson was responsible. But then who was?

I let go of the leaf, letting it drop to the grass. I couldn't seem to figure anything out.

Yawning, I decided I needed to make up for my lack of sleep with a second dose of caffeine. It wasn't yet noon, but I also had a hankering for something chocolatey. A mocha latte would hit the spot, I decided, so I walked over to the coffee shop and ordered one. As I waited for the barista to prepare my drink, I turned my thoughts to the Inkwell and all of the pub-related tasks I needed to take care of over the next few days. I had some invoices to pay and some supplies to order, but I also needed to prepare for the first mystery book club meeting that would take place next month.

Thinking about the book club buoyed my spirits. The mystery genre was my personal favorite, and I was hoping the first meeting of this club would be as successful as the one for the romance club. Before that could happen, however, I needed to choose the first book for the members to read. There were so many great options that I hadn't yet settled on a particular one.

Maybe I'd take some time to browse the shelves and look for inspiration at Primrose Books, Shady Creek's only bookstore. That idea raised my spirits even more. In my mind, there were few things better than being surrounded by books. I'd visited the bookshop several times since I'd moved to Shady Creek, and I'd never managed to leave the store without at least one or two purchases. Not that I minded. I didn't think there was such a thing as owning too many books, and with shelves in my apartment as well as in the Inkwell, I had plenty of space to store each treasured volume.

With a trip to the bookstore on the horizon and time to enjoy the festival that afternoon, I was able to offer a genuine smile when the barista handed me my mocha latte. The happy expression remained on my face as I passed Eleanor Grimes, seated alone at a table near the front window. She stared at me as I went by, her eyes anything but friendly.

My smile faltered. Not sure what else to do, I pushed open the coffee shop's door, ill at ease and eager to get away, but even as I left the woman behind, I could still feel the icy touch of her glare on my back.

CHAPTER 21

I strolled around the green as I sipped at my mocha latte, trying to shake off the edginess that had settled over me as I'd left the coffee shop. I had no idea what Eleanor Grimes might have against me, but I didn't want to let her drive my spirits back down. I greeted some of the locals as I walked across the grass, receiving friendly responses from all of them, and that helped me to all but forget about Eleanor's frosty glare.

As soon as I'd finished my latte, I returned to the Inkwell and carried the coolers over to the tent. Aunt Gilda met me there shortly before noon and ushered me out of the tent with instructions to go and enjoy myself. Although I intended to stop in at the bookstore and check out the parts of the Autumn Festival that I hadn't yet experienced, I had a prior commitment to attend to first. It was the day of the pumpkin pie baking contest, and I needed to show up for my judging duties in less than half an hour.

Across the green from the tent where I'd left Aunt Gilda in charge of my cocktail samples, a long table had been set up beneath a white canopy. Earlier in the day, the white-clothed table hadn't held anything other than some clipboards.

Now, however, as I approached that end of the green, I could see close to two dozen pies lined up in two rows.

"Oh, good, you're here, Sadie," Betty said as soon as she saw me.

"Am I late?" I asked with surprise. I thought I'd arrived early, but Betty seemed a bit harried.

"No, no," she rushed to assure me. "I just wanted to take some time to familiarize you with the judging process. The other judges have been doing this for years now, so I'll bring you up to speed before they arrive."

She handed me a pen and a clipboard with a judging form attached to it.

"As you can see, all entries will be anonymous to ensure that there won't be any bias." She pointed to a column with the heading ENTRY NUMBER. Then she drew my attention to the other columns. "The pies are judged on three criteria—overall appearance, crust, and filling. Each of those is given a score out of five, with five being the best. For the crust and filling, I suggest you consider things like the texture and integrity as well as the taste."

"Sounds straightforward enough," I said.

"Oh, good. I'm sure you'll do a great job."

"I'll try my best."

Betty patted my shoulder. "We'll be starting shortly. Louie's about to set up the perimeter."

"Perimeter?" I echoed with confusion. I spotted

Louie stringing caution tape from one tent pole to another. "Is that really necessary?"

"We've learned over the years that it's definitely for the best. It's rather distracting for the judges if the contestants are hovering behind them. Plus, this way none of the competitors can whisper to the judges which pie is theirs."

"Would anyone really do that?"

"That and so much more."

"Really?" I said with disbelief, but Betty had already turned away to greet a man and a woman who'd ducked under the caution tape.

Fellow judges, I assumed, since Betty handed each of them a clipboard and pen. While Betty spoke with them, I waved at Louie and wandered toward the edge of the canopy. Several people had gathered outside the caution tape over the last couple of minutes. Most were women, but a couple of men were there too.

"Hey, Sadie," one of the men said as I wandered past him.

He'd been at the Inkwell a few times, but I couldn't remember his name.

"Do you like cheese?" he asked.

"I love cheese," I replied, unable to hide the fact that I was puzzled by the question.

"I own the Caldwell Cheese Company." He tapped his blue baseball cap, and I saw that the logo was the one for his company. "I can make you up a basket of all your favorites."

The woman standing next to him jabbed him hard in the ribs with her elbow. "Bert Caldwell, you should be tossed out of the competition for attempting to bribe one of the judges."

"Is that what you're doing?" I asked Bert, shocked.

He gave me a sheepish grin. "No harm in trying."

I was about to distance myself from the onlookers so I wouldn't fall victim to any further attempts at bribery, but then I noticed a familiar face heading my way.

"Are you one of the judges?" I asked Grayson when he reached the tape barrier.

"Nope. A contestant."

"You bake?" I said with surprise.

He smiled. "What? You thought my double-wall ovens were just for show?"

I could feel the warmth rush to my cheeks at the reminder of my snooping. I decided to ignore the question, especially since that thought had crossed my mind as I'd peered through his kitchen window. "You're not going to try to bribe me, are you?"

"I don't need to."

I raised my eyebrows. "You seem awfully sure of yourself."

"That's because I bake a mighty fine pie, if I may say so myself."

He reached up and touched the side of my

head, rendering me momentarily speechless. When I realized he was disentangling a clump of cobwebs from my hair, I felt my cheeks flush again. How unkempt did I look to him?

I didn't want to know.

"Did you sleep last night?" he asked once he'd managed to shake the cobwebs from his fingers.

I caught sight of two women off to the side, whispering to each other as they watched me and Grayson. Coming up with more rumors to spread about us?

"Sadie?" Grayson drew my attention back to him.

"A little," I said, trying to ignore the whispering that was still going on. I met his eyes and once again found myself speechless. They were so blue, and the way he was so focused on me sent my heart skipping. I gulped and gathered myself together, saying the first thing that came to mind. "I'm sure there are plenty of mighty fine pies in the running."

"No doubt," he agreed, "but I came in second last year, and I've tweaked my recipe since then to make it even better. I like my chances."

He grinned at me again, and my heart decided to dance a tarantella. Annoyed by my reaction, I frowned. Amusement sparkled in his eyes. I hoped it wasn't because he knew the effect he was having on me.

I decided I'd better make a quick escape. "I

guess we'll both find out soon enough if your confidence is justified."

"I guess we will."

He reached toward my face, and a flock of butterflies took flight in my chest. He brushed my hair back over my left ear and produced another clump of cobwebs. His grin widened, and I quickly turned my back on him, my face burning. I joined Betty under the canopy, fighting the urge to run my fingers through my hair in search of more cobwebs. I was relieved by the distraction when she introduced me to my fellow judges, Marnie Wilson and Clive Holbrook.

"Any questions?" Betty asked once we all had our clipboards and pens in hand. When the three of us judges answered in the negative, she clapped her hands together. "Perfect. Then let's begin."

My stomach grumbled in anticipation as we approached one end of the table. The scent of pumpkin and spices was making my mouth water, and I couldn't wait to get started on the tasting. Betty sliced the first pie for us, and we each dug our forks in for a sample.

When the first bite hit my tongue, my taste buds practically sighed with happiness. I had to remind myself to pay close attention to the subtleties of the sample, rather than just diving back in for more. The crust was a bit on the crumbly side, I decided after some thought, but the filling was delicious. I gave it a solid four on my scoresheet and went on to assign scores for the crust and appearance.

The next pie looked beautiful, with pastry maple leaves decorating the top, but I found the filling to be a bit on the grainy side. We continued on along the table, tasting each pie and making notes on our scoresheets. By the time we had only three pies left to taste, I had a clear favorite in mind. None of the pies had been terrible, but some were only average, while a couple had amazed me with their scrumptious flavors.

When I tasted the third to last pie, however, I almost got weak in the knees. Marnie's and Clive's eyes went wide as they tasted the sample, as mine must have done.

"Sweet Sherlock!" I said once I'd swallowed. "That's the best pumpkin pie I've ever tasted."

"Do you think anyone would notice if I stole the rest of it?" Marnie joked.

"*I'd* notice," I told her.

"So would I," Clive said. "Hands off."

"I at least need another taste or two," Marnie said. "Just to be sure about what score I should give it."

"Same here," I chimed in, and Clive agreed.

We dug our forks into the pie again.

After another couple of tastes, we managed to pry ourselves away from that pie to taste the remaining two. The first had a hint of caramel that seemed to enhance the pumpkin flavor. It wasn't quite as outstanding as the previous one, but it was my second favorite at that point.

The final pie wasn't quite up to scratch. The crust was decent, but the filling was a bit on the sloppy side, and it looked and tasted underbaked.

Marnie, Clive, and I spent a few minutes completing our scoresheets before handing them over to Betty so the numbers could be officially tallied. Once my judging duties were complete, I sidled back along the table to my favorite pie. Marnie and Clive weren't far behind me.

"I'm guessing we decided unanimously on the winner," Clive said as he sank his fork into the pumpkin filling.

"Mmmm," was all I could say, since my mouth was full of pie.

By the time we'd all had our fill, only a third of the pie remained. The only reason I'd stopped eating was because my stomach was getting uncomfortably full.

I set down my fork and sighed with happiness. "I need the recipe for this one."

"Good luck with that," Marnie said. "Competitors are usually very protective of their recipes. Missy Filbert has won four times in the past six years, and the rumor is that she keeps her recipe locked in a safe."

"You're kidding."

"Nope."

"She's right," Clive assured me. "There are bakers in this town who wouldn't give up their secret ingredients on pain of death."

"But I really need to eat this pie again sometime." I eyed the remains with longing.

Marnie patted my shoulder. "Then I suggest you sign up to be a judge again next year."

"I'll put my name down right now."

Betty hurried over and asked us to join her at the bandstand. "It's time to announce the results."

We followed her across the grass, the crowd of spectators bunching around us, many with eager looks on their faces.

"I'm sure my new recipe will be a winner this year," a woman with curly gray hair said to the person next to her.

"I adjusted my Great Aunt Lou's recipe," a rail-thin man in denim overalls announced. "I made the best even better."

"If it's the best, how come you didn't even place last year, Isaiah?" a short and stout woman asked.

"Because Fanny Dawes sabotaged my oven."

"I did no such thing!" a voice piped up.

A petite woman in her seventies—Fanny Dawes, I assumed—elbowed her way through the crowd toward her accuser.

All around me, figurative feathers were ruffling.

I feared the situation might escalate to fisticuffs, but then Betty spoke into a microphone from the bandstand.

"May I have your attention, ladies and gentlemen? I'm pleased to say it's now time to announce the winners of the annual pumpkin pie baking contest."

Fanny muttered something under her breath, but she and her companions turned their attention to Betty instead of continuing their bickering.

I let out a sigh of relief. Apparently Shontelle hadn't been exaggerating when she'd hinted that the contest would be far from drama-free.

"But before I announce the winners," Betty continued, "I'd like to say a heartfelt thank-you to this year's judges, Marnie Wilson, Clive Holbrook, and Sadie Coleman."

My fellow judges and I smiled at the crowd around us as people applauded.

"And now for the results," Betty said when the clapping had died down. "In third place, we have Bert Caldwell."

Everyone burst into applause again. Bert appeared out of the crowd, a big smile on his face as he stepped up to the bandstand. When Betty presented him with his ribbon, he beamed at her and gave her a hearty handshake. Maybe he'd hoped he could bribe his way to first place, but he seemed happy enough with third.

"Congratulations, Bert," Betty said as he

returned to the crowd. "And in second place we have Fanny Dawes."

"Second?" Fanny said with distaste.

Someone gave her a gentle push toward the bandstand. Her nostrils flaring, she walked over to Betty and accepted her ribbon without ever cracking a smile or anything close to a pleasant expression. Clearly she wasn't satisfied with second best.

"And finally, with the best pie of the competition, we have Grayson Blake in first place."

My eyes went as wide as they must have been when I'd first tasted the winning pie. Grayson had created that heavenly concoction?

I wiped the surprise from my face as Grayson stepped up to the bandstand to accept his ribbon and trophy. I clapped along with the rest of the crowd, noting that some people seemed genuinely pleased for him, while others were obviously unimpressed because they hadn't won the top prize.

"And that concludes the pumpkin pie baking contest for this year," Betty said once she'd handed over the trophy and ribbon. "Thank you so much to everyone who participated. I hope you'll do so again next year."

I clapped some more and then put a hand to my pocket when I felt my phone buzz against my leg. I checked the device and saw that Rhonda had sent me a text message.

I don't think I can tell the police about Frank after all. I'll feel like a rat!

That wasn't good. I understood where Rhonda was coming from, since she worked for the guy, but the police needed to know what she knew.

Do you want me to tell them for you? I wrote back.

Her response came right away. *Would you? Thank you!*

They'll probably want to talk to you at some point, I warned her.

As long as I'm not the one to tattle on him, I'll feel better, her next message read.

It looked like I'd be getting in touch with the police yet again. I wasn't keen on that idea, but I wanted them to have the information, and I wanted to help Rhonda feel better about the situation.

I made my way through the crowd, intending to contact Detective Marquez right away, but when I spotted Grayson nearby I made a detour in his direction.

"Congratulations," I said with a nod at the trophy he had tucked under one arm.

"Thank you," he said. "I appreciate that you and the other judges enjoyed my pie."

"We more than enjoyed it. I'd go as far as to say it was pie ecstasy." I almost sighed with bliss as I recalled the taste. "The flavor was delicate with a hint of mystery, and the texture of the filling was so smooth . . . like silk sheets against my tongue."

When I saw the amusement in his eyes, I realized what I'd said.

Oh, for the love of Dame Agatha, why was I talking to this man about ecstasy and silk sheets?

I knew I was about to blush fiercely, so I hurried to say something more in the hope that he wouldn't notice. "Any chance you'll share the recipe?"

"Sorry," he said, not looking very apologetic. "It's top secret."

"You won't even hint at the ingredients that make it unique?"

"I'm afraid not."

I couldn't help but frown with disappointment.

"But maybe I'll bake one for you sometime."

My frown faded.

Several people surrounded Grayson then, everyone trying to praise him at once, inadvertently shoving me aside. He accepted their congratulations, but as he shook hands, his eyes met mine, and he sent a smile my way.

My heart resumed the crazy dance it had started earlier.

I turned away, trying to calm my heart as I walked across the green.

I am not falling for Grayson Blake, I told myself. *I'm really, really not.*

Deep down, I knew that was a lie.

CHAPTER 22

I had to wait twenty minutes at the police station before Detective Marquez was able to see me. When she finally appeared in the reception area, she led me to a large room with several desks, only two of which were currently occupied. One officer was on the phone, while the other was focused on his computer screen, typing away on the keyboard.

Marquez offered me a chair next to her desk, which was neat and tidy, a small potted plant sitting at one corner. Judging by its healthy green color and lack of dust, Marquez was a far better plant caretaker than I was. Many a houseplant had died under my watch. I always felt guilty when I lost one, so now I avoided bringing any home.

"I understand you have some information to share about the fire at the antiques shop," Marquez said once we were both seated.

"It *might* have to do with the fire," I qualified. "I'm not sure, but I thought you should hear about it."

"I appreciate that."

I told her about my conversation with Rhonda and how Frank had lied about not having plans for the piece of property destroyed by the recent fire. As I recounted the information, I watched the detective's face, trying to assess her reaction to what I was telling her. As usual, however, I couldn't read much at all from her expression.

"It seemed odd that he would lie about that," I said to finish. "Don't you think?"

Marquez tipped her head to one side in a barely perceptible movement. "A lot of people lie about a lot of things. That doesn't mean they're criminals."

"I know that," I said, trying not to get annoyed. "But it seemed suspicious. And the fire happened around the same time as Eric was killed. Maybe there's no connection, but I thought that should be for you and your colleagues to determine."

"Again, I appreciate that. Truly."

"So you'll look into it?" I pressed.

"I will."

"Rhonda was uncomfortable about tattling on her boss, so that's why I'm here in her place. I warned her that you might want to speak with her at some point, though."

"If that's necessary, we'll do so when Mr. Fournier isn't around."

I relaxed with relief, knowing I could reassure Rhonda with that news. I asked Marquez if she could share any new information about the murder investigation, but I wasn't the least bit surprised when she replied in the negative. After I thanked the detective for her time, I went on my way, texting Rhonda to bring her up to speed as soon as I was out of the police station.

It was the middle of the afternoon by then, and I was itching to stop by the tent to see how Aunt Gilda was doing. I also wanted to get over to the Inkwell to see how things were going there. I knew Mel would phone me if there were any problems, but I didn't like to be away from the pub for long when it was open. At the same time, with Mel at the Inkwell and Aunt Gilda taking care of things at the festival, I had more freedom than I would the next day, when I'd have to be either in the tent or at the pub all afternoon.

While it was good to know the police would be looking at Frank Fournier as a suspect, that didn't put my mind completely at ease. What if he was the arsonist and the killer but the police didn't find enough evidence to charge him?

I couldn't get that thought off my mind. I sent a quick text message to Rhonda, asking if Frank was back in the office. While I waited for her response, I wandered over to the nearest food truck, deciding to indulge in a funnel cake topped with powdered sugar. When I had the tasty treat in hand, I took a large bite and savored the delicious flavors.

This wasn't exactly my healthiest day of eating, considering that I'd filled up on pumpkin pie a short time ago, but I'd at least started the day out well with oatmeal . . . and chocolate chips.

Hopefully I could balance out my indulgences with a few more bike rides during the week.

With my funnel cake in one hand, I checked my phone.

He's here, Rhonda had responded. *Why?*

I tapped out another message with my thumb. *I thought I'd check out his place . . . see if I can find any clues.*

Are you sure that's a good idea? she wrote back. *Maybe you should leave that to the police.*

She was probably right, but I asked her for Frank's address anyway.

I didn't receive a response right away, but by the time I'd finished my funnel cake, she'd sent me the requested information. Fortunately, Frank didn't live too far away, so I set off toward Willow Street.

The weather was no longer as bright and welcoming as it had been earlier in the day. Gray clouds had rolled in, obscuring the sun, and a chilly wind whipped my hair into my face. I really needed to start remembering to wear gloves when heading outdoors. I'd at least put on a jacket before leaving the mill, but I had to tuck my hands inside my sleeves to keep them from going numb in the wind. I didn't let the weather deter me from my plan, however. That probably would have taken torrential rains or a hailstorm.

Although I knew it was unlikely that I'd find a bloody sword lying on Frank's back porch, I wanted to take a look around anyway. As far as I knew, the police still hadn't found the murder weapon, so it had to be somewhere. If Frank had killed Eric, maybe he was too dumb or too confident to have disposed of the weapon somewhere nobody would ever find it.

Maybe.

Realistically, I didn't expect to find anything, but I couldn't leave any stone unturned.

When I arrived on the right street and approached the small but well-kept gray-and-white house, I slowed my steps. Ideally, I would have approached the property from a back alley, reducing my chances of being seen by someone, but there was no such back access to the lot.

Time for Plan B, then.

I glanced around and noted with relief that I was the only one out and about on the street. Doing my best to look as though I had every right to be on Frank's property, I followed the narrow concrete path to the gate at the side of the house. While the front lawn was tidy and free of debris, on the other side of the gate, weeds poked their way up through the cracks in the pathway, and fallen leaves from a tree in the next yard lay scattered about.

I moved quickly but cautiously toward the back of the house, trying to avoid the driest of the fallen leaves, not wanting to make any noise that might draw the attention of Frank's neighbors. When I reached the backyard, I was glad to see that a couple of tall trees helped to shield me from any potential prying eyes.

The back porch was my first destination. I crept across it and over to a window. Shading my eyes, I peered through the glass and into Frank's kitchen. A newspaper lay on the table, and a coffee cup sat on the counter by the sink, but otherwise everything was neat and clean.

It occurred to me that I didn't know if Frank was married or not. I should have asked Rhonda if anyone else might be at the house even though her boss was at the office. Since she hadn't warned me of any such thing, I hoped it was because Frank lived alone.

I moved over to the next window, this one larger than the last, and leaned close to the glass. This time I was looking in at a small den with a leather couch against one wall and a large television mounted above a gas fireplace. As with the kitchen, there wasn't much to see. A closed laptop sat on the coffee table, but there were no swords in sight. In fact, there wasn't anything remotely suspicious within view.

I was about to draw back from the window when dry leaves crunched close by. I whirled around, my heart leaping up into my throat, expecting to find myself facing an irate Frank Fournier.

"Do you make a habit of peering in people's windows, Parker?"

Grayson stood by the corner of the house, without his trophy now, but with an amused light in his eyes.

"What are you doing here?" I practically hissed at him, annoyed by the nickname and by the fact that he'd caught me snooping again.

"Probably the same thing you're doing. Looking for incriminating evidence."

"Keep your voice down," I admonished in a whisper as I descended the porch steps to approach him. "So you think Frank Fournier could be the killer too?"

He shrugged. "It's possible. He could have burned down the antiques shop, hoping to get rid of his tenant and collect the insurance money. If your ex saw him starting the fire, Frank might have killed him."

"That's what I'm thinking too," I said, forgetting my annoyance for the moment. "You mentioned that Barry had some antique swords in stock. Frank could have grabbed one and used it to kill Eric."

"That's what I thought."

Barely hearing him, I rested my hands on my hips. "But that still doesn't explain why Eric's body was all the way over by the creek."

"Maybe Fournier chased him a ways before catching up to him and killing him."

"That could explain it," I agreed.

"So, did you find anything while you were snooping?" Grayson asked, inclining his head toward the back windows.

"You're here to snoop too," I reminded him. "If I'm a nosey Parker, so are you."

"Fair enough."

"But, no," I said once we had that straight. "There's still that shed, though." I pointed to a small structure in the back corner of the yard.

We crossed the grass together. Grayson tried the shed's door, but it was locked, so I moved around the side to take a look through the small window. That didn't prove very helpful. The glass was covered with dirt and cobwebs on the inside, making it impossible to see much other than shadows.

"I can't see anything," I said quietly as I returned to the front of the shed.

I stopped in my tracks when I saw Grayson open the shed door with one hand while slipping a credit card into his pocket with the other.

"You picked the lock?" I was half surprised and half impressed.

"I'd have no idea how to do such a thing," he said, feigning innocence.

"Yeah, right."

Once again, I wondered about his supposedly

criminal past. He'd laughed at the rumor, but maybe there really was some truth to it.

He was about to step into the shed, but I slipped in ahead of him. It didn't do me much good. There wasn't much to find inside the small space. The shed housed a lawnmower, a couple of rakes, and a weed whacker, but nothing else. No swords, bloody or otherwise, were tucked away in the corner.

"Not much to see here," Grayson echoed my thoughts.

He was standing so close behind me that his breath tickled my ear.

"I guess it was always a long shot," I said, trying my best to sound composed and completely unfazed by his nearness.

Dry leaves crunched beneath someone's feet again, the sound drawing closer as it repeated. I spun around, my eyes wide.

"Someone's here!" I whispered.

My first instinct was to hide, but Grayson grabbed my hand and tugged me out into the daylight just as a thin woman with gray hair rounded the corner of the house. She couldn't have been more than five feet tall, and she was slight and bony, but she still managed to look as intimidating as heck. Maybe it was the deep scowl on her face, or maybe it was the fact that I already felt guilty for getting caught where I didn't belong.

The woman pointed a gnarled finger at us. "Who are you people, and what are you doing in Frank's yard?"

I stared at her like a deer in a car's headlights, trying desperately to come up with some sort of innocent explanation for our presence. It was only when Grayson squeezed my hand that I realized he was still holding it.

"We're looking for our cat," he said smoothly, sounding completely innocent and believable. "He's been missing for two days, and we were walking around looking for him when we saw a cat like him disappear into this yard."

"That's right," I added quickly. "Only we haven't found him."

Some of the woman's suspicion faded, though not all of it. "What does your cat look like?"

"He's black," Grayson said, just as I was about to say, "White."

"We call him Binx," Grayson added.

"As in Thackery?" I asked.

He squeezed my hand again, and I realized what I'd done.

"As in Thackery Binx," I said, this time making it a statement rather than a question.

The woman eyed me like she thought I was odd, which she probably did. "I don't know what that means, but I haven't seen a black cat around here lately."

"We'll try the next street over," Grayson said.

Still holding my hand, he led me toward the gate. He held it open for the elderly woman. "Is that your house next door with the beautiful garden out front?"

For the first time, the frown left her face. "It is. It's not at its best right now, given the time of year. You should see it when the roses are in bloom."

Grayson latched the gate. "It must be spectacular then, because it looks incredible now."

The woman beamed at him. "I've got a garden around back as well. Stop by sometime in the spring or summer and I'll show you around."

I noticed she only looked at Grayson when she extended the invitation.

"I'd love that," he said, giving her a smile.

I almost expected to see animated hearts pour out of her eyes. From the way she was gazing at Grayson, it was clear she was completely smitten with him.

She pressed a hand over her heart. "Good luck finding your cat."

"Thank you."

I thanked her as well, but I doubted she'd heard me.

Grayson bestowed another smile upon her before we turned to leave.

We were halfway down the street when I realized that my hand was still in his. I tugged it away, suddenly self-conscious.

"You seem to have a new member of your fan club," I said as I tried not to think about how I missed the warmth of his hand over mine.

"I wasn't aware I had a fan club."

"Made up of half the town. Although a few have probably dropped out since you beat everyone in the baking contest."

"What about you?" he asked, sounding both amused and curious.

"What about me?"

"Are you a member?"

"Hardly."

As soon as the word was out of my mouth, I realized how rude it sounded. I shot a glance his way, but he didn't appear the least bit insulted. On the contrary, his eyes practically danced with silent laughter.

I should have been relieved that I hadn't offended him, but instead I only felt a familiar prickle of annoyance creeping over my skin. Why did he find me so amusing?

"That was a waste of time," I grumbled, wanting to change the subject.

"It wasn't too likely that Fournier would leave incriminating evidence lying around his yard."

"I know that," I said, even more annoyed now. "But I had to check, just in case. You clearly wanted to do the same."

He didn't respond to that, and we crossed the street toward the village green in silence. I caught sight of a flash of red hair and realized that Cordelia was hurrying toward us.

"Oh, good. You found her," she said to Grayson. "I left your trophy in the tent like you asked."

"Found me?" I said before he could thank her. My suspicion meter had gone from zero to a hundred in half a second.

"He lost you in the crowd here on the green," Cordelia told me. "I mentioned that I'd seen you heading off that way." She pointed in the direction we'd just come from.

I swung around to face Grayson. "You *followed* me?"

"You had a look on your face, like you had something planned," he said, not anywhere near as sheepish as I thought he should be. "I wanted to keep you from getting into trouble."

"I'm perfectly capable of keeping myself out of trouble, thank you very much," I fumed, choosing to ignore the fact that I'd been caught both times I'd gone snooping.

He held up his hands in surrender. "I was just trying to help."

There was so much I wanted to say in response, but I was determined not to lose my temper so I bit my tongue. Literally. When I felt sure I could control the words that would come out of my mouth, I eased up on my tongue and kept my voice even.

"I appreciate your concern, but I don't need a keeper. Or a sidekick."

A muscle in his jaw twitched at that last word.

I smiled at Cordelia, who'd watched our exchange with wide eyes. "It was nice to see you again."

Without another word, I struck off across the green, glad to leave Grayson Blake behind me.

CHAPTER 23

It wasn't until I'd reached the far end of the green that I managed to shake off my irritation. When I entered the tent, I forced myself to stop scowling, not wanting to scare off any tourists, but Aunt Gilda and Juliana were the only people present. I took over the Inkwell's table for a while so Gilda could have a break, but only a handful of visitors wandered in while I was there. Aunt Gilda returned half an hour later, shooing me off to the Inkwell, ensuring me that she'd be fine for the rest of the day.

The windy, darkening weather had scared some of the tourists away, and there was still half a bottle of each cocktail remaining, so I didn't need to worry about getting refills of the samples. When I stepped outside again, a fat raindrop hit me right on the top of my head, and several more followed after it. By the time I reached the footbridge, the rain was pouring down. I ran the remaining distance to the pub's front door and ducked inside, smoothing back my damp hair with one hand.

As the door drifted shut behind me, the sky rumbled with thunder. With the worsening weather, it wouldn't have surprised me if Aunt Gilda didn't get any more visitors to the tent that day. I wouldn't have been eager to wander around the festival during a storm. I much preferred being in the Inkwell, surrounded by its cozy character, my book collection, and friendly faces.

It turned out that a good number of tourists and locals felt the same way as I did. As the thunder continued to rumble and the rain pelted down outside the windows, the pub grew more crowded until we had a full house. The place was so busy that Mel ended up staying an extra hour after her shift ended. At least the roaring business meant I could afford to pay her for the extra time.

After darkness had fallen and Mel had left for the night, the crowd slowly thinned out. Most of the tourists had left, leaving a scattering of locals. When I returned to the bar after delivering a tray of pints to a table, I noticed Joey Fontana sitting on one of the stools.

"Sadie." He saluted me with a pint Damien had served him.

"Joey," I said with a hint of wariness.

"I heard your windows got egged."

"You heard right." I poured scotch into a glass and delivered it to a man at the other end of the bar.

"Between that, the gas can, and your tires getting slashed, it seems like someone doesn't much like you," Joey said when I returned. "Any idea who might have it in for you?"

"Not really." I recalled the venomous stare Eleanor Grimes had aimed at me in the coffee shop and wondered—not for the first time—if she had some sort of grudge against me.

"Nobody's seemed less than friendly since you arrived in town?" Joey pressed. From the way his dark eyes pierced into me, I wondered if he was trying to read my thoughts.

"I'm not going to publicly accuse anyone, if that's what you're hoping for." I piled dirty glasses onto a tray and took them into the kitchen, loading them into the dishwasher before going back out to the bar.

Joey's eyes zeroed in on me as soon as I reappeared.

"You know what goes on around this town," I said to him. "Do *you* have any idea who might have something against me?"

"I have some thoughts on the matter."

"Such as?" I pressed when he didn't continue.

He flashed me a smile. "You know how this works. I can't give my information away for free. I'll need something in return."

"Like what?" I asked warily, although I could easily guess the answer.

"That interview. About your ex."

"I'm not going to help you dish out dirt on Eric."

"I'm not looking for dirt. More of a human-interest angle. Plus a bit about you finding his body." When I hesitated, he added, "Of course, maybe I'd be better off going to his family for information."

"The last thing they need right now is for you to be hounding them."

He shrugged, unconcerned. "There's an easy way to avoid that."

I gave in reluctantly. "Fine. You'll get your interview. Now what do you know?"

He lowered his voice. "At first, I thought Grayson Blake might be the guilty party, but his feelings toward you seem to have changed in recent days."

"We sorted out our differences before my windows were egged, so I've scratched him off my suspect list too."

"What else have you two been sorting out?"

I narrowed my eyes at him. "What's that supposed to mean?"

He grinned. "Rumors."

"What is it with this place and rumors?"

"Small town. What do you expect?"

"Whatever the rumors are, you should ignore them," I advised. "Any other suspects?"

"Eleanor Grimes."

So I wasn't the only one who'd noticed that she didn't much like me.

"What's up with her?" I asked. "I don't even know her, so why would she have something against me?"

"The Shady Creek Museum is Eleanor's life. You'd think she'd given birth to it, the way she's so devoted to it."

"So?"

"So, when this building came up for sale, she wanted the town to purchase it so it could be the new home for the museum. But she didn't have a chance to do anything about it before you snatched up the place from under her nose."

"I didn't snatch up anything from under anyone's nose," I said. "It was on the open market. I bought it fair and square."

He held up a hand in surrender. "I know that, but Eleanor had her heart set on moving the museum here. At the moment, it's in a nondescript building a couple of blocks off the green. This place, with all its history and character, would have been perfect."

"It's also perfect as a pub."

"I happen to think it's even *more* perfect as a pub." He raised his pint glass in a salute and took a sip. "But, like I said, the museum is Eleanor's life. And to top it off, she's a teetotaler. So you can be sure you're not on her list of favorite people."

"But how do we find out if she's responsible?" A light bulb went off in my head as soon as I asked the question. "Whoever the culprit is, they must have bought an awful lot of eggs recently."

Joey nodded as if he'd been thinking along the same lines.

"We could ask at the grocery store if anyone's bought an unusual number of eggs lately," I suggested.

"That's the first step," Joey agreed. "But it might not get you any answers."

"Why not?"

"There are plenty of people just outside of town who sell fresh eggs on their farms. Heck, whoever it is with an ax to grind might raise their own chickens and not have to buy them at all."

My spirits deflated.

Joey drained the last of his beer and set down his glass. "But it's a good place to start. And I know pretty much everyone in town. I'll ask some questions."

"Just remember that I'm not accusing anyone," I said as he slid off his stool.

He gave me a two-fingered salute as he slapped some money onto the bar. "I'll be by for the interview tomorrow."

I wasn't looking forward to that. Talking about Eric would be difficult, considering how we'd parted and the terrible end he'd met here in Shady Creek, but if it meant sparing his family from the badgering of at least one reporter, I'd find a way to get through it.

Even though Joey planned to ask around about the eggs, I itched to get out there and ask the same questions myself. Maybe I would, first thing in the morning. Until then, I'd enjoy my time here at the Inkwell.

First thing in the morning turned out to be more like mid-morning. Aunt Gilda had come over to the pub near closing time and waited while I finished up work and gathered up Wimsey so we could spend the night at her place again. With Aunt Gilda to feed him breakfast, Wimsey didn't bother waking me up until almost nine o'clock.

By the time I'd showered, dressed, and eaten a bowl of oatmeal, the first two tour buses of the day had arrived in town, their passengers spilling out onto the green. Although it wasn't currently raining, the sky was thick with dark clouds, and the rain had pounded against the roof of Aunt Gilda's apartment all night long. No doubt the green was rather soggy now, but from what I could see out Gilda's front window, that wasn't stopping anyone from checking out the festivities.

Since Wimsey was sound asleep on the back of the couch when I was ready to leave, I decided to let him stay there instead of taking him back to the mill for the day. I stopped in at the salon for a few minutes to let Aunt Gilda know that Wimsey was still upstairs, and to chat with her and Betty. I didn't linger as long as I might have under normal circumstances because I was eager to get to the grocery store.

Although I was tempted to drop in at the Treasure Chest for a visit with Shontelle, I simply waved at her through the front window of her shop and kept going. She had several customers in her store at the moment anyway, so I figured we'd be better off catching up another time.

I did, however, stop at the bookstore on my way past, since I'd never made it there the day before. I'd left a sign-up sheet for the mystery book club with Simone, the shop's owner, and I was happy to see that three people had added their names to the list. There were four other names on my list at the Inkwell, so the group now had seven interested parties—a great number to start with.

All I had left to do was to choose a book for the first meeting, set a date, and send out an e-mail to all the members with that information. Setting a date would be easy. Picking a book would be a much tougher task.

Despite my eagerness to get to the grocery store, I spent some time in the bookshop's mystery section. No matter how much of a hurry I was in, I couldn't leave a bookstore without at least a bit of browsing, and I really did want to choose a book for the club's first meeting. The problem with that was the long list of great choices.

I'd go with a classic, I decided. The club's

meetings would take place in the Agatha Christie room at the Inkwell, so it seemed fitting to choose one of her books.

Ten minutes later, I finally settled on *Murder on the Orient Express*. Simone approved of my choice and assured me that she'd order in some additional copies so it would be easy for the club members to get their hands on one. With that task complete—and with a copy of Ellery Adams's latest cozy mystery in my purse for my own enjoyment—I finally managed to get myself to leave the shop.

My plan was to set off to the south to visit the grocery store, but as soon as I stepped out on the sidewalk, I heard someone calling my name from the opposite direction. Rhonda, I realized, when I saw her waving at me. She headed my way, so I met her halfway along the street.

"Morning, Sadie."

"Morning," I returned. "What are you doing out and about at this time of day?" Normally, she'd be at work.

"Mr. Fournier sent me to get some coffee."

"You're not going to the Village Bean?" That's where everyone in town got their takeout coffee, but she was going in the opposite direction from the coffee shop.

"Oh, I mean coffee to brew. Our supply at the office is almost gone. Mr. Fournier likes to be able to offer coffee to his clients." She glanced around, but we were alone on the sidewalk. "Speaking of Mr. Fournier, did you find anything at his place?"

"Not a thing," I said, not bothering to mention that my snooping mission had been cut short. Even if I'd had another hour to look around, I doubted I'd have found anything.

"So maybe he's innocent?" She sounded hopeful.

"Or just not dumb enough to leave evidence around that could be used against him."

Her face fell.

"Have the police talked to you since I told them about Mr. Fournier?"

"No." She bit down on her lower lip. "Could I really be working for an arsonist and murderer?"

"I don't know, but hopefully we'll find out one way or the other before much longer."

"Yes, either way, it'll be best to know for sure."

"If you're in search of coffee, we're probably going to the same place," I said.

"You're going to pick up some groceries?"

"Actually, I'm hoping to pick up a clue. If the person who egged my windows bought a lot of eggs at the store, maybe someone will remember them."

"I heard about that incident."

"Want to walk together?"

"Sure."

We'd only taken a step or two when a frantic

shout rang out somewhere behind us. I glanced over my shoulder and saw several people running in the direction of the village green. The looks on their faces sent a hum of alarm through me.

"I wonder what's going on." I abandoned my plan to visit the store and jogged toward the green.

I heard Rhonda following me at first, but then she fell behind. I didn't slow my pace, and when I reached the green, I noticed that the festivalgoers had gathered in bunches, all of them focused on something to the north. When I looked over their heads, I noticed a dark cloud billowing up toward the sky.

I went cold all over, and my heart jumped into overdrive.

It was a cloud of black smoke, and it was coming from the direction of the mill.

CHAPTER 24

I darted around the crowd in front of me, splashing through puddles and over soggy grass. When I had a clear view of the mill, I saw dancing flames beneath the smoke.

I ran as fast as I could, charging across the street toward the footbridge.

"Sadie!"

Someone grabbed my arm and pulled me to an abrupt stop.

"Don't go any closer," Cordelia begged, still holding onto my arm. "It's too dangerous."

"But the fire!"

"I called for help. The fire department's on the way."

Sure enough, a siren wailed nearby. A second later, the first truck turned onto Creekside Road and rumbled toward the mill.

I remained frozen in place, unable to tear my gaze away from the fire engulfing the shed next to the pub. The walls were made of stone, but the fire was burning hungrily through the roof, sparks flying as the flames popped and crackled. The trees and grass were damp from the night's rain, but I was still terrified that the fire would jump to the mill.

At least Wimsey was safely at Aunt Gilda's.

"Sadie!"

I turned to see Shontelle running toward me.

"You're okay?" she said. "You're not hurt?"

I shook my head, struggling to get my numb mind to work. "I just got here. I spent the night at Gilda's."

"Wimsey?"

"Still at Gilda's."

Firefighters hurried past, and one yelled at us to move farther away from the fire. Even from across the creek, I could feel the heat of the flames, and the smoke was fouling the air with its acrid smell.

I allowed Shontelle to lead me across the street to the green, Cordelia following along next to us. Aunt Gilda appeared out of the crowd, her face pale, her eyes wide with fear.

"I'm okay," I assured her when she rushed over to me. "It's just the shed."

For now.

"Thank God." Aunt Gilda pulled me into a fierce hug. "How did this happen?"

"I don't know," I said.

That was the truth. I didn't know for certain how the fire had started, but I had a strong suspicion that it wasn't accidental. Whoever was behind all these incidents, they were getting bolder, the acts more dangerous and menacing. I shuddered and leaned against Aunt Gilda when she put her arm around me.

It was terrible, standing there watching the fire while fear kept my stomach churning. Every minute felt like an hour, but at last the firefighters extinguished the flames. There wasn't much left of the shed—just a blackened stone shell— but at least the pub was safe, and my apartment too. And nobody was hurt. That was the greatest blessing.

With the fire now out, the crowd slowly dispersed. The fire crew kept working, dousing the remaining embers, with me unable to look away.

"Come on, honey," Aunt Gilda said, her arm still around my shoulders. "Let's go to the salon so you can sit down for a bit."

Her voice helped to free me from the numbness that had settled over me. "Just a moment."

Cordelia had started up the street toward the inn, but when I called her name, she turned back.

"You were the first one on the scene," I said. "Did you see anyone near the shed?"

"No, I'm so sorry. The only people I saw were over on the green."

Disappointment weighed heavily on my shoulders. "Thank you for calling the fire department."

She reached out and squeezed my hand. "You're welcome. I'm glad the fire didn't do any more damage."

"Me too."

She went on her way, and I allowed Shontelle and Gilda to lead me across the green to the salon. Shontelle had to return to the Treasure Chest, and Aunt Gilda and Betty both had clients waiting at the salon, so I slumped into one of the chairs in the salon's waiting area, not sure what else to do with myself.

Aunt Gilda made me a cup of tea before she got to work trimming her client's hair, and I sipped at it slowly as the conversations in the salon blurred around me. Halfway through my cup of tea, I realized that I hadn't prepared the cocktail samples for the day. I almost forced myself to get up and go over to the pub, but in the end, I didn't bother. Maybe it wouldn't hurt to miss one day of the festival.

Once I'd finished my tea, I decided I needed to get moving, festival or no festival. The day's soup would be delivered to the pub soon, and after that it wouldn't be long before it was time to open the Inkwell. Before leaving, I spent some time upstairs with Wimsey. I was so relieved that he was safe and sound that I didn't want to be away from him, but after putting up with my cuddling for a few minutes, he squirmed until I released him. Reluctantly, I said good-bye to him and left him there in Aunt Gilda's apartment.

When I returned to the mill, only a couple of firefighters remained, cordoning off the area around the shed with tape. A silver car was parked next to my white Honda in the parking lot, and as I crossed the footbridge, the driver's door opened and Detective Marquez emerged. I stopped briefly to thank the firefighters for their work and then led the detective into the pub.

She didn't have many questions for me this time, and I didn't have many answers, so her visit was short. I hoped one of us would figure out who was behind all the recent incidents before much longer. Now that the shock from earlier in the day was wearing off, I was getting mad. Whoever the culprit was, they'd gone too far, putting my home and business at risk.

I didn't have time to get to the grocery store at the moment, but hopefully Joey would make it over there and get back to me with whatever he found out. I'd mentioned my plan to ask about recent egg purchases to Detective Marquez, but I couldn't tell if she thought that was a smart idea or not. Maybe someone on the force had already asked the question and she just wasn't letting on. I wasn't going to sit back and hope she figured everything out for me, though. I'd put so much into establishing my new life in Shady Creek. I wasn't about to let it all be taken away from me by some devious person with a grudge against me for who knew what reason.

Once the vat of soup had arrived and Mel had shown up for her shift, I unlocked the front door and flipped the CLOSED sign to OPEN. It took less than five minutes for the first customers of the day to arrive. Naturally, everyone wanted to talk about the fire. Over the next few hours, I lost track of how many times I answered questions about whether I knew how the fire had started and if it was related to the fire at the antiques shop.

No, and I don't know, were my respective answers. I didn't mind the questions, though, and I had a chance to ask several people if they'd seen any suspicious activity near the shed before the fire broke out. Unfortunately, nobody had noticed anything until the fire was well underway.

Despite the fact that I didn't come up with any clues while I worked, I took comfort in being at the Inkwell. As I mixed cocktails for tourists and explained the inspiration behind them, I relaxed and even managed to smile now and then. In the evening, Shontelle arrived, settling on a free stool as I pulled pints for other customers.

"How are you doing?" she asked me with concern.

"I'm all right," I assured her. "A bit angry at whoever's behind all this, but otherwise okay."

"I heard someone grabbed you on your way home from my place the other night. This is getting to be too much, Sadie."

"I agree one hundred percent."

I delivered the pints to waiting customers, and when I returned, I asked Shontelle if she wanted something to drink.

"Not tonight, thanks. My mom's with Kiandra, but I promised I wouldn't be long. You're staying with Gilda again tonight, right?"

"Yes. It looks like I'll be there until whoever's out to get me is behind bars."

"Good. I wouldn't be able to sleep if I thought you were here on your own in the middle of the night." She reached across the bar and gave my arm a squeeze. "Let me know if the police make any progress?"

I promised I'd tell her anything the police told me, although I wasn't expecting that to be much.

Soon after she left, Joey showed up for the interview I'd promised. He asked about the shed fire as well, but he knew as much as I did about it. Talking about Eric left me emotionally drained, but I survived the interview and was glad to have it over and done with.

Later on, Damien helped me close up and get the place tidied for the next day. He insisted on walking me over to Aunt Gilda's place afterward, and I appreciated his concern and his company. The streets were deserted by that hour, and if I'd been on my own, I would have expected attackers to leap out at me from every shadow and darkened doorway.

I wasn't the least bit surprised when I had trouble falling asleep. Even when I did start to drift off, I'd start awake again, worried that I'd smelled smoke or heard flames crackling. Then

I had to tiptoe to the window and stick my head out into the cold night air to get a look at the mill. Every time I checked on it, the place looked still and undisturbed, but that didn't do much to reassure me.

Whoever was behind all of the incidents directed at me had to hate me with a passion, and that was unsettling. Why would someone feel so strongly about me?

I'd mentioned to Detective Marquez that Eleanor Grimes was a suspect in my mind, but the slightest lift of one of her eyebrows had left me feeling like she didn't think much of that theory. Whoever the guilty party was, I didn't doubt they'd strike again, and that thought kept me from getting anything more than a couple of hours of restless sleep.

In the morning, I got up earlier than usual, sick of lying in bed, tossing and turning. I cooked myself a bowl of oatmeal and joined Gilda at the table as she ate some toast with grape jelly.

"What are you up to today?" Aunt Gilda asked.

"The same as usual," I replied as I stirred melted chocolate chips into my oatmeal. "I'll mix up some cocktails to start. Mel's going to look after the table at the festival today. Other than that, I might try to get out for a walk before the Inkwell opens." And swing by the grocery store while I was at it, I added, only in my mind.

I would have loved to get out on my bicycle, but the fire had destroyed it, along with the catapult, my lawnmower, and a few other items.

"Please don't go walking along any lonely roads," Aunt Gilda said. "You need to be careful until the police catch the nutjob behind all these terrible things."

"I'll stay in town," I assured her, and she seemed satisfied. "Can I leave Wimsey here for the day again?"

"Of course. Both of you are welcome here for as long as it takes to get things back to normal."

I got up from the table to give her a hug and a kiss on the cheek. "I don't know what I'd do without you."

"Right back at you, sweetheart," she said. "So you need to make sure you stay in one piece."

"I'll do my very best," I promised.

Once I'd finished my breakfast and brushed my teeth, I set off for the mill. The first thing I did was stand before the ruins of the shed, surveying the mess left over from the fire. So much for entering the catapult competition.

Fortunately, Damien hadn't left any of his own tools in the shed the last time he worked on the catapult. The only ones destroyed were those that had come with the property when I bought it—a hammer, a wrench, a screwdriver, and a few other basics. Those would be easy enough to replace. My bicycle was a different story. I wasn't sure if

I could buy a new one in town or if I'd need to go farther afield.

Finding out about that would have to wait for the time being. As much as I already missed my bike, I realized I was more in need of tools at the moment. I backtracked across the footbridge to the wooden sign set on the grass between the road and the creek. The sign itself was fine—which was lucky since I'd paid a lot to have it made—but one of the two posts it was affixed to was broken. I hadn't noticed if the sign was damaged the day before, but I figured it probably got broken at some point while the firefighters were on the scene.

There was a second, much smaller shed on the property, near the forest, hidden from view from the road by the mill itself. It was home to my stash of firewood for my woodstove and a few other odd pieces of wood. I sorted through them and found one that would work as a replacement for the signpost, at least until I could find one that matched the other post better.

All I needed now was a hammer and a couple of nails. Thanks to the fire, I didn't have either of those things, and the hardware store wouldn't open for another hour. I was about to leave the task of fixing the sign until later when I realized I might be able to get what I needed elsewhere.

I cut across the parking lot—empty except for my own car—and up to Rhonda's front porch.

She was an early riser, so I wasn't worried about waking her. I knocked on the door and peered through the sidelight, but there was no sign of movement from within, and no answer to my knock. I wandered around the back of the house, thinking she might be out in her yard, but she wasn't. There was a small shed attached to the house, and when I tried the door, it opened with a creak. I knew Rhonda wouldn't mind me borrowing what I needed, but all I found in the shed was a lawnmower, a stack of firewood, plenty of cobwebs, and a large spider.

I backed out quickly and shut the door. Maybe Harvey could lend me a hammer. He only lived two doors away from Rhonda, next to the Creekside Inn, so I was able to walk to his place in under a minute. I knocked on his door twice but received no response. As I'd done at Rhonda's place, I wandered around the back of the house. A large shed—probably more of a workshop—sat near the far edge of the property, the creek gurgling along behind it.

Harvey was a handyman, so I knew he owned lots of tools, but there was a good chance he kept them locked up.

Or not.

When I tried the door of the workshop, it opened easily. That surprised me, although maybe it shouldn't have. I was in Shady Creek, after all, where some people didn't even bother to lock their houses.

Inside the door, I found a light switch and flicked it on. A bank of overhead lights came to life, allowing me to see that a workbench ran along one wall of the shop, an array of tools hanging from pegs on the wall above it. A table saw and a drill press took up much of the middle of the workshop, and lumber, ladders, and all manner of other bits and bobs were stored up against the back wall.

I aimed my sights on the workbench first. A hammer lay on the surface in plain sight, but I had a feeling the tools on and above the workbench were Harvey's best ones. Maybe he wouldn't mind me borrowing those, but I decided to take a look around for some spare tools. I spotted a dusty metal toolbox on the floor by the back wall, partially hidden by two-by-fours and a cardboard box full of plastic garbage bags.

The dust on the top of the toolbox had been disturbed recently, but not by much, so I figured there was a good chance Harvey didn't use its contents very often. I picked up the toolbox and set it on the workbench before opening the lid. The box was heavy when I lifted it, so I expected it to hold several tools, which it did. What I didn't expect to find was jewelry mixed in with those tools.

Strange, I thought as I picked up a gold chain

with a heart-shaped pendant hanging from it. Why the heck would Harvey store jewelry in an old toolbox?

He wouldn't, I realized, unless he was trying to hide it.

I dropped the necklace, and it fell back into the toolbox with the other pendants, brooches, bracelets, and rings that were tucked among the hammers and screwdrivers.

I took a step back from the workbench, my heart thudding so loudly I could hear it beating in my ears. I was no expert, but the necklace and all the other pieces of jewelry looked like they could be antiques.

Sliding my hand into the pocket of my jeans, I fingered my phone. I considered calling the police, but maybe I was overreacting or jumping to conclusions. Leaving my phone in my pocket, I moved to the back wall of the workshop, opening another metal box. It held nothing but an assortment of drill bits and some long nails. I closed the lid and shifted aside some pieces of lumber. Nothing but dust and cobwebs hid behind them. Still, I kept searching.

When I reached one of the back corners, I peeked behind some two-by-fours leaning against the wall. Something was tucked behind them, wrapped in an old burlap sack. My mouth went dry, and I had to fight the urge to run out of the shed and all the way back home. I grabbed the object, the feel of it in my hand making my heart boom even harder.

I carefully unwrapped the burlap sack, already knowing what I'd find. I froze when I had part of the object exposed, not needing to see any more. The blade of the sword gleamed in the workshop's artificial light. A wave of nausea hit me when I noticed a dark smudge on the blade.

Dried blood.

I swallowed hard, quickly rewrapping the sword and setting it back behind the two-by-fours. At least I hadn't touched anything but the burlap sack. Hopefully that meant I hadn't contaminated the evidence.

No longer able or wanting to fight the urge to escape from the workshop, I hurried toward the open door, pulling my phone from my pocket as I went. As I dashed outside, a shadow moved to my left. I tried to turn in that direction but didn't get a chance. Something hard struck the side of my head, and the world around me dissolved into darkness.

CHAPTER 25

My head ached something fierce.

That was the first thing I noticed. I wanted to touch a hand to the sorest spot, but I couldn't get my arm to move. I winced as I bounced and jolted about, every bump briefly intensifying the pain in my head. My neck was bent at an uncomfortable angle, my arms and legs stuffed up against my body.

I wanted to complain, but all that came out of my mouth was a quiet whimper. My eyes didn't want to open, but I forced my eyelids up anyway. I regretted it right away, the gray daylight far too bright and only making my head hurt more. I was tempted to let my eyes close again, but when another jolt shifted my body to the left, I realized that something was terribly wrong.

I struggled to bring myself more fully awake. Tree branches crisscrossed overhead, some evergreens, others with colorful leaves. As I bounced and shifted about, I took in my more immediate surroundings. I was stuffed into the tray of a wheelbarrow, I realized—a rusty and dirty wheelbarrow that was currently being pushed through the forest.

Although it made the pain even worse, I tipped my head back to get a look at Harvey. Only it wasn't Harvey pushing the wheelbarrow. It was Rhonda.

A small sound escaped from me, a mixture of surprise and pain. Rhonda glanced down at me, only for a second, her face grim as she struggled to get the wheelbarrow up a small rise.

"Rhonda? What are you doing?"

The wheelbarrow crested the top of the small hill. Stopping for a moment, Rhonda wiped her sleeve across her forehead.

"I think you can figure that out," she said, gripping the wheelbarrow's handles again.

I winced as the bouncing and jolting started up again. The pain in my head made it hard to think clearly, but my mind was growing less hazy by the minute.

"You're getting rid of me." As I said the words, fear settled heavily in my stomach. Together with the ceaseless pain in my head, that fear brought on a wave of nausea.

"Got it in one," Rhonda said.

"But I didn't know you were the killer. I thought Harvey—"

"Harvey? He hasn't got the gumption."

In my mind, that was a good thing, but Rhonda made it sound like a shortcoming.

"I thought it was best to hide the sword and jewelry in his workshop until I could get rid of them, though. I didn't want anyone finding them at my place."

"But you had me fooled. Why not let me go on thinking Harvey was the killer?"

"You would have figured out the truth before long," she said. "Harvey had no motive, and if you'd asked about the eggs at the grocery store, you'd have known."

"You did that too?" I put a hand to my head as the wheelbarrow hit something solid, coming to an abrupt halt.

Rhonda grunted with effort as she backed up a couple of steps and then charged forward. The wheelbarrow shot past whatever had momentarily blocked it. I gripped the sides to keep myself from sliding around, noting that my limbs were working now.

"Of course I did," Rhonda eventually replied.

"But why?" As I asked the question, I glanced around, trying to assess my situation.

"Because I wanted you gone, that's why," she said. "I wanted you to put the pub up for sale, hopefully for a lower price than you paid for it."

"You wanted to buy it," I said, suddenly understanding.

"That pub is my life. It should be *mine*. But you had to come from away and ruin my plans."

"But your father owned it. If you wanted it so badly, why didn't he sell it to you?"

"Because he wanted more than I could pay him, and he wanted it sooner than I could get any financing. He was so freaking eager to retire to

Arizona with his fancy new wife." Her words practically sizzled with the heat of her anger and resentment.

I swallowed hard, trying not to let fear and panic smother me. I needed to escape, but I was in such an awkward position that Rhonda would be able to grab me before I could even clamber out of the wheelbarrow.

Keeping my movements stealthy, I touched my hand to the pocket of my jeans. It was empty. Rhonda must have taken my phone or left it by Harvey's workshop. I forced myself to stay calm and think. I needed to keep Rhonda talking to give myself more time.

"Even if I put the mill up for sale, there are other people who'd want to buy it," I said.

"Like Eleanor Grimes?" She snorted. "She doesn't have the money, and the town's not about to buy the place when the museum already has a perfectly good home."

"Grayson Blake would want to buy it too."

She snorted again. "Figures. You newcomers show up and think you can take over the whole town."

Through my fear, I felt a pang of sadness. I'd thought Rhonda was my friend, but now I could see that what I'd mistaken for kindness and friendship was really just her attempt to stay involved with the pub she loved so fiercely. No wonder she'd only set fire to the shed and not the mill. She wanted to scare me off, not destroy the business or the main building.

"But why burn down the antiques store?" I asked as I surreptitiously looked left and right, searching for anything that might help me escape. "Why kill Eric?"

"I wanted Frank to get fingered for the fire. All those years I worked for him, all the time I dedicated to him and his business, and he laughed in my face when I asked for a raise. He deserved to get tossed in jail. I knew he was planning to tear the place down and put up his boutique hotel. I figured if people knew about that, they'd think he'd burned down the place to collect the insurance before rebuilding."

The wheelbarrow jolted over a large bump. I tightened my grip on the sides, slowly and carefully moving my legs into a better position, one that might allow me to spring out of the wheelbarrow if I got the chance.

"As for your ex . . ." She paused as she pushed at the wheelbarrow. "He saw the light of my flashlight when I was in the shop taking a few things to sell for extra cash. He tried to stop me, so I grabbed the closest sword and went after him when he ran away."

I closed my eyes briefly, picturing the terrible scene in my head—Rhonda chasing Eric through the night, catching up to him near the creek, driving the sword through him.

Had he yelled for help, with no one around to hear him? Had he suffered or had he died quickly?

The wheelbarrow rammed into something hard and tipped to the side. I clambered out of the rusty metal tray and to my feet. I charged past Rhonda, running as fast as I could, heading back the way we'd come, hoping that would get me out of the woods to safety. My head throbbed, but I barely noticed the pain. Fear and adrenaline drove me onward.

I stumbled, my grogginess still not completely gone, but I grabbed onto the nearest tree trunk to save myself from a fall. There was no need to waste time looking back to know Rhonda was after me. I could hear her crashing through the forest behind me.

I screamed for help, knowing there likely wasn't anyone nearby to hear me. I kept calling anyway, my voice shaking as I kept running.

Trees and more trees filled my vision. I couldn't see the edge of the forest, but that only made me run faster. I tripped on a tree root and went sprawling, landing face-first in a pile of soggy leaves. My head hurt more than ever, so much that tears formed in my eyes. I struggled to my knees, knowing I had to keep moving.

Before I could get to my feet, something large and heavy plowed into my back. I lurched face-first into the ground again. Rhonda had tackled me. She rolled off my back and grabbed me, hauling me to my feet. I tried to fight her off, but my efforts were feeble and clumsy. Dizziness had joined my pain and nausea, and I didn't have the strength to do much of anything. I kept struggling anyway, but Rhonda tightened her hold on me and easily dumped me back into the wheelbarrow.

I knew I needed to stay awake, to attempt another escape, but the world kept fading away around me. I struggled to stay conscious, but that only brought me more pain and nausea. When the wheelbarrow bounced to a stop, I realized that my eyes had closed despite my best efforts to keep them open. I forced my eyelids up and saw nothing but gray clouds above me. We were out of the forest.

How long had I been unconscious?

Terrified, I pushed myself up, searching the area for any sign of someone who might be able to help me. We had arrived at a grassy meadow not far from the edge of the woods. The forest bordered the field on two sides, a rocky hillside jutting up on the third side, a line of sugar maples on the fourth, half their colorful leaves shed. I thought I spotted a building beyond the maple trees, but I couldn't be sure.

I screamed for help anyway.

Rhonda grabbed me and roughly hauled me out of the wheelbarrow before pushing me to the ground. I heard a strange clunk, and then she grabbed the back of my shirt and yanked me up off the damp grass. She pulled me a couple of feet to the left and gave me a hard shove. I put out my hands, hoping to break my fall when I hit the grass again, but the ground had disappeared.

Flailing, I fell into a pit of darkness.

CHAPTER 26

I landed with a splash and a simultaneous shock of pain and cold. A loud thud boomed over my head, and the shaft of gray daylight shining down on me disappeared, leaving me in complete darkness. I gasped with fear. Splashing around frantically, I tried to clamber up toward the place where the daylight had been moments before. In my haste and panic, I lost my balance and fell back down to where I'd started, making another splash.

Stay calm, I told myself.

That was hard to do when my mind was reeling with fear, when I didn't know where I was or what would happen next.

My breaths were still coming in great gasps, and the sound of them—so loud and raspy—was what snapped me out of my panicked state. I forced myself to stay still and calm down. I needed to assess my situation, to figure out where I was so I could find a way to escape.

I wouldn't let myself consider that I might not have time, that Rhonda's next move might put an end to my life before I had a chance to try to save myself.

Carefully, I felt the space around me, moving my hands here and there. I was sitting on a set of stone stairs, I realized. No wonder my elbow and hip had hurt so much when I landed. They still ached, though not quite as fiercely as my head.

I continued my investigation. On either side of the stairway were brick walls.

My legs were completely soaked, and when I moved my foot down another stair, it splashed into water.

What was this place?

I sat still and listened, trying to detect any sign that Rhonda was still nearby. All I could hear was a steady drip-drip-drip from somewhere nearby. My teeth chattered, and only then did I realize that I was shivering, that I was freezing from my unintended dip in the icy water below me. I hugged myself and closed my eyes in the darkness, trying to keep the cold and pain from overwhelming me

When I opened my eyes again, I tipped my head back, looking at the darkness above me. I blinked, wondering if my eyes were playing tricks on me. They weren't, I realized a moment later.

A tiny sliver of light punctuated the darkness. Placing my hands on the brick walls to steady myself, I climbed up three stairs until my head bumped against something solid. I felt around the sliver of light. My fingers pressed against solid wood.

A trapdoor, maybe?

That would make sense.

I pushed at it, tentatively at first and then with more force. It wouldn't budge. I pounded my fists against the wood, but still it held fast, and I only succeeded in getting a splinter in my hand. I sank back down to sit on the stairs, resting my head against my knees, fighting off another wave of despair.

I was shivering more than ever now, and I realized that Rhonda might have no intention of coming back, of doing anything further to me. She wouldn't need to. Stuck down here, my jeans soaked with cold water, I wasn't likely to last long. How many hours it would take for hypothermia to set in, I didn't know. But I did know that I didn't want to wait around to find out.

Forcing myself to move, I tried pounding on the trapdoor again. Then I bent over so I could press my back and shoulders against it. Still it wouldn't budge. I braced myself against the brick wall and awkwardly kicked at the wooden hatch. I screamed for help, over and over, until my voice grew hoarse and my throat scratchy.

The temptation to sit down on the stairs and cry was almost irresistible, but I refused to give in to despair. I wouldn't let Rhonda win, wouldn't let her get away with doing this to me, doing what she'd done to Eric.

With a fresh surge of determination, I decided

to try a different approach. I balked at the thought of entering the water below me, not knowing what lurked beneath the surface, but I needed to find out if there was another way out of my underground prison.

Tentatively, I descended the steps. Icy water closed around one foot and then the other, creeping up toward my knees before I reached the bottom of the stairway. Slowly, moving my hands out to the front and side of me, I inched forward. My hands didn't touch anything, so I stopped. I reached farther to my left, and then to my right. On both sides, my fingers touched brick walls again. I put one hand above my head and found that the walls curved over my head in an arch. I was in some sort of tunnel.

I inched my way forward again, grimacing at the cold water. When I stubbed my toe against something, I give a shriek of surprise.

After a moment of blind examination, I realized that I'd run into a wooden rack holding kegs, the bottom of the rack submerged in the earthy-smelling water.

As soon as I realized what I was touching, I knew where I was.

The abandoned cellar on Grayson's property. The one prone to flooding during rainy weather.

Knowing my location brought me a small measure of relief, but only for a second or two. Since the cellar wasn't in use, Grayson and his employees would have no reason to come here. I thought I'd caught a glimpse of a building through the stand of maple trees before Rhonda shoved me down in the cellar, but it was a long way off. Nobody there would hear my screams. There was even a chance that my body would never be found if I succumbed to hypothermia.

"Not going to happen," I said out loud, my voice sounding strange in the confines of the watery tunnel.

Despite my fears of what slithering creatures might be hiding in the water, I continued my progress through the tunnel, constantly checking the walls and ceiling for anything remotely like an escape route. I reached the end of the tunnel a few minutes later and found only a dead end. Shivering uncontrollably now, my legs almost numb, I headed back the way I'd come. When I reached the bottom of the stairway, I searched with my hands until they made contact with the wooden slats of the rack holding the kegs.

I tested the slats until I found one that felt a little looser than the others. I tugged and pulled and wrestled with it, until it finally broke free. Keeping a tight grip on it, I splashed through the water and made my way up the stairs. I pulled my wet sleeves down over my hands to protect them from getting more splinters, and then got a firm grip on the broken piece of wood.

Drawing on whatever strength I could find, I

rammed the makeshift tool against the trapdoor. I did that over and over again, pausing once in a while to readjust my grip on the splintering piece of wood. Then I resumed my attack on the hatch, channeling all my fear into the onslaught.

Eventually, I collapsed onto the stairs, breathing hard. My efforts had helped to warm me up a bit, but now I was exhausted. My head throbbed so hard that I felt ill all over, and I had to lean against the brick wall to stop myself from feeling like the world was spinning around me in the darkness.

When I caught my breath, I looked up above me. At first, I thought all my desperate work had done nothing, but then I realized that the small sliver of light was no longer quite as small. With renewed energy, I pushed myself back to my feet and pressed my fingers against the trapdoor, trying to squeeze one through the crack in the wood. Only my pinky finger would fit, but if I kept hitting that spot, maybe—just maybe—I'd be able to make a bigger hole. And if I made a bigger hole, I might be able to reach through and unlock the trapdoor.

Motivated by that thought, I went back to ramming the wooden slat against the hatch. I didn't know how much time had passed while I worked, but when I collapsed onto the stairs for a second time, the wood next to the hole had splintered slightly.

I wanted to get up and try again, but a wave of nausea hit me so hard that I had to close my eyes and focus on breathing to keep myself from vomiting. When the worst of it had passed, I staggered to my feet and attacked the trapdoor once again. But I didn't have much strength left and only managed feeble strikes.

The piece of wood fell from my hands, and another bout of dizziness sent me staggering into the brick wall. I thought of Wimsey, Aunt Gilda, Taylor, and the rest of my family. I couldn't accept that I might never see them again.

The first tear I'd allowed myself to shed trickled down my cheek.

"Hello?"

I froze, thinking I'd imagined the voice.

"Hello? Is somebody there?"

No, I definitely hadn't imagined it. It was closer now.

And it was a man's voice, not Rhonda's.

"Help!" I yelled.

I used the last of my energy to pound my fists against the trapdoor.

"Help! I'm down here!"

I heard the sound of a sliding bolt, then a click.

The trapdoor lifted upward, and beautiful gray daylight shone down on me.

CHAPTER 27

"How did you get down there?" Jason asked as he pulled me easily out of the hole and onto the wet grass.

I collapsed into a heap, no energy left to stay on my feet. "Rhonda Hogarth pushed me down there."

"Rhonda who?" he sounded as confused as he looked.

"The woman who burned down the antiques store and killed my ex."

The confusion fell away from his face. "Where is she now?" he asked.

"I don't know. I've been down there a while, but I don't know how long." I barely got the words out through my chattering teeth.

Jason shrugged out of his large jacket and wrapped it around my shoulders. I burrowed into it as he whipped out his cell phone. His first call was to someone at the brewery, a terse two-sentence message.

"We've got a situation at the old cellar. Bring one of the golf carts and blankets."

He hung up before the person on the other end could ask any questions. Then he called the police.

"I don't know exactly what happened," he said

to the dispatcher after making his initial report. "All I know is that I've got an injured woman here who says there's a murderer on the loose."

"Rhonda Hogarth," I supplied again. "They need to find her before she disappears."

If that was her plan. Maybe she hoped that with me out of the picture she could go on living her life in Shady Creek, no one knowing the truth about her.

Jason repeated Rhonda's name to the dispatcher. After that, I tuned everything out until I heard a low hum of a motor approaching. I hadn't realized that I'd closed my eyes, but when I opened them, I saw a golf cart trundling our way at high-speed. There were two people on board, and one jumped from the passenger seat before the cart had pulled to a complete stop.

"Sadie? What's going on?" Grayson's gaze went from me to Jason.

"She was trapped in the cellar." Jason gestured at the open trapdoor.

"Rhonda Hogarth locked me down there." I touched the sore spot at the side of my head. "She knocked me out and brought me here in a wheelbarrow."

It only took a second for Grayson to absorb that information. He grabbed a gray blanket from the golf cart and tucked it around my legs while I sat there on the grass, still huddled inside Jason's jacket.

"Does your head hurt?" Grayson asked as he tried to get a look at my injury.

"Does it ever."

"Are you dizzy? Nauseated?"

"A little of both."

"Do you think you can get in the golf cart? That way we can meet the ambulance up in the brewery's parking lot."

"I don't think I need an ambulance," I said as I tried getting to my feet.

"I think you're getting one anyway."

Grayson grabbed one of my arms, and Jason took the other, both of them helping me to stand. I returned Jason's jacket to him with thanks and wrapped the blanket around my shoulders.

"How did you find me?" I asked him. "I didn't think anyone would come out this way."

He nodded toward one of the closest trees. "Security camera. When I checked the live feed, I saw a woman heading into the woods with an empty wheelbarrow. I wondered what she'd been up to, so I decided to take a look. When I got close, I heard a thumping sound over here by the cellar."

"Thank goodness for you and the camera. You probably have footage of Rhonda tossing me in the cellar."

"Probably," Jason agreed.

That was good. More evidence to give to the police.

"We'd better get you to the parking lot," Grayson said, putting a hand on my back to guide me over to the golf cart.

For once, I had no desire to argue with him. I climbed into the cart next to Grayson's employee, who was still at the wheel. Grayson and Jason piled into the back, and off we trundled, leaving the site of my near demise behind us.

"You need to rest," a young female nurse told me as I sat up in my hospital bed.

Less than half an hour ago, I'd been transferred from the emergency department to a ward where I was to spend at least one night.

"I can't," I said, although I leaned back against the pillow. "Not until I know the police caught the woman who did this to me."

"At least try to relax," she said. "Worrying won't do you any good."

That was true, but it wasn't exactly easy to relax when I knew a murderer could still be on the loose, a murderer who'd tried to do away with me only hours earlier.

Shortly after we arrived at the brewery's parking lot, two police cruisers had appeared, followed closely by an ambulance. I provided the police officers with a brief account of what had happened, and then the paramedics had taken me into their care. Once we were at the hospital, the attending doctor had ordered an X-ray of my painful left elbow, which I'd struck on the stone steps of the cellar, and a CT scan.

The final conclusion was that I had a concussion and a badly bruised—but thankfully not broken—elbow. I had a few other scrapes and bruises, but considering what I'd been through, I thought I'd come out of it quite well. My head hadn't even required stitches, though I was glad to put an ice pack on it.

My headache wasn't quite as intense now, and my nausea had disappeared, but I was still experiencing some dizziness, and the doctor didn't want me going home until at least the next morning. I didn't argue with her, but I couldn't help but feel antsy. I wanted news of Rhonda, and I wanted to see Aunt Gilda.

I still didn't know where my phone was—hopefully in Harvey's backyard so I could recover it at some point—but someone at the hospital had called Aunt Gilda for me, and I knew she was on her way. I was eager to see a familiar, friendly face, but it wasn't until Aunt Gilda appeared on the ward that I realized just how desperately I wanted her there.

"Oh, Sadie, honey," she said as soon as she saw me. She hurried over to my bed, and I sat up carefully. "Can I hug you without hurting you?"

"Yes," I said. "It's my left elbow and my head that hurt the most."

She wrapped her arms around me and held me tightly for a moment.

"When I got the call from the hospital saying you'd been injured, I nearly had a heart attack," she said when she pulled back.

"I'm sorry. I should have talked to you myself, but they sent me off to get my elbow X-rayed."

She pulled up a chair and patted my leg. "It's all right. As soon as I hung up, Grayson Blake called me and filled me in on all the details he could."

"He did?" I said, surprised. "That was good of him."

"It was, but I nearly had another heart attack. Rhonda Hogarth is the one who killed Eric? And she tried to kill you?"

"Yes. And what if she's still out there?"

"No, no," Aunt Gilda said quickly. "I should have said right away. I stopped by the police station on my way here."

"And?" I said, hardly daring to hope for good news.

"Rhonda is in custody."

I sank back against the pillows, so relieved that I couldn't speak for a moment. "Did she try to get away?" I asked when I found my voice again.

"Apparently not. She was raking leaves in her backyard as casually as anything."

So she really had thought she could simply go on with her life once I was out of the way.

"It's really over?"

Aunt Gilda squeezed my hand. "It really is."

The exhaustion I'd been fending off ever since I arrived at the hospital hit me like a bag of bricks. "Can Wimsey stay with you until I get home?" I asked sleepily, fighting to keep my eyes open.

"Of course he can." Aunt Gilda squeezed my hand again. "You sleep now, honey."

It was good advice, so I took it.

CHAPTER 28

The final day of the Autumn Festival dawned clear and bright, the sky a brilliant and cheerful shade of blue. A lot of leaves had fallen from the trees in recent days, but there were still enough remaining on the branches to keep the town looking like a picture-perfect autumn post-card.

I dressed in jeans and my favorite long cardigan before giving Wimsey a good-bye kiss and leaving the mill. The creek gurgled happily beneath the footbridge as I crossed it, and I smiled at the sound, feeling equally happy myself.

It was a beautiful day, and I was alive. What could possibly be better?

I hadn't completely recovered from my con-cussion yet, but I was doing well and ready for my first stretch of time away from home since I'd been released from the hospital.

Aunt Gilda met me on the other side of the bridge, and together we walked past the green and down a couple of streets until we reached the field behind the elementary school. A good-sized crowd had already gathered, but Aunt Gilda found a free bale of straw and instructed me to sit down. She was determined that I wouldn't overdo it on my first day out and about.

I had a good view, I realized, as I settled on the straw bale. My seat was only a stone's throw from the spot where each catapult would be set up in preparation for its pumpkin launch. I also had a clear view of the large wooden target that had been built at the opposite end of the field, painted to look like a castle wall. Whichever team got their pumpkin to hit the castle wall closest to the red X at the center would win the competition. Already the crowd was abuzz with excitement.

Aunt Gilda had disappeared to talk with someone in the crowd, but I didn't mind being on my own. I studied the people around me but didn't spot Harvey anywhere. I'd have to check in with him soon. Shontelle had spoken to him while I was still in the hospital and had told me that he wasn't doing so well. That wasn't surprising. Not only had the woman he loved turned out to be a murderer and arsonist, she'd also put him at risk of being implicated in the crimes when she'd hidden the sword and jewelry in his shed.

From my seat, I watched as the first contraption was rolled into place. This one was more of a giant slingshot than a catapult or trebuchet. The team members readied their pumpkin, and a moment later it went sailing through the air. The crowd let out a collective sound of disappointment as the pumpkin fell short of the castle wall, but everyone applauded as the first team rolled their slingshot away to make room for the next one.

"How's the head?"

I looked up to see Grayson standing next to me.

"A lot better, thanks."

"Glad to hear it."

"How's your catapult?"

He grinned. "Ready to wow the crowd."

"You don't think you've got this competition in the bag too, do you?"

"I think my team's got a pretty good chance." When he saw the skepticism on my face, he added, "I was right about the pumpkin pie contest, wasn't I?"

I tried to scowl at him, but that was hard to do when I was remembering how heavenly his pie tasted.

"I was sorry to hear your catapult got destroyed," he said, interrupting my pie reverie.

"Really? Because with the Inkwell's team out of the competition, you have a better chance of winning."

"I think we had a pretty good chance even before you guys had to pull out."

This time I did scowl at him.

That only made him grin all the more. "See you around, Parker."

"Don't call me that!" I groused, but he'd already disappeared into the crowd.

I managed to forget about Grayson Blake as I watched the competition progress. Two teams had managed to hit the outer edges of the castle wall by the time an hour had passed. All the rest had fallen short of the target.

"Next up," the announcer said into his microphone, "we've got the team from the Inkwell pub."

I sat up straighter as everyone applauded. "But we had to pull out," I said, although no one heard me over all the clapping.

I was about to get up and explain to the announcer that the Inkwell didn't have a catapult, when Mel and Damien came into view, pushing a contraption that looked almost exactly like the one that had burned in the shed. They both had big smiles on their faces when they saw me watching, and I realized that I must have looked absolutely gobsmacked.

"What do you think?" Mel asked me.

"But it burned," I said, still stunned.

"I built another one," Damien said.

A big smile spread across my face. I clapped and cheered as Mel fetched a pumpkin and set it in the trebuchet's sling. Damien released the counterweight, and the pumpkin went flying.

Forgetting that I was supposed to take it easy, I jumped to my feet, watching the orange missile cruise through the air. It drew closer and closer to the castle wall.

Then it hit the target with a smack.

I cheered wildly. The pumpkin had hit closer to the center mark than any previous one. The Inkwell's team was in the lead.

"And now we have just two teams remaining," the announcer said.

I high-fived Mel and Damien after they'd moved the trebuchet out of the way. "You guys are amazing."

"We didn't want you to miss out on a classic Shady Creek experience," Mel said.

I thanked them both again, but then we all focused our attention on the competition. The Spirit Hill Brewery was up next, and I watched closely, suddenly far more invested in the outcome than I was minutes before.

Grayson and Jason rolled their catapult into place, and Juliana carried over a pumpkin. They got everything ready and then let the pumpkin fly.

Smack!

It hit the castle wall, just to the right of the center.

I sank down onto the bale of straw with a groan as Grayson sent a triumphant grin my way.

Darn him. His team had beaten the Inkwell's.

"Don't worry," Damien said. "There's always next year."

But winning over Grayson Blake would have been so sweet.

The last team rolled their contraption up to the line. Kiandra gave me an excited wave as she moved the catapult with the help of two adults and several other girls around her age. I gave her two thumbs-up.

She and one of her fellow Girl Scouts hauled a pumpkin over, and one of the troop leaders helped them get it ready. I cheered them on as they let the pumpkin loose. As it arced through the air, everyone fell silent, but anticipation crackled through the crowd like an electric current.

A second later the pumpkin hit the castle wall.

Dead on center.

I jumped to my feet, cheering like a crazy woman as people around me whistled and applauded.

"And we have our winners!" the announcer declared as the Girl Scouts jumped around, hugging each other with glee.

I kept clapping, a huge smile on my face. I caught sight of Grayson out of the corner of my eye. He was grinning too.

He made his way over to me. "It looks like the best team won."

"I'd say so," I agreed, still smiling.

"So what do you think of Shady Creek's annual tradition?" he asked.

I watched as the announcer handed over the

trophy to the Girl Scouts, who continued to jump around in triumphant excitement.

"I think," I said, "that I'm very much looking forward to next year."

COCKTAILS & RECIPES

Huckleberry Gin

2 oz. gin
1 oz. huckleberry syrup
4–5 oz. tonic water
Twist of lime

Fill a cocktail shaker ¾ full with ice, then add gin and syrup. Shake vigorously and strain into an ice-filled glass. Top with tonic water and add the twist of lime. Makes one cocktail.

Huckleberry Gin Mocktail

1 oz. huckleberry syrup
4–5 oz. tonic water
Twist of lime

Add tonic water and syrup to an ice-filled glass. Stir vigorously. Add the twist of lime. Makes one mocktail.

Happily Ever After

2 oz. coconut rum
6 oz. pineapple juice
4 oz. lemon/lime soda

Put some ice in a glass. Add the rum, juice, and soda and stir. Makes one cocktail.

Carrot Muffins

1 cup unsweetened applesauce
½ cup sugar
⅓ cup vegetable oil
3 eggs
1½ cups flour
½ teaspoon salt
1½ teaspoons baking soda
2½ teaspoons baking powder
1½ teaspoons cinnamon
2 cups grated carrots

Preheat oven to 420°F.

Mix together the applesauce, sugar, and oil. Add the eggs, one at a time, beating after each addition. Sift together the dry ingredients and add them to the egg mixture. Mix well and fold in the grated carrots. Fill the muffin tins to the top.

When you place the muffin tins in the oven, reduce the heat to 375°F and bake for approximately 18 minutes. Remove from the oven and let sit for 5 minutes. Take the muffins out of the tins and allow to cool before serving. Makes 12 muffins.

ACKNOWLEDGMENTS

I'd like to extend my sincere thanks to several people whose hard work and input made this book what it is today. I'm truly grateful to my agent, Jessica Faust, for helping me bring this series to life and to my editor, Martin Biro, for taking a chance on this series and for his enthusiasm and guidance. Thank you to Sarah Blair, Jody Holford, and Nicole Bates for reading my early drafts and cheering me on, and to all my wonderful friends in the writing community.

Books are produced in the United States using U.S.-based materials

Books are printed using a revolutionary new process called THINKtech™ that lowers energy usage by 70% and increases overall quality

Books are durable and flexible because of Smyth-sewing

Paper is sourced using environmentally responsible foresting methods and the paper is acid-free

Center Point Large Print
600 Brooks Road / PO Box 1
Thorndike, ME 04986-0001 USA

(207) 568-3717

US & Canada:
1 800 929-9108
www.centerpointlargeprint.com